13 Again

edited by A. Finnis

SCHOLASTIC

Scholastic Children's Books
7–9 Pratt Street, London NW1 0AE, UK
a division of Scholastic Publications Ltd
London ~ New York ~ Toronto ~ Sydney ~ Auckland

Published in the UK by Scholastic Publications Ltd, 1995
This anthology copyright © 1995 by Scholastic Publications Ltd

ISBN 0 590 55914 1

All rights reserved

Typeset by TW Typesetting, Midsomer Norton, Avon
Printed by Cox & Wyman Ltd, Reading, Berks.

10 9 8 7 6 5 4 3 2 1

CONTENTS

Acknowledgements

All of the stories are original and appear for the first time in this volume.

The following are the copyright owners of the stories:

"Anjelica's Room" copyright © 1995 Laurence Staig
"Foxgloves" copyright © 1995 Susan Price
"The Ultimate Assassin" copyright © 1995 Malcolm Rose
"The Rattan Collar" copyright © 1995 Garry Kilworth
"Boomerang" copyright © 1995 David Belbin
"The Delinquent" copyright © 1995 Maresa Morgan
"The Ghost Trap" copyright © 1995 Lisa Tuttle
"Close Cut" copyright © 1995 Philip Gross
"Grandma" copyright © 1995 Colin Greenland
"Vampire in Venice" copyright © 1995 John Gordon
"Picking up the Tab" copyright © 1995 Stan Nicholls
"Evidence of Angels" copyright © 1995 Graham Masterton
"Hospital Trust" copyright © 1995 Dennis Hamley

ANJELICA'S ROOM

Laurence Staig

A COBWEB HUNG ACROSS A CORNER OF THE WINDOW. For a moment it trembled, bowing and shimmering from the breath of a soft breeze. The estate agent from Ashton-Tate blew sharply into its centre, and then out of nowhere a spider scuttled into view. It paused, sensing it had been tricked. A wave from his hand cleared the silvery skein with a single sweep.

"Nice property," sniffed the agent. "It'd be a shame if we have to give it away. So, I thought, let's give it a bash on the open market first, do it up a bit. Spot of paint here, spot of paint there – you know, nothing too flash."

He turned on his heels and peered over the top of his round wire spectacles. An easy white-toothed smile spread across his face. The light from the window shone like thin golden butter across his grey suit. There was too much gel on his hair, and the sun picked out the excess globules, making them sparkle like tiny uncut diamonds.

"Nothing too complicated, you understand ... nothing too expensive." He winked at Mark, whilst gently rubbing his thumb and forefinger together.

3

The spider scuttled along the floor in front of him, and he crushed it with a single step forward.

"We'll give you a good deal, Mr Hart," said Mark. "My assistant is red hot. She has a real design sense."

"Oh, red hot eh? Wow, wouldn't want anything less Mark, wouldn't want anything less."

"You should see her pictures – her paintings. She's an artist – or wants to be an artist, that's what we do at college."

"Don't want no Van Goghs – I just want the place clean and tidy, attractive, nice for a first-time buyer, or a couple maybe. It'd be a shame to let it go to auction."

"Yeah. It's a nice house."

He knew that he had lied.

There was something about the place that made Mark uneasy, an unusual sensation for him. Perhaps it was the smell: there was a sense of oldness, and the atmosphere seemed to hang like a musty shroud. But it wasn't just that, it was something else. Speckles of dust floated through the air. Mark felt as though he was moving through an ever-thickening silence. He dusted down his jeans with a snort and looked up at the ceiling. There were some cracks, but nothing that couldn't be fixed with a bit of filler. Sarah could handle that, it would be a bit bodged, but this character in his smart shiny suit wouldn't notice – or care for that matter. Weren't they just in it to make some money, all of them? Him especially. No, he smirked, Sarah would do it for love.

The estate agent frowned and rubbed away a clear patch in the speckled grime, which smeared the window pane like vaseline. He sniffed and pulled a face. Then he moved his head slowly, like an inquisitive bird. For a moment he seemed concerned.

"Somebody's out there, I think. It's the farmer, must be. The neighbouring farmland backs on to the rear of the garden. I've asked his wife if he'd smarten the boundary hedge up a bit. Never know, it might make a difference – people like a tidy garden, place for the 2.4 kids to play. Yeah – that's the farmer, that's Mr Favor, you can tell by his overalls."

He waved and tapped on the glass with a grin, then, satisfied that all was well, he turned to Mark. The agent ambled across the floor and put his arm around his shoulder. With his other hand he rearranged the sunglasses that were hooked over the front of his breast jacket pocket.

"It's Robin! Let's not be formal, call me *Robin*."

"Well, Robin," Mark said quietly, still unsure of his ground, "I think we can do a deal."

"Great. That's fine." The agent slapped his hands together and stared about the room. The dust swirled within a brown-stained shaft of sunlight. "When could you start?"

"I expect we could have a go next week. Perhaps I can call you to confirm?"

"Sure, sure," sang the agent. He patted the side of his nose with a finger. "I know what it's like being students, need every penny, eh? Tight budgets. You

5

can use some of the paint that the other decorators left, if that helps."

"Pardon?"

"There's tins left, quite a few. Just white – that'll do, paint it white everywhere. People can do anything with white, can't they? Makes the place seem all fresh, don't it? White's OK. Nice colour."

Mark nodded.

He walked out of the bedroom and on to the landing. He took out a large handkerchief and held it to his nose for a minute and coughed. Although most of the house had been cleared, there were still some items of furniture around. There was a broken hall table by the door, and inside another room Mark could just make out part of a wooden chest of drawers. He ran through the *To Do* list. The hallway would be difficult – but they could put rollers on broomsticks to reach the awkward parts. Hell, he thought, she'll love it here, my money-making slave, my little Miss Eager-to-please.

Mark's gaze stopped at the hall table. Something was propped up against an ornament. It was a photograph, but it seemed very old. The edges were mustard coloured and parts of it were faded from having been in the sun. He thought it might be the front of the cottage; it showed a family scene. A man and a woman stood in the garden and between them was a small child – a little girl. He held it closer to his face. The girl was dressed in a party outfit, with ribbons and bows. The adults had grim, set faces and the girl was smiling. He wondered what their problem was. With a half-hearted shrug he replaced the picture on the table.

He glanced back into the main bedroom. The estate agent stood silently in the centre of the room. He looked peculiar, standing there on his own. Different, somehow. His hands were clenched into fists and his head was tilted as if he were listening. Perhaps he was sniffing the air. Suddenly, he turned and caught Mark staring at him. His smile returned. But an ice-cold shiver shot down Mark's back.

The agent looked at him harder.

I wonder whether he feels it too, the strangeness – the atmosphere? thought Mark. He spoke up. "The house. Have you noticed it, there's an odd smell?"

The agent coughed and ignored his remark.

"How much, then?"

"What?"

"To do the house, Mark. Wakey, wakey. How much? Ball park figure. Bottom line, there's others I can go to – but students … I like to help them. When I got your flyer through our door I thought right then, give them a go."

Mark wished he'd kept his mouth shut about the place. There was no nonsense now, the man meant business.

"It's out in the sticks, too," said Mark. "I mean, there's the cost of petrol, it's miles from anywhere, I have to take that into account…"

"Secluded, desirable spot," said the agent. "Bring sleeping bags. That's OK. You'll be on your own – just the pair of you." He skipped across the room and turned. "Make a kind of holiday out of it. Have some fun."

Mark nodded.

"And there's one room where the paper needs stripping off – looks a tough job." Mark struggled to continue. "That will be extra. I need to take another look, a proper look. It's covered in a sod of a thick paper and…"

The agent fixed Mark with his eyes.

"You mean the end room, the one at the end of the corridor?" He had snapped back with the suddenness of a slammed book. He glanced to the side, almost embarrassed by his abruptness.

"Yeah – the one with the brown wallpaper," repeated Mark.

"Forget it." He looked up, straight into Mark's face and smiled. "You don't need to touch that room, not at all."

Mark turned towards the doorway. A false laugh tumbled from the agent.

"That was the straw that broke the camel's back. Better to tell you, I suppose. We fell out with the previous contractor, he said that room was going to cost, needed more work than we wanted, than we were prepared to pay for. The paper is really stuck on in there, see, and between you and me, if you were to pull it off, the walls would probably crumble.

8

Just leave it. Can't deal with structural problems if any crop up. The other feller, he kept upping the price. I mean a deal's a deal. Told him to get lost, that's what I did – told him straight."

Mark nodded. The room might need a lot of work, but he had only glanced inside, the agent having pulled him away during their tour.

"Come on, Mark." The agent marched out into the hallway. "A quick lick of paint for the whole house. How much?"

Mark sucked through his teeth as he had seen professional builders do. He pulled himself up straight.

"OK – £2,000."

The agent shook his head and shuffled his feet. He sighed.

"Mark. Come on – it's me you're talking to. I just want it cleaned up – not done up like Buckingham Palace. I want to sell the house quickly, not live in it; my boss has promised a nice earner."

"£1,750," said Mark. "For doing the whole lot, less the wallpapered room."

The agent stopped shuffling his feet.

"Finish it in a week and I'll bung you £1,400. That's a lot for students."

Mark winced. The man was good, he had to admit it. He was a slug in silver grey, but he was successful in every way that Mark so badly wanted to be. The agent's hand shot out, Mark hesitated, but only for a moment, and they shook on the deal. The agent

9

pulled the doors shut, and followed him back downstairs.

"Oh, Mark?" said the agent. His eyes sparkled, a mask of ill-concealed humour breaking through. "What about the girlfriend then, the er, *assistant* – Sally or Sarah, wasn't it? Do you need to show her the job first?"

He swallowed. "Sarah? What about her? She'll do what I tell her, I'm the business man after all, she works for me." He paused for a moment. "If we have an agreement you deal directly with me, OK? That's £1,400 to finish in a week."

"Sure, Mark, sure," said the agent. "Take it easy."

"I' did hear you right earlier? I mean, we only get £1,000, to paint the entire house?"

Sarah's incredulity showed on her face. Her small elf-like features, her eyes and smile, which were usually irritatingly bright and smiling, were now dulled.

She had stopped the car half-way down the lane which led to the house. The engine gently ticked over as she leant forward over the wheel and peered through the windscreen. Raindrops had begun to make a gentle tattoo on the screen, but she had not switched on the wipers.

Mark gave a snort. He pushed the remains of his sandwich into his face, screwed up the cellophane wrapper and pushed it into a corner of the glove compartment. Sarah watched him with a sigh.

"Mark, please don't do that – it's my mum's car, don't trash it. We couldn't do all of this without her. I mean it's kind of her to lend it to us."

He rolled his eyes upwards.

"Give it a rest!" He gave another growl of irritation.

"You said it was a small cottage," she said, reaching out to hold his hand.

He snatched his hand away and reached forward to wipe the windscreen with a rag.

"Look Miss Dim, put the wipers on. We're not there yet, you can't see it properly from this angle, we're not even inside."

She tried to force a smile, but deep down she wondered whether he would ever get anything right. But it didn't matter, he would change, he would learn. She leant over and gently took his hand. This time he let her.

"Look. Why don't you let me come with you when you give estimates – you said we were partners. I'm sorry Mark, but I think you've well undersold us this time."

He pulled his hand out of hers and grabbed her tightly by the wrist. His eyes became large, his words were spoken through gritted teeth. He frightened her sometimes when his temper was roused.

"Lay off me, I know what I'm doing – you've got to charge a keen price. There's a lot of competition out there!"

"Mark, you're hurting me!" she cried.

He let go of her wrist. With a disgruntled sigh he leant back in his seat and tossed his hair back. Curse his temper. He was annoyingly attractive. If only he was just a bit *nicer.* She wiped away a tear. She would change him – it would just take time.

"I'm sorry," he said, and leant over and kissed her lightly on the cheek. It was almost sincere. She rubbed her wrist and sniffed.

"That's all right. Perhaps I am jumping to conclusions. We'll take a look inside."

She eased off the handbrake and let the car creep down the lane. After a few moments they had arrived outside. Sarah rolled down the window and gazed across to the house.

It was set within its own garden, the front wall a colourful mixture of browns and greys, dry stone built with patches of bright green moss. A brand new estate agent's board, fixed to the iron garden gate, bowed under the occasional gust of wind. An overgrown front garden hid most of the front aspect. There were a tangle of rose bushes and ivy and Russian vine, which had become attached to the right hand side of the building, almost obscuring the top and bottom windows.

"It is empty, isn't it?" asked Sarah.

"Of course."

"And it was lived in until recently? It's just that it looks as if it might have been abandoned."

"It's not that bad," said Mark sharply, getting out

and slamming the door. He searched in his pocket for a moment and produced a large old black-stained key. He held it up for her to see.

"Don't see keys like this any more, eh? Are you coming or not?" He crossed the lane and pushed the gate open.

Sarah forced a smile and joined him, catching herself on the bushes and brambles as they made their way up the short front path to the timber-framed porch. Fixed above the door was the sign: Rose Cottage.

Within moments he had unlocked the front door; he stood to one side and bowed, gesturing that she should enter. The door opened wide with a rasping yawn that set Sarah's teeth on edge. The presence of the house, the full weight of its atmosphere bore down on her. Crane flies buzzed with house flies above her head, but the sudden stillness once the door had settled came as a shock. She caught her breath.

Mark waited for a moment, and then gently pushed her forward. The stairs met the front door. There was a sitting room to the left and what might be a dining room to the right: an old gate-leg table had been left in the centre. The passage beside the stairs led down to the back of the house, where an old iron stove stood, with hanging rails like a dryer. She presumed this to be a kitchen.

"See," said Mark, "it's only a cottage, and think of all that dosh. I told you it would be a cinch. I won't even take commission for getting us the job."

Sarah said nothing. She suddenly felt an urgency inside, a need to be held. She turned and gazed up into his eyes and then pushed her face into his chest, holding him tightly.

"You ... you do care for me, don't you, Mark?"

She looked up into his face, her eyes lost and lonely. He laughed and then he cradled the back of her head in his hands.

"Of course, of course I do. I wouldn't have asked you to be my business partner otherwise, would I?"

"It's just that..."

He didn't let her finish. Instead he swept down the corridor, pulling her behind him.

"Come on – the kitchen's tiny – bet you could do that in a morning. Come on!"

She snapped out of her sudden spate of gloom and allowed herself to be dragged around the house.

"See," he gushed, pointing like some excited tourist. "Almost all the walls are plain plaster. They've been painted with this dingy magnolia colour. So you see, you don't have to worry about stripping down paper, or lining or whatever. Touch of plaster filler here and there – lick of paint. I can undercoat – you can top coat and emulsion..."

"Mark! Slow down." Then she broke into a laugh. He put his arm around her and squeezed her to him. "Look," she continued, "there's more to this than you realize. I mean it may be plaster, but to cover some of this we may have to prime the walls, then there's – oh, there's so much. You don't think!"

He let go of her and glanced away.

"Yes, I do. If it wasn't for me we wouldn't have the job."

He was in danger of sulking.

"I'm sorry. I guess you're right," she said with resignation. "So where's the owner?"

"The bathroom's downstairs," he said, and walked through to a back room. "The owner? The agent said that she'd gone abroad, an old girl apparently, had lived here for years. She asked them to auction the place – the move was sudden. This agent's boss wanted to have a go at selling it on the market first, get a better price. That's where we come in. If we can crack this one then we may not even need to stay at college. Do the rounds with the other estate agents. We've got to be competitive, Sarah."

"But £1,000? I mean, for goodness' sake."

He ignored her comment; they'd been there before with that one. Instead, he turned away from her and moved the palm of his hand across the wall. He moved his face closer to the plaster – smelling it. The surface felt cold to the touch, yet smooth like marble. His hand roved, then stopped. There was something by his fingers, a black mark. He pulled his head away and squinted at the wall. There was an outline, a drawing or something similar in black marker or ink. At first he wasn't certain what it could be, then he realized it was the figure of a woman. She had long hair and a triangle that was supposed to be a dress, but there was something

15

wrong with the mouth – it was too wide and the teeth were large. Sarah stepped forward and peered at the drawing.

"Did a child live here?" she asked.

Mark was becoming impatient.

"No. Maybe. Hell, I don't know!"

Sarah stared past him and noticed a stack of white tins by the back door. He caught her look as he turned to face her.

"Oh those – well that's in the arrangement, we've even been left some paint. See – it was a great deal. They had to pull the other decorator off the job, some dispute. Left the paint, so..." He shrugged his shoulders.

"OK – I must be mad. Let me take a look upstairs."

"Of course, look round. I'll move these tins into the front room: we can use it as the base room for our stuff. Glad you've seen sense. Let's get this show on the road. Then I'll shoot into the village for some extra rollers and brushes. I told you we'd need them."

She turned abruptly on her heels.

"Mark."

"What? What is it?" He froze; she suddenly looked pale and startled. "Sarah?"

"Don't ... don't leave me here alone."

She noticed a smell, something sharp, sweet and sickly, just detectable.

"It's only the village, not the other side of the world. What on earth's the matter?"

Although he had asked such a simple question, somewhere inside of him a nagging understanding resurfaced.

She swallowed hard. A pair of fat bluebottle flies danced into her hair, causing her to flinch. He tried to smile.

"Don't get spooked – it's an old house. I felt a bit, well – you know, a bit off when I first came here, too. There's this odd smell sometimes, too: you get that where old people have lived, don't you?"

He lowered his voice.

"We'll get used to it."

He retreated down the corridor to the stack of paint cans.

"Mark?" Her voice carried after him, but he kept on walking.

She whispered under her breath, *"Don't be so stupid, Sarah. You don't want to lose him."* She decided to make a big effort: their start had not been good.

"I guess we should start bringing the stuff in from the car? Yeah?"

He turned around, almost surprised at her remark. That was more like it.

"Yeah – sure. I'll do it after I shift these cans. Yeah. You go and have a look round upstairs, start to put a plan together, about how to tackle all of this. I'll get the gear in. Oh, by the way, there's a small room upstairs with this thick wallpaper. No need to touch that. What's the stuff called – anaglypta?"

17

"Why leave it? I mean if we're going to do a proper job."

"Just leave it, Sarah. It's a big job, been varnished too, taking the stuff off will pull away the plaster and it can't be painted over easily."

"But, I like to do a proper job and..."

He gritted his teeth.

"Sarah, shut it! Just get on, will you. It's only an old spare room – a box room."

"OK." She found it hard to sound enthusiastic.

She tried a light switch and was surprised to find that it worked. The corridor changed from an ill-lit shadowy tunnel to a vinegar coloured cave. Beneath the glow of the low-powered light bulb, the drawing looked different somehow – almost like a prehistoric cave painting. She found it difficult to take her eyes off the thing. For a moment she crouched down and looked at the figure.

"Move it!" called Mark, as he started to re-emerge from the end of the corridor. He was loaded with cans of paint.

She stood up, startled, and without a further word returned to the foot of the stairs. He pushed past her without apology. Nervously, she climbed the stairs, up to the bedrooms. Stopping half-way, she felt the wall with her fingers. This too was painted in a magnolia colour. She hoped that it was emulsion: if it was water-based paint the job would take half as long again. But no residue of powder came away.

"Whoever lived here seemed to like a world of

gloom," she said.

She received no reply. Mark was outside unloading the car.

At the top of the stairs there were two bedrooms which led off from the small landing, and to the right there was a short corridor which mirrored the one on the ground floor. She stepped into the larger of the rooms.

The first thing Sarah noticed was how grimy the windows were, though the bright light outside glowed through a wiped area. She managed to twist the window lock and opened one of the frames. She peered out. The garden below had been orderly and managed at one time, there were small signs; but now it had become overgrown, a jungle of greens and browns. Someone had made a start at clearing a corner: a wheelbarrow and a rake stood on a stone flag path. All of a sudden the figure of a man popped up from behind the rear hedge.

Sarah gasped, then she laughed; the figure had frightened her. The man was almost like a scare-crow, dressed in a pair of dark green dungarees or overalls. He was quite plump, stood with a slight stoop and was wearing a huge straw hat.

"Hello!" Sarah called.

The man stood perfectly still.

She called out again, and this time leant through the window and waved. He raised his arm as if acknowledging her greeting. He was holding a scythe, or something similar. Sarah took this to be a wave in response and was about to commence a conversation when he disappeared again, down behind the hedge.

"Suit yourself," mumbled Sarah.

She left the window open and turned. The opposite wall had already been painted a brilliant white, and the cover had been good. An adjacent wall had a first coat applied and was thinner, the brush marks showing.

"Must have been the previous decorator," she said to herself. "But I wonder why he left? A dispute? What about, though?"

Mark called up from below.

"I'm off to the village – I'll not be long!"

She caught her breath: she wanted him here.

"No. Stay, please. There's somebody outside."

"That's the farmer," Mark called back. "He's working on the hedge. That's OK. Just get on, start a plan, we'll start work tonight, but I'll have to leave you to it tomorrow, I've costings to do from some punter enquiries."

"Here we go," she said beneath her breath. "Leave me to do it all, as usual."

She raised her voice. "Don't go yet!" Then she added, "Please!"

She found herself staring at the whiteness of the wall. It was like a vast emptiness, reminding her of the wall of a hospital. The front door slammed; he was gone.

For a moment a huge silence filled the loneliness

of the place. She looked about her. A trunk stood in the corner. There was a lamp on the lid, with a mottled leathery brown shade, opaque like skin, and it was speckled from splash marks.

Like skin. For some reason the notion stuck for a moment.

Suddenly, a warm current of air blew through the room, the window creaked wider on its hinges and the door gently batted back against the wall, making a tapping noise. Sarah shuddered. Her eyes flicked up to the ceiling. A coat of white had already been applied here too, but the cracks showed, making a jagged mosaic pattern around the light fitting like a lightning fork frozen in time. The smell of the paint still lingered but an older more pungent smell hit her: it was like home-made glue. For a moment she felt nauseous.

Sarah ran from the room, out on to the landing. There was a card on a table further along the corridor. Taking a deep breath, she went towards it and picked it up.

It was the same photograph that Mark had discovered. She stared at the family group for several moments then turned it over. There was writing on the back, in a blue ink scrawl: *Mummy and Daddy with Anjelica, June 1935*. She flicked it back over and slapped it face down on the table.

"Anjelica," she hissed the name. "Who was Anjelica, then?"

From further down the hall the breeze blew once

again, carrying a brief snatch of the strange odour.
This time it seemed different. Why was her imagination playing tricks? Why was it so rich and
pungent, with the same sweet sickly sting?

Beyond the table at the end of the corridor was the
brown room, the room they didn't need to touch. The
door was ajar and a small puddle of auburn light
spilled out on to the floorboards. For a second Sarah
wondered whether the smell wasn't coming from
that direction, but no sooner had the idea occurred
to her than the smell vanished with another waft of
breeze.

"Let's take a look," she said to herself.

It was a very small room, with a tiny window
recessed into a strange shaped gable which
reminded her of an eye. The window was slightly
open; the glass had been cleaned recently and a
decorator's rag was stuffed beneath the stay. She
looked out. As with the other bedroom, it overlooked
the garden. The farmer still stood in the field. This
time she thought he might be looking up at the
window, and was tempted to wave again – but didn't.
The door slammed, and she twisted round.

For a brief second she thought the aroma had
returned. Perhaps Mark was right about it just being
an old person's house. In the corner of the room was
a bucket and a paper scraper. Somebody had already
tried to soak the wallpaper. There were scratch
marks to allow the water to soak in more easily, and
scraps of paper lay in a pile beside a half-filled bin

liner. The first eighteen inches or more of paper had already been cleared from one of the walls.

She crouched down and tore another strip of paper from the wall. It came away with difficulty. It didn't look as though it had been stuck with paste.

"They didn't want this to come off, did they?" she said. She smelt the paper. "It's an animal glue of some kind; my God, it's rock hard."

She reached down and pulled away some more paper. Then stopped.

"I wonder if that's what I can smell? Why put up a paper like this in such a small room, and why weld it on to the walls?"

Was someone watching her? She glanced over her shoulder again, but there was nobody there. There was only a small basket, like a picnic hamper, next to the door. Another lamp stood beside it, almost a matching item to the one in the other bedroom. It had been speckled with paint.

She shuffled across to the basket. There was a small label, crumpled and old, tied to one of the carrying handles. She peered at the writing. In faded ink it read: *Anjelica's*. She lifted the lid. A jumble of items lay in the basket and at first glance they all appeared to be toys. Reaching in, she smiled as she saw the face of a toy doll with long blonde hair. It was lodged between something furry – perhaps a bear – and a parcel of postcards which were tied up in string.

She pulled at the doll. It was stuck, but after a

moment of persistence it soon came loose. Only the head came away in her hand. It was a funny thing to happen, but she did not laugh. Pulling the postcards to one side she foraged further into the basket. There were other dolls, too.

She pulled the furry toy out first. It was a bear, but it had no eyes and the head was about to come away – like the doll's. She noticed that the rest of its body had been damaged. The chest was covered in lots of small cuts, and some of the woolly stuffing was poking through. She looked back at the basket and pulled it into a better light. Now she could see the other toys more clearly. The rest of the dolls were broken in some way too.

Gradually, she laid the pieces out beside the basket. There were arms and legs and heads: it was a bizarre collection, but there was something particular that worried at her. Splodges of red paint had been applied to the ends of the arms and legs, and as she now noticed, at the neck of the doll's head. Were they supposed to look like stumps, like injuries? Carefully, she lifted one of the dolls into the air, to see it better. It was missing an arm, and the blue chequered dress was torn. But it was what she thought she saw within the tears in the cloth that bothered her.

She looked hard. Surely not?

"Why? This must have been an accident," she whispered.

She tugged at the rest of the dress and finally

managed to pull it away. Now it was plain to see.
Marks covered the doll's body like a strange
grotesque rash. She wondered what they were and
looked closer. In places the marks had been the
result of gouging as though with some kind of sharp
instrument, but it was what had been done to the
marks that particularly puzzled her.

"Someone's tried to hurt them, someone's tried to
make the dolls look as though..."

The teddy bear rolled over, and something bright
like a blade peeked through the stuffing near his
neck.

A wave of nausea, almost a dizzy sensation
overcame her. The sweet smell returned. She fell to
one side and reached out to steady herself. Her hand
brushed against the lamp shade and she let out a
small cry. The room turned around the shade, the
dark reddish brown marks which speckled the cloth
seemed to shudder like stars. Paint splashes? The
decorator had used *white* paint – not red.

Sarah picked up the doll again. The question
wouldn't leave her. Why paint red weals into the
gouged slits? Why give your toys such vicious-
looking wounds? She tilted the doll and the eyelids
shot open. In place of the usual glass blue eyes,
there was bright red sightless softness: it was cotton
wool stained red. The effect was horribly realistic.

"Sick!"

She threw the doll to one side in disgust. With a
sudden urgency she pulled at the string on the

postcards. They tumbled out into her hands. Some were photographs mixed in with letters and seaside holiday scenes. Some were of the man and woman in the picture she had seen earlier, others showed the same little girl, Anjelica. It was the photographs of the family group which troubled her most: she wasn't certain what it was exactly, but the group just didn't work. She looked closely at the faces of the mother and father. Were they afraid of their own daughter?

With a frown she looked back at the area which the decorator had started to strip. Peeping out from beneath the torn edges, as though below a curtain, were black lines reminiscent of the marks downstairs in the hall. She reached forward for the wallpaper scraper.

"Let's see what's here." She swallowed hard, fighting back a growing sense of fear. She slid the blade beneath the bottom lip of the wallpaper. There was something there, she was certain of it.

Gradually a line drawing began to appear. Sarah worked methodically. It had to be a child's drawing of a woman or girl: first of all the legs were revealed, then there was a dress and after a moment it became clear that she was holding something in her hand. Impatient, Sarah reached forward and tore away the remaining strip of paper. It came away in a single pull.

It was a child's drawing.

Her fingers shot up to her mouth, she bit on the tips to stop them trembling. In one hand the girl held another smaller figure, obviously a doll, but it had no head. Instead the head was held in the other hand, and a red wash of colour, that was meant to represent blood, flowed from the dismembered neck. It had been drawn with inks, black for the outline – but with an over-generous use of red.

But it was the wide smile on the face of the girl that Sarah couldn't take: it was supposed to be of a happy figure – a *very* happy figure.

"Sarah!" a voice echoed out in the hall.

"No!" Sarah screamed. "This is a sick house, I'm not staying here a moment longer."

She sobbed back tears and tugged at the handle on the front door. Mark pushed the door shut again.

"Just the work of kids, that's all. You're over-reacting. What about the money, the job? You can't pull out."

"I can and I am."

She pulled the door open again.

"But I've got us some extra! Whilst I was out I called the agent. I've agreed an extra £150 for us to do up the nursery. It'll be easy, you'll see."

"Do up the nursery?"

A curtain of silence dropped between them; even the birds in the garden stopped singing.

"*Nursery?*" said Sarah. "You mean the room with the brown wallpaper? It's a *nursery*?"

"Yeah," said Mark quietly. "So, so what?"

Her hand shot up to her mouth.

27

"Then what kind of child played there, Mark, answer me that! What kind of child?"

She pushed past him, out into the front garden. The cloying atmosphere of the house vanished. He stood in the doorway, almost shaking with rage.

"You know what you are?" he yelled back at her. "You're neurotic, that's what you are, a neurotic cow!"

She swung the garden gate open and glanced up at the estate agent's sign. He noticed her doing so.

"That agent's near here, isn't he?"

"Why, what are you going to do – I do the business side."

"Bull!" she snapped back. With that she jumped into the car and started the engine.

"Damn it – I'll do the room myself!" Mark stepped back and slammed the door behind him. She'd be back, she'd better or else.

As Sarah drove away the farmer, who was working in the rear field, cried out to her. She glimpsed him from the corner of her eye.

The office of Ashton-Tate, Estate Agents, appeared to be in turmoil. Sarah pushed the smart glass doors apart and for a moment wondered where to start. An elderly woman carrying a wicker basket was almost shouting at a young man behind the desk. The man kept pulling off his spectacles and running his fingers through his over-gelled hair. Behind him, an office girl was frantically pulling files from a cabinet; another was speaking to a man in a suit who carried a notebook and a mobile phone.

"Do you handle Rose Cottage?" asked Sarah.

Her question silenced the room.

The older woman turned abruptly. The man behind the desk lifted his hand to his face.

"Er, yes."

"Who lived there?"

"Who are you, please?"

"I'm 80 per cent of the pair that are painting the damn place for you. The woman who lived there, what was she like?"

"Hello love," said the woman. "I was just explaining – more *trying* to explain to Mr Hart here, about my husband's bad back. I know he was supposed to clear up the hedge for you all at the Cottage – but he's been laid up for weeks, flat on his back. Not his fault."

Sarah felt the blood drain from her face. The *farmer*?

"You are..."

"This is Mrs Favor," said the agent. "Her husband farms the field at the back."

"Sounds like there's quite a to-do on now," said Mrs Favor, "what with Miss Waterstone having escaped an' all. An' that decorator chappie running off the job for some reason or other."

The agent pushed his face into his hands.

"Miss Waterstone?" asked Sarah. Her voice had become high, almost a cry.

Mrs Favor shuffled over to her.

"Exciting, ain't it? Anjelica Waterstone, the crazy person that lived there before they locked her up."

"Er, Mrs Favor, let's go out the back," said the agent.

Sarah's face turned to stone. She held Mrs Favor by the arm. "You knew her?"

"All the locals did. Sad story."

"Tell it," said Sarah.

"I beg your pardon?"

"Tell it! Please!"

Mrs Favor looked uneasy. "Well, she was born and brought up in that cottage. Then when she was only seven both her parents were found murdered, they were done in their beds. Stabbed to death – horrible. Never caught who did it, but *she* was never right afterwards. Anjelica – she could never speak about it, was looked after by her aunt, who wasn't too right upstairs either, if you know what I mean." She tapped the side of her head. "After she died, poor Anjelica had nobody; there were talk of the odd stranger staying there, kind of housekeepers I think – but they never lasted and she kept herself to herself, they always moved on." She went quiet and whispered her last words: *moved on*. "Anyhow, they locked her up and now they want to sell her house."

Sarah found it difficult to speak. "Where ... where is she now? I mean, you said she'd escaped?"

"Can you help us, Miss?"

The man in the suit with the notebook and the

phone, who had been speaking to the woman, stepped forward.

"I'm Detective Constable Collins. Anjelica Waterstone escaped from a secured hospital ward a week ago. She's just a harmless old lady, but we *do* need to find her."

Sarah felt the office spin around her.

"Harmless? Oh my God, I don't think so. Oh my God."

She could hear her own heartbeat, thudding in her head like a hammer.

"What was she wearing when she went missing?" Sarah's eyes were wide.

The policeman flipped over his pad.

"That's easy, Miss. Not exactly designer wear – a kind of green jump suit – like overalls, hospital issue. She was working in the garden, see."

As they approached Rose Cottage, Sarah observed the activity in the lane as though she was watching scenes under water. Everything seemed to slow down, almost to freeze in time, but in reality it was chaos. They passed the flashing light of an ambulance, and a string of police cars parked close to the opposing wall. As the car pulled to a halt, Sarah leapt out.

"Miss!" called the policeman. "Don't go in!"

By the gate a policewoman and two policemen were leading away a plump figure in green overalls. It was the farmer who wasn't a farmer, the *he* who

31

was a *she*. No longer wearing the straw hat, her long grey hair hung wildly about her shoulders.

She turned to Sarah and smiled, but her eyes were wide and rolled like marbles.

"They were my pictures, Missie, and they should have stayed hid. Jus' like auntie said. Auntie put up the nice dark paper – mustn't get found out, eh? Auntie said get smack otherwise. Get smack."

"Mark!" yelled Sarah.

"Stop her, for heaven's sake!" cried a voice.

But the police were unable to stop her as she rushed into the house and up the stairs. She pushed open the door to the nursery, and stared in disbelief.

Mark had made a start – the brown paper was almost stripped off one wall. But it wasn't clear, not like a stripped wall should be. Instead of plain plaster the surface was covered in the same kind of drawings she had seen before. They were clearly the handiwork of a young child – but it was a macabre mural: hundreds of drawings of smiling figures with huge eyes stared out at her, and every one showed a dismembered body strewn with knife wounds. Knives were drawn in black ink – and there was a deep, awful red – and it was everywhere.

Somebody groaned behind her.

She turned and heard a scream.

He was dead: the groan was just expelled air. Mark hung there, just like one of Anjelica's dolls, pinned to the wall by the bright chrome arc of a scythe.

"Get her out, now!" somebody said.

She never heard the comment, or the one made out in the hall. The scream came again.

"That smell, sir, I think you're right, there's a false wall in there."

There was only the scream.

It was only much later that she realized: the scream that wouldn't stop was her own.

FOXGLOVES

Susan Price

"OH, GIVE ME A BREAK!" SEAN SAID. "IT'S TOO HOT TO argue." It was almost one in the morning, but all the windows stood open, and the flimsy curtains hardly moved.

Penny, sitting on the settee, folded her arms and turned away. Her mouth was tightly shut.

"I went over and said a few words. I used to work with her. What d'you want me to do – ignore her?"

"Oh! You weren't ignoring her!" Penny said.

"She was a *friend*!"

"Oh, yes. *Very* friendly."

"I can do without this," Sean said. "I'm going home, get some sleep." He started out of the room and down the hallway. He heard someone move on the landing overhead: Penny's mother or father eavesdropping.

Penny came out of the room behind him. "And I can do without you! Don't bother coming back here – ever again!"

Sean opened the front door and stepped out into the thick summer dusk. The warm air folded around him like a soft blanket, scented by the roses in

Penny's front garden. Feeling as if he was amongst those roses, scratched and sore, he shouted back into the house, "I *won't* bother coming! What's the point? You've sulked all night just because I spoke to a friend, you stupid – ! Good riddance!"

Penny came out on to the step and shouted after him, "Drop dead! I hope you drop dead! Just drop dead!" Before he could shout anything back, she'd slammed her front door shut.

He hurried down the road, half-running, until he had to stop because his head was swelling with heat, and his shirt was sticking to his wet body. His throat was sore with thirst, and tight, and he felt half-choked. The hot, still air was as difficult to breathe as wool. It was mid-summer – literally. It was Midsummer's Eve, and it had been hot for weeks, the nights seeming hotter than the days. The last thing he wanted to do was walk three miles home in that heat, but he had no choice. The last bus had long gone. All because he'd hung on with Penny, hoping that her bad mood would pass. Anger helped him walk faster. Replaying the argument in his head, muttering aloud, he hurried past hedges and walls and windows with drawn curtains.

He took a short cut – a narrow gully between two streets. Overgrown bushes grew high on either side, and bindweed climbed through them, the white of its flowers shining in the dusk. His footsteps, loud and clear in the early morning quiet, echoed back from the walls and returned to his ears as shuffling steps that seemed now ahead of him, now behind. He turned and walked a few steps backwards as he checked the path behind him. No one was following him. Turning again, he caught a glimpse of something whisking into the tall nettles and weeds beside the path. Two green lights flashed briefly from the undergrowth – cat's eyes, probably.

Had it been a black cat? It was lucky to have a black cat cross your path. A pity it couldn't have crossed his path earlier that evening, though.

He walked on a pace or two, and turned in a circle to check on some slight noise behind him. Whatever made it, he couldn't tell. There was nothing to see. He hurried on, to get out of the gully and back to the street. Walking alone, late at night, wasn't one of his favourite things. He didn't like the state of prickly alertness which made him twitch at every little sound and movement, and then feel a fool because there was nothing to be afraid of.

Midsummer's Eve, too – an unlucky night to be out. It was one of the "turning days" of the year, according to his granny, like Hallowe'en, Christmas Eve and May Day. They were the days when the year turned from winter to spring, from spring to summer, from summer to autumn, and then to winter again. They were different from other days... More open. The nights were even more so. Ghosts walked on those nights that couldn't walk other nights; things were seen on those nights that couldn't be seen on other nights... On those nights,

39

magic worked. According to Granny.

He turned in a circle again, to check on the normality of the hedges and lamp-posts around him, the parked cars, and paving stones and gates.

His granny was full of such stories. Whenever he went to see her, she seemed to remember another that he hadn't heard before, and she would swear that they were all true. Ghastly stories of the ghosts of stillborn babies coming to call away their still living but pining mothers; or the story of the ghost his great-grandad had seen when he'd been out late on Midsummer's Eve.

Ghoulies and ghosties and long-leggety beasties, he thought, trying to laugh himself out of the nervous mood that was settling on him. But that mood fed on itself, and there was no shaking it off. He turned to look behind him again. Obviously some passing ghoulie had put a jinx on him, and inspired him to give Cassie a kiss while Penny was watching. It was so stupid. He and Cassie had worked together for nearly two years, and had got on really well, always had a laugh and a joke – but he'd never been out with Cass. She was older than him, and still had the same steady boyfriend she'd had when he first met her. He couldn't honestly say that he'd never fancied Cass, just a little bit, but it had never been serious. He'd just given her an affectionate, friendly kiss on the cheek. And, because of that, Penny had gone into a major sulk that had lasted all evening, and had told him to drop dead. He hadn't realized she could be so jealous. It was flattering, he supposed... He would give her a day to calm down, and then ring her...

He came to the place where he could take the little track that led along the side of a closed fish and chip shop, and on down to the river – or he could go on along the road and through the town centre. He teetered on his feet, leaning first towards one way and then towards the other.

It would be quicker to follow the river, but from where he stood he could see the darkness that the track led into, the overhanging arch of whispering, leafy branches. The river way was also lonelier, and darker, and there would be countless little rustlings and shiverings in the undergrowth, to make him jump and sweat.

He turned towards the road, grey and drab in the street lights, but hesitated again. Always walk where it's well lit, the police said, but it was such a long, dreary trudge through the town-centre – and even at that time in the morning there would be people about. Drunks. They could be more dangerous than rustlings in the undergrowth.

He was angry with himself at his cowardice. Take the shortest way, he told himself. Get home and get to bed. The river was the shortest way. He turned down the side of the chip-shop, following a track which became a hard-trodden, narrow strip of gravelly earth with tall grass and nettles growing on either side. The trees began to lean in from the sides, and he had to duck beneath the branches. Cool leaves touched his neck. A spider's web spread its stickiness across his mouth. He wiped it away with his hands, and his fingers were plastered with a mess of sticky fibres, dust and trapped insects.

In the river lived Megs Greenteeth. Another of his granny's stories. Megs Greenteeth, with her long hair that looked like weed floating on the water, who lurked under the water near the banks of the river, and seized hold of small children who went too close. Down under the water she would drag them, and hold them there while they drowned, and then she ate them with her big green teeth. Every year she drowned two boys and two girls – had to, or she would die herself. So she never relaxed, she was always waiting... And it was Midsummer's Eve, so she would be there. Such monsters were always more alive on the year's turning nights. On Midsummer's Night, Old Megs would be able to clamber right out of the river on to the bank... And there she would be, waiting for him in the half-dark ... a hunched, crouching figure, dripping water and weed, her grin showing her big, green teeth...

He was actually scaring himself. He paused where the track came out on to the river-bank. It was cooler there, under the leaves, and darker than it had been on the road. The air was full of the green scent of leaves and grass, and of the rattle and brush of grass-heads against his clothes. Ahead of him the water of the river shone with a dull grey sheen, like pewter. It was so warm that smoke-clouds of gnats still danced in the air above the water.

He peered up and down the river-bank. There was no sign of anyone or anything waiting, nor of any large head breaking the surface of the water. He laughed at himself, but it came out as a thin, nervous giggle. Of course he didn't believe that a monster named Megs Greenteeth was hiding just out of sight below the river-bank – but in the whispering quiet under the trees he had a sense of something waiting.

He set out briskly along the river path and, as he went, his hip brushed a tall foxglove and set it swaying. He glanced back at it. In the dusk its pale, fresh pink glowed, and he could even see the darker spots in the throats of the flowers. Foxgloves... Midges whirled about his head and fluttered against his face as he walked through the haze of them hovering under the trees. There was something about foxgloves, some other story his granny had used to tell him when he'd been little... She'd made silly jokes about foxes making gloves out of the flowers, but there'd also been something about woods where foxgloves grow being lucky – or unlucky. A sound of splashing in the river made him turn sharply and peer into the darkness behind him. Megs Greenteeth was coming for him!

He waited tensely, studying the darkness for any movement, and listening. And when he moved on, he was still uneasy. White moths fluttering above the grasses and shining in the dusk drew his gaze sharply. A sudden fish rising in the dark on the river's other side made him jump on his heels with fright. The assurances he tried to give himself were hollow, and only made his unease deeper. Something in him – something that made the hair shift on his arms and his neck, something that had made his heart beat quicker and his breath come faster – knew that there was reason to fear on the shadowed path under the trees.

A thick stand of hawthorn cast a stretch of the path into dense darkness, starred with a few late white blossoms. Their scent was spread wide by the warmth of the night and the dampness of the river, but he wasn't in the mood to hang around sniffing flowers. He stretched his legs and hurried to get past the bushes – and so walked hard into someone who stood in the darkness, and who reeled back with a little gasp and said, "Oh, you scared me!" A girl's voice.

Sean backed off. A pale face glimmered in the dark. "Sorry," he said. "You scared me, too. Are you all right?"

"I'm scared," she repeated and he felt again that shiver over his own skin – but before he could wonder about it, he was surprised to recognize her as Penny. He was walking on, slowly, and she walked with him and, as they emerged from the shadow of the hawthorns into the twilight of the more open path, he looked at her and saw that she wasn't

Penny. Of course she wasn't – how could she be? Again there was that trickle of apprehension through his mind, which he tried to ignore. He couldn't be scared, not in front of a girl.

A pretty girl, too. It was even more impossible to be scared in front of a pretty girl. She was about the same height as Penny and had long hair like her – which explained his mistake. He tended to see Penny everywhere, mistaking any girl of similar height and colouring for her.

This girl's face shone pale in the dusk as she turned towards him. Her chin was very pointed as she lifted her face to look at him. Her mouth opened softly and her eyes seemed huge and black in the darkness. Her hair fell in heavy dark curls on to her shoulders. The dark top she wore was low-cut, and her throat and breasts gleamed too. She had a fuller figure than Penny. "Can I walk with you?" she said. "I'm feared. Let me walk with you."

To his own surprise, everything instinctive in him said, "No!" He wanted to step away from her, to hurry past her, even to run away. His reason told him that was ridiculous. She was just a girl. "What are you doing down here on your own?" His tone of voice was harder than he had intended. Her boyfriends are waiting in the bushes, he was thinking. She's been sent to bring you along to them.

In a thin little voice, she said, "I'm feared. Can I walk with you?"

The voice, and the whimper in it, instantly

appealed to him. Was she simple-minded, he wondered. There was no possibility of leaving her if she was. " 'Course you can," he said.

She startled him then by suddenly hugging his arm in both of hers and leaning against him, close and warm and soft. Her hair fell over his shoulder and brushed against his neck. Again that shiver of fright – or revulsion – quivered through him. He found himself struggling with two distinct sets of thoughts. One set – cowardly and childish – was telling him to shove her away and run, leave her, get away. The other set – adult and reasonable – was telling him not to be so stupid, and asking him, how could he leave a frightened girl – a simple-minded girl – alone in the dark?

If she wasn't simple-minded, she was very bold. She was rubbing her chin against his shoulder and hugging his arm tight (so you can't get away!). He wouldn't want Penny, or his little sister, to behave like this.

"You're all right with me," he said, "but you should be careful who you talk to at this time of night."

She looked up at him, her face pearly in the dusk, her eyes huge. With a little wrinkle of her nose, she said, "I could see you were nice." An accent of some kind lilted from word to word.

A confusion of feelings filled him: that dread again, the sense of warning which urged him to run; but also a foolish pleasure which made him grin despite himself. "I am nice. Very nice. And so are you." She looked up at him again, and gave a little rub of her cheek against his shoulder. He'd only known her minutes. But it was nonsense to suspect her of meaning him any harm. Why should she? "I'm Sean. What's your name?"

"Essylt."

"What? That's different. Are you from abroad?"

She shook her head and her dark hair rippled and floated around her face. "No. I'm – I'm Welsh."

"Oh, that's the accent!" She was so very pretty that he was strongly tempted to try kissing her – except that he shivered at the thought. Anyway, he'd told her that she was safe with him – and what if she *was* simple-minded? Then it would be wrong of him to try anything on with her. It was nobility, he told himself, that kept him from kissing her, not fear. The path where he turned off into the back streets of Brierley wasn't far ahead.

"Where do you live?" he asked.

She drew a soft breath and hesitated before saying, "Not far."

She sounded like a child. "I'm only going as far as the dairy," he said. It was a reminder to himself as much as a warning to her, in case he should be overcome by chivalry and offer to walk her to her door. He refused to admit to the relief he felt at the idea of soon being rid of her. "Can I get you a taxi? I'll worry about you getting home otherwise."

She raised her pointed face and smiled at him. "Walk with me."

He felt a revulsion, as if at some slyness or insincerity. Glancing ahead, he saw the wall of the dairy through the trees. That was where he turned off. "There's a cab-office on the way. We can get you one there." He ducked into the darkness of the trees overhanging the path, and she went with him, clinging to his arm and pressing warmly against his side. Straightening, he walked out on to the wider track that led into the factory estate. The dairy's chain-link fence was on one side and, on the other, a little wilderness of bushes, brambles, tin cans and litter. As his feet trod on the hardness of tarmac, he felt a draught at his side, and lost the touch of her. She was gone.

He turned in a complete circle, looking all around him, at the drab concrete and tarmac, at the bushes and litter, at the dark, overhanging trees of the river-bank. Essylt was nowhere.

He opened his mouth to shout her name, and then closed it again. She had not let go of his arm and gone away... When he had ducked under the trees, she had been close beside him, holding on to his arm. There had been no slackening of her hold, no moving away. She had been there – and then she had not been there. The night around him had that curious, flat feeling – that somehow threatening feeling – that tells you a house is empty.

He turned his back on the river-bank and ran, ran with loud feet through the empty roads and past the empty buildings of the factory estate. The hot air was hard to breathe, and he choked for breath. His head swelled with heat, his body ran with sweat, but he forced himself to stumble on until the pain in his chest and side was so bad that he fell against a wall and leaned there, gasping.

He was in a long street of small terraced houses, all of dirt-darkened brick, all with small windows and coffin-sized doors. From where he leaned he could see them stretching on and on along a dark pavement. Cars were parked at the kerb, the street-lights shining on the curves of their roofs. A ripple of light, reflected from the lamp-posts, ran down the long line of windows.

His breath roared in his ears and scoured his throat. His legs shook under him. I've seen a ghost! he thought. A Midsummer's ghost. He didn't know whether to laugh or start running again. As he was in no state to run, he laughed, a little, shaky, breath-less laugh. You coward, you fool! he said to himself. Running off and leaving the girl like that, when she'd only gone back under the trees for a moment ... Maybe she dropped something.

But however his brain reasoned, his body knew that he had been right to run.

He hadn't fully recovered his breath when he started walking. He didn't want to hang about there. Sweat had soaked his shirt, and he took it off as he walked, and tied it around his waist by its sleeves. His footsteps were loud and clattering in the open street, but every few feet he passed the mouth of an entry leading to the yards behind the houses. The entry caught the sound of his walking and made it boom. The entries, with their echo and their darkness, made him nervous, and he took to walking as far from them as he could, close to the cars. He set off one over-sensitive alarm, and its shriek made his heart thump again, just when it had been beginning to slow down.

A ghost! He'd really seen a ghost, just like his grandad. Not everybody could say that. Just the same, he looked behind him and – with a start – into an entry he suddenly discovered himself to be passing. Seeing ghosts might be something special, but it wasn't an experience he wanted to repeat.

Not that it had been a very frightening ghost... His body didn't agree. His skin shivered again at the mere thought of the thing he had met down by the river. Get home! Get home, as soon as possible, to brick walls and locked doors, curtained windows and electric light. He hurried on.

He reached the main road, a broad dual-carriage-way, where lorries were still passing. He waited for one to pass and ran across the road, vaulting the barrier in the middle. And then he had a choice. He could go the long way round by the road – a long, dreary trudge through empty streets, which would add an hour or more to his journey. Or he could cut through the wood.

It wasn't a natural wood, but a new plantation on derelict land, an "Urban Reforestation Project". It

50

made a long, black shape in the midsummer dusk, but something pale glowed against its darkness – a tall foxglove, swaying at one of the arched entrances to the wood. Was it lucky or unlucky to walk where foxgloves grew?

He stood on the pavement before the wood, considering. A whisper of wind through the leaves made him jump, and shiver, and turn to look behind him. What to do? He didn't want to go into the darkness of the wood – (wolves and witches sneaked through the fairy-tale woods of his mind) – even if it was only a little, tame, Council-planted wood. But if he took his short way through the wood, and hurried, he would only be among the trees for a few minutes, and then he'd be home in half an hour, at most.

If he went the long way round, by road, it would be a long hour of silent streets, and stealthy noises, and looking behind him.

He took a step towards the wood, and then stopped again. He'd met *her* under trees...

Come on, he said to himself – as he turned to look behind him again – make up your mind instead of standing here. What's it to be? A quick trot through the wood, or a long trudge by road?

The wind was still, and the leaves hung limp, making no sound. With one last look at the grey, empty road behind him he entered the wood by one of its many hard-trodden little paths, passing through an archway of trunks and leaves. He kept his hands out of his pockets, ready to act. The shortest path would take him through the wood in less than five minutes.

Just inside the wood the paths were wide, though grooved with the flow of water and uneven with roots, and he was able to walk briskly. It was darker under the trees, as their canopy of leaves shut out the light of the street-lamps and moon, and gathered in the dusk. It was much cooler, too, and there was a smell of earth and damp. The shadow of the trees had preserved puddles and muddy hollows even through the long, hot, dry spell.

But once away from the main road, where many people entered the wood, the paths became narrower, and then Sean was reminded that it's never easy to walk through a wood at night, and impossible to walk quickly. There were hollows filled with leaves to send him stumbling, and fallen branches to roll under his feet. Thin whippy branches, blended into the greyness of the dark, smacked his face or poked him in the eye. Briars snagged his clothes and, in the dark, were painful and difficult to remove. He began to curse himself for ever having come into the wood but, by then, it would have taken as much time and effort to go back as to go on.

So he went slowly, one hand held before his face to fend off branches, which projected suddenly even into broad and well-trodden paths. A narrower path turned off to his left, in the direction he needed, and he followed it. Ahead the trees were closer and darker, and he was constantly ducking or brushing leaves or twigs from his face. A booming, crashing sound from above, and a snapping of twigs made him halt, his heart thumping in his chest – he had scared up some roosting birds, which now rebuked him with the wood-pigeon's cry of, "You fool you! You fool you!"

He agreed with them, and pushed on. The path seemed to be closing ahead of him, until he found himself trying to shove his way through bushes, and being showered with dirt, his bare arms and chest thwacked with branches, or scratched. He wiped his hot face, smearing it with bark dust, and reluctantly started back the way he had come. Obviously he'd taken the wrong path. He hadn't realized that the wood was so big. He swore as he went, striking out at bushes. Just the time to get lost (on ghost-haunted Midsummer's Eve). He could have been home by now (and safe).

He found his way back, not to a broader path, but to a clearing he had never seen before. It wasn't a place easy to forget. Moonlight filtered down through the opening in the leaves above, and showed – all black and silver – an immense fallen trunk, grooved and split and grown with fungus. Another tall tree stood at the clearing's centre, its black trunk and branches glimmered over with white flowers. I'm lost, he thought, completely lost. A little cold dread crept into him and settled under his breast bone. Such huge old trees as that didn't grow up in a few years, after being planted by an Urban Reforestation Programme.

He wandered around the clearing, peering along the paths that led from it – paths that led into a thick grey of dusk and faded into darkness. His arm had been badly scratched, and he licked it, and stumbled on uneven ground, and briefly wondered if it would be best to lie down and sleep there – but no, not in that place. He couldn't sleep there. Not in that place, on that night.

A voice spoke from the darkness, and it was no imaginary voice. The sound vibrated softly against his ear-drum. "Can I walk with you? I'm feared."

A pale tower of foxglove flowers swayed as she stepped from the darkness of the bushes at the edge of the clearing. He recognized her voice, and the shape of her, the gleam of her face in the dim light, and the dark fall of her hair... The river, where he'd last seen her, was more than a mile away. He tried to back away from her, but she moved more surely in the dark than he could.

She came close, her head tilting as she looked up at him. "I'm lost and feared. Can I walk with you?" He shivered as if her voice was a feather drawn over his skin. Her manner held no hint that she remembered him, or that she remembered speaking those words before.

She came closer still and tried to take his arm, but he violently shook it free of her and took a clumsy step back. A bush behind him jabbed its many sharp twigs and branches into his back, and he had to stop. He opened his mouth to tell her to get away from him, but then remained silent. He was afraid to speak to her, as if beginning any kind of talk with her might trap him.

She came close again, and he couldn't back further, and had to stand still as she leaned against him. The touch of her body was soft and warm against his skin; not at all as he had always supposed the touch of a ghost to be. The thickness of her hair brushed his chin, and a scent came to his nose – a sweet, honey-scent of flowers, gorse-flowers. Yet he stood braced and tense against her, too scared of her even to shudder.

"I'm cold," she said, as if anyone could be cold on that night. "Keep me warm." Her head tilted its heavy, warm weight on to his shoulder, and her hair was soft on his neck. "Put your arms round me and keep me warm."

Revulsion and fear made him act. He shoved her away from him, so that he could move away from the bush and into the open space of the clearing. She was solid and warm, like a living body, and swayed away from his push like a real girl – but the shivering of his skin and the sickness in his gut told him that she wasn't. Whatever she was, she wasn't a living girl.

She moved after him: he could see the paleness of her face, throat and breast in the dusk. "Don't you like me?" she said, and her little voice, which hardly disturbed the silence, was so sad that it tugged at the pity in him. He had to make an effort to take another step away from her, and to hold out a hand to fend her off.

"I want to get to the road," he said. "That's all. You go away!"

She tried to catch hold of his hand. "Let's lie down here and keep each other warm."

Never! he thought. He was trying to watch where he put his feet, feeling for each step in the dark, fearing to stumble and fall. He kept turning his head slightly, trying to hear the sound of traffic. The wood was surrounded by roads; they must be near one. He could hear nothing but the sound of the breeze in the leaves, his own breathing, the sound of his own movements.

"You're tired," her voice came whispering. "Lie down and sleep with me. We'll keep each other warm till morning." She made a snatch and caught one of his hands between both of her own. Her hands were small, but their grip – he couldn't get free. Her fingers were clenched as tightly around his as a tree's roots clench around a stone. It was horrible enough that she – the thing – was touching him again, but he sweated with panic as he used all his strength and still couldn't break her grip. She was pulling him towards her, her pale face gleaming in the dark and her voice whispering, "Lie down with me, lie down with me—"

"No!" With his free hand, he tried to wrench her

fingers open. "What are you?"

Still clinging to his hand, holding him still, she said, "I love you, I love you – Stay with me, I love you–"

"Let go!" He shook their linked hands violently. "Get away from me!"

She stilled suddenly and straightened, a dark shape against the dark background of trees. But still she clung to his hand. Her voice, when she spoke, was louder, and harder. "Don't you like me?"

"Let me go."

"Am I ugly?" she said.

He paused, remembering how pretty she had been by the river, and seeing her now, all soft in the moonlight. So like Penny, but prettier. "You're beautiful," he said, "but you're not real – are you? What do you really look like?"

"Do you refuse me?" she said.

"Let me go. I don't want you. I want to go."

She swung him from her, releasing her grip on his hands, so that he went staggering away from her. "Go then!" she cried. As he passed her, he felt a solid blow thump on to his spine, between his shoulder-blades, and her voice shrilled, "And that to take with you!"

The blow was so hard that it sent quivers of impact through his body, and knocked the breath from him. His mouth gaped as he turned back towards the girl, but he could no longer see anything of her. She might have been standing among the black shapes of the trees, watching him, but he couldn't catch even the pale sheen of her face.

He crooked one arm behind his back, straining to reach the spot between his shoulders where she'd struck him. He feared that he'd been stabbed, but he touched no knife, and could feel no wound or blood. Yet the blow went on aching, and his flesh felt bruised at every slight movement, not only on his back, but inside his chest. The pain even seemed to have seeped into bones, and spread up his neck into his head.

He had stumbled into one of the narrow paths leading from the clearing, and he reached out for support to the trees on either side. His chest was heavy, tight. His feet were disconnected from his control, and sent him half-running, staggering, almost falling. Every breath took such effort that sometimes he had to stop and lean on a tree while he dragged in air. His heart was stifled, sometimes beating ponderously slow, sometimes skittering in panic before being overcome by the solidness of his chest, which was so hard to move, it seemed to be turning into wood.

His eyes glazed with light and, finding no tree where he reached for support, he fell. The hard ground thumped him in the chest, but he had no breath to lose. He tried to get up but his wooden lungs pinched out his life.

A man on his way to work on Midsummer morning

took his usual short cut to his bus-stop through the little patch of woodland. Lying in the middle of the broad path he found the boy, lying face down, his shirt tied around his waist, and a big blue-black bruise between his shoulder blades. His head, lying at the edge of the path, nudged a tall foxglove, its pale pink flowers glowing in the morning light.

THE
ULTIMATE
ASSASSIN

Malcolm Rose

THE SEMICIRCLE AT THE END OF THE PLATFORM LOOKED like the gateway to a tomb. Occasionally Kate's mum and dad glanced towards it as if they expected the dead to rise and flow from the hole. Kate sat between her parents, and waited. She was nervous but her head felt luxuriously empty and clear.

Further along the platform, to Kate's left, a hunched and withered woman stood motionless like a grotesque waxwork figure from a bygone age. She was dressed in rags. She could have been part of the archaic scenes painted on the wall behind her but, every few seconds, she issued signs of life by muttering to herself. Kate shuddered. The old lady gave her the creeps. Nearer, there was a middle-aged man, erect and dressed in a suit. He carried an umbrella and a briefcase. He looked vaguely familiar. To her right, there was a group of four young women, probably going home after an evening on the town. Chatting amongst themselves and giggling incessantly, they took no notice of anyone else.

With a clunk, a coin fell from the trouser pocket of

a man as he emerged from one of the passages in the human warren. The pound coin rolled towards Kate and instinctively she leaned forward and picked it off the floor. She held out her hand to return the money. When she looked up at the man, she wished immediately that she hadn't been so honest. He was a skinhead, built like scaffolding. His bare arms stuck out threateningly from his massive upper body. Intimidated, Kate shuffled in her seat as he scowled at her. He snatched back the money and grunted with disdain at her good deed. He thudded down the platform in his heavy boots before grinding to a halt like a soldier on sentry duty. Kate's mum glanced at her daughter and shrugged.

Beyond the group of girls, there was another man. Clutching the neck of a bottle, he was clearly drunk. He stood upright in one place for just a few moments then staggered and almost fell, as if someone had pulled a rug from under his feet. Once he'd regained his equilibrium briefly, he repeated the pitiful performance. That late in the night, the line wasn't busy. There was only one other traveller. A tall thin man in a green raincoat leaned against the mural, just a few metres from Kate and her parents. He seemed to be the most normal of the passengers.

Every so often, the skinhead whistled a refrain of "Land of Hope and Glory". Somehow, he made it sound menacing. The whistle seemed to fill the station as if he were claiming it as his own property.

Opposite Kate, there were large notices about fare

dodging and posters advertising the Science Museum, a brand of lager, and a newspaper. Between each of the billboards, there were no-smoking signs and a red circle, severed by a blue band. Across it was written Charing Cross.

Kate's father looked at the black tunnel and then at his watch.

Her mother said, "We're OK, aren't we? We won't miss the train?"

"No," he answered. "Plenty of time. Just that I'd like to get out of here. It's…"

"Claustrophobic? Eerie?" her mother suggested.

"Yes. Something like that. I just don't like it."

They were headed for Euston station and the overnight train to Edinburgh. And her father was feeling uncomfortable. Kate guessed that he ached to be above ground in the open air.

Kate thought that it was a bit spooky, deep underground late at night, but she was also content to be closeted in a vault, well below the streets of London that still buzzed with revellers. Even if it was sinister, like a deserted excavation, it felt restful. It was the first time she'd experienced real peace and quiet since she'd left the hospital's isolation room. Now, the subterranean chamber offered a respite from the dreadful hustle and bustle of everyday life. Temporary relief until the specialist near Edinburgh, Dr Stead, could cure her for good. At the age of thirteen, she craved the fresh start that he promised.

Suddenly, they became aware of a subtle change. A ripple in the air. Kate's father hesitated, then declared, "It's coming." The three of them got up eagerly and took a pace towards the edge of the platform, nearer to the long line of posters.

An evil wind emanated from the tomb, like the sickly breath of a furious waking demon.

The gaunt man had detached himself from the wall painting and focused his attention on something beyond Kate. The drunk remained unaware of the impending arrival but the leathery woman shuffled slightly and ceased her mumbling. The girls continued their chaotic conversation. The skinhead, still glowering, strode to the edge as if he intended to'claim the train as his own as well. From the new angle, Kate recognized the man in the suit. She couldn't remember his name but she'd seen his face on the news recently. He was an MP and he'd made himself unpopular by airing the dirty linen of some of his colleagues. He was probably on his way home after a late-night sitting in Parliament. Waiting at the edge, he stared at the advertisements on the opposite wall.

Then there was another change. This time, though, only two of the travellers seemed to notice it. There was no real evidence that something new had come uninvited into the station but its force was undeniable and overwhelming. It was not physical. It didn't ripple the atmosphere like the foul gust from the tunnel but it traversed the cavern like an invisible beam of light – radiation beyond human perception. When it penetrated Kate's head, it became an urge, a compulsion. And it was irresistible, like an addict's need for drugs.

Not entirely conscious, Kate mumbled, "The poster. Got to take a closer look."

"What?" her dad cried.

Kate walked forward, her toe over the edge of the platform. "The posters," she repeated blankly. She began to take another step, as if she were driven by autopilot. Further along, the politician mirrored her mechanical, mindless movement. Both of Kate's parents yelled, "No!" Instinctively, they grabbed their daughter before she toppled on to the electrified rails.

The demon screamed as it burst from its burrow.

The politician did not jump in front of the approaching train. Like a zombie, controlled by some unknown evil force, he simply strolled off the platform as if he hadn't noticed the edge. He fell over, out of sight, until the train tossed his body playfully in front of it, like a bull goring a matador.

Roused from her daze, Kate could not distinguish her own scream from the squeal of the brakes. Sparks flew from the train's wheels and the clattering carriages shuddered to an abrupt halt.

The engine stopped near the drunken man. Vaguely aware that something had happened, he hiccuped loudly. The four young women peered sheepishly over the edge of the platform and then, groaning, turned away in disgust.

The wind had blown itself out. The shock provoked utter silence.

Kate, a stunned parent still clinging to each arm, turned her head slowly towards the gaunt man. "He did it," she breathed.

Her mother looked into her daughter's face. "What did you say?"

The man in the raincoat headed towards the exit.

Kate released her arm from her father's grasp and pointed at the retreating man. She was certain that he was the source of the invisible disturbance. "He did it," she insisted firmly and loudly.

At the corner of the subway, the gaunt man hesitated and looked back piercingly at Kate. He saw her pointing accusingly at him.

"Don't be silly," her dad admonished her. Embarrassed, he added, "He heard you."

The tall man disappeared down the tunnel, his face expressing a curious combination of anger, exhaustion and gratification.

More sympathetically, Kate's mum whispered, "It's just the shock, love. He wasn't anywhere near. The poor man just stumbled."

Defiantly, Kate shook her head but did not reply.

In a matter of moments the silence was broken. The driver and other officials were scuttling everywhere, taking the names of witnesses, shepherding passengers away. The commotion filled Kate's head with its intensity. She was relieved when they were led back into the tunnel and redirected to Euston via the Bakerloo line and Oxford Circus.

Despite the diversion, they reached the main-line station just before midnight, in time to catch the sleeper from one capital to another. They had reserved sleeping compartments but before they settled into them for the long journey, they took a nightcap in the lounge car. Kate sat on one side of the table, facing forwards, and her parents sat opposite as they sped out of London, away from the rat race, the rancour, and the death of a hated politician that would be regarded as suicide.

"Try not to think about it," Kate's mum advised while they waited for their drinks to cool.

Kate was not sure if her mother was referring to the MP or to the purpose of their journey. For Kate, the trip was an adventure. More importantly, though, it represented hope. It had raised her expectations so much that she could not dismiss it easily from her mind. She was excited and anxious at the same time.

Her mum's eyelids drooped and her dad sipped his drink. Calm descended on the train as it hurtled north through the black night. Kate finished her tea, sighed and shut her eyes against the dim lighting. The noises in her head had diminished almost to nothing.

*   *   *

At school, Kate did not get on well. She could not concentrate on her work when her brain pounded with the noise of her companions. She had never dared to admit the problem till she went to secondary school. There, the importance of education was drummed into her and so, when she failed to progress, she explained tearfully that the ceaseless racket stopped her working. She was not popular with the other kids because she complained about them and at first she was not taken seriously by the teachers. After all, she reported that Mr Patchett's History lessons were too turbulent even though no one in the entire school dared to utter a word in his class. As a formality, the nurse examined her ears and gave her a clean bill of health. But the noises did not go away. When her parents assured the Head that Kate was not in the habit of lying, a hospital check-up was arranged. The first doctor confirmed that her hearing was fine. He was unable to offer a reason for the horrendous noises that brought tears to her eyes in the hushed hospital waiting room.

Things got worse at school. She was a loner, bullied, and educationally she was going backwards. She grew more and more haggard and unhappy. The only relief that she seemed to enjoy was late at night. A couple of weeks ago she saw a second doctor at the hospital – a specialist. Dr Thompson examined Kate thoroughly and came to the same conclusion as her colleagues. Yet she also recognized a tortured soul. "When you're in school," she asked, "do you hear just noise, like discordant background music, or actual voices?"

"Both," answered Kate.

"And are they happy voices or sad?"

"Both," Kate replied again.

"And you say it's particularly bad in here. In the hospital. What are you hearing now, Kate? Happy sounds or sad?"

Kate was on the verge of breaking down. "Sad," she stammered. "Despairing voices. It's awful. Like the screams of a thousand tragedies," she sobbed.

"Mm." Dr Thompson kept her thoughts to herself but told Kate to follow her.

They went down long corridors that rang loud with distress. Then, turning one corner, the tumult in Kate's head transformed. She could still hear the cries of agony but she also detected other emotions. Pausing, the doctor asked, "What now?"

"It's strange," Kate said. "There's still a din. Still the sound of aches and pains. But I feel ... joy, wonder. Shock as well."

"Yes," Dr Thompson replied as if she expected that answer. "Come on. Not far now." She led the way through the maternity ward and into the isolation wing. Pushing open the doors to one empty room, she drew Kate inside and asked her to sit on the bed for a while. "Well?" she prompted. "Noises gone?"

She did not really have to ask. Kate's face said it all. "It's quiet," she murmured blissfully. "I've never known such..."

"Serenity?"

Kate nodded. She looked at the doctor and said, "You believe me, don't you? My ears might be OK but the noises are real, aren't they? I'm not imagining them or using them as an excuse."

Dr Thompson smiled. "No, you're not imagining it."

Another wave of well-being flooded over Kate. "What's wrong with me?"

"Not a diagnosis I can write on your record, Kate. Not without jeopardizing my career or making you a medical curiosity."

"What do you mean?"

The doctor hesitated, then remarked, "I once had a colleague, Dr Stead. Best junior doctor in the business, he was. But he despised the way we went about medicine. Too much reliance on this." She placed a hand on some intricate, computerized machine by the bed. "Technology," she announced. "He opted out, more interested in treating the whole body, not just the science of disease. Do you follow me?"

"I think so," Kate replied.

"He has a practice in St Andrews now – near Edinburgh. Alternative medicine and all that. I think he might be able to help. I'll write to him about you. We need to persuade your parents to take you to him for a day or two. I can't do anything for you, but he might."

"Yes," Kate mumbled, "but what's wrong?"

"I don't know how, Kate, but you're hearing the emotions all around you. We're here, isolated from people and you hear nothing. Out there," she said, pointing towards the door, "you somehow pick up the silent cries of our patients. You must be unusually receptive to the emotions of others. What you hear," she concluded, "is the bustle of other people's lives and thoughts."

It made sense to Kate. And because a doctor had pronounced her problem, it became official, even if it couldn't be categorized neatly as some common disease. At a stroke, Kate had been vindicated. She wasn't a liar, a whinger or a cheat. She had a condition. She was ill. With that knowledge, it almost became bearable.

Hardly anyone in the lounge car noticed as the train pulled out of Watford Junction. Hoping to get a few hours' sleep before arriving at Dr Stead's surgery in the morning, Kate decided to retire to her cabin. She stretched her legs and realized that first she needed to go to the toilet.

There were only a few passengers left in the lounge coach, like a dormitory just before lights-out. As Kate made for the end of the carriage, the stragglers stirred lazily before cloaking themselves in sleep. A nun sat with bowed head. She could have been dozing or praying. Round a table that was littered with empty plastic cups and burger boxes, three men whispered the dregs of a discussion. A

fourth companion snored irregularly. In another
seat, a drowsy woman slouched over a whisky and
her sleepy son leaned against her.

As Kate neared the door, it slid aside suddenly and
she jumped with surprise. She shook her head and
frowned at her own sensitivity. It was an automatic
door. Nothing to be scared about. Leaving the coach,
she looked round for the toilet. There was an axe
encased behind a sheet of glass, a fire extinguisher,
and three doors. It seemed simple enough to locate
the toilet but at once Kate was bewildered. She went
to open the door on her left but something told her
that it was the wrong one. She was compelled to
turn and stride up to the door that seemed more
likely.

Outside, the world rushed past at incredible speed.

Unable to find the handle, Kate put both hands on
the strip of metal across the top of the window and
pulled it down. She remembered that on trains the
handles were on the other side of the doors. With the
window down, a vicious squall flung her hair across
her face. Ignoring it, still convinced that she was
trying the right door, she pushed her arm out of the
open window. Her sleeve billowed. Even on tiptoe,
she struggled to reach the handle. She thrust her
head and shoulder out of the window as well so that
she could finally get a good grip on the handle. She
pulled and pushed but nothing happened. Leaning
on the door, she twisted it instead and felt it yield.
Abruptly, there was a rushing noise and the door

began to swing open. Below her, the sharp stones on the track and another rail were visible. The speed of the train resisted the opening door. Kate had to put all her weight behind it to make it budge. She was determined to get through.

Her feet were on the edge of the step and her hands clung to the lip of the window. She was bridging the coach and the open door when a passing guard, aghast for a second, dashed to the door, leaned over her and firmly slammed it shut. He grabbed Kate and yelled, "What do you think you're doing? You could have killed yourself!"

There was a thump at the open window and the carriage lurched as they were hit by the shock wave from a passing train, powering towards London.

"See?" the guard said. "You wouldn't have stood a chance."

Her legs buckled with delayed fright and the guard gripped her more tightly. He asked, "Are you all right? Are your parents on the train?"

Holding her head as if freshly coming out of a trance, she murmured, "Yes. Down there."

"OK, let's go and have a word."

Before he marched her back into the coach, she glanced into the next one. She recognized the green coat and the back of the head of the gaunt man as he retreated down the narrow corridor.

Of course, her parents were horrified. Her mum whispered, "She's had a terrible shock tonight. Witnessed a suicide. I think it's affected her."

"She looked as if she might be sleep-walking to me," the guard proposed.

To end the embarrassment of letting everyone overhear what had happened, her dad responded, "You might be right. But it's OK now. We'll take her to her sleeper. Then she can't get up to anything else."

The guard did not seem entirely satisfied but, after muttering his uneasiness, he left Kate with them.

Her mum called softly after him, "Thanks."

Outside, it began to pour. The train was moving so fast that the drops of rainwater raced in horizontal lanes across the window.

When her parents started to lecture Kate on safety, she interrupted, saying, "He's on the train."

Her parents were taken aback. "Who is?"

"That man. The thin one. The one who made the MP walk off the platform."

Exasperated, her father snapped, "Don't be silly. Pull yourself together. We know you've had a shock and this journey has got you unsettled but even so..." He ran out of abuse.

Her mum added, "Even if he is on the train, it doesn't mean anything. He was probably on his way to Edinburgh as well. And you know he can't have pushed that man."

"I didn't say he pushed him," Kate objected.

"So how could he ... you know?"

Kate's head slumped. It was hopeless, she knew.

She couldn't explain it and, even if she could, no one would believe her. "It doesn't matter," she muttered. "As you said, I must be confused, that's all."

Her mum smiled sympathetically. "Time for bed. The sooner we get to this doctor's, the better. Perhaps he can give you something to help."

In her cramped quarters, Kate could not sleep. She could not even rest. She was too scared. When she closed her eyes in a fruitless attempt to block out the world, her mind replayed the sickening fall of that politician. Even more, she recalled the intrusion on her mind. It seemed so harmless, that implanted instruction to walk up to the posters. Its innocence had distracted her from any notion of the danger that lurked between the platform and her goal. Apparently the MP had felt the same effect. Somehow the order had come from the tall man. He was responsible for the death. And, having disposed of the politician, now he wanted to kill Kate. She was convinced that she'd opened the wrong door on the train because the gaunt man had infiltrated her mind again and lured her blindly towards it. She shuddered at his power. Simple, undetectable and effective. She understood why he needed to silence her. She was a threat to him because she was the only one who knew that he was a murderer. He had only to eliminate her and he was in the clear.

Kate groaned inwardly. She felt threatened and alone. All too easily she could imagine him standing outside her locked door, waiting for his next opportunity. Everyone already regarded her as a crackpot – even her mum and dad. If she told anyone her suspicions, they'd put her away for good. If there was a solution to her predicament, she'd have to discover it for herself. Without much conviction, she turned on the light and tried to read a book. Her eyes skimmed the words on each page but she did not really absorb the story. It seemed neither real nor relevant.

By the time that the train cruised into Edinburgh Waverley, it was dawn. Half-past six. The light had dispelled some of her fear but the clamour of the waking capital produced a loud and perverse dawn chorus in her head. Before she stepped off the train, she glanced along the platform. There was no sign of the tall man in the green coat.

Waverley station was a tangle of shops, roads and platforms. Her father went to track down the hire car that he'd arranged for them. He wanted to break their journey at Edinburgh so that, if there was time on the way back, they could explore the city. Shortly, he returned in a new white Escort and they clambered in. Driving up the ramp, her dad said, "Look out for signs to the Forth Road Bridge and the M90. That's where we've got to go."

Kate peered out of the window. At least the rain had stopped. On her right, the shops of Princes Street were still devoid of life. In front, she could see Edinburgh Castle, perched snugly at the top of a hill. Yet she wasn't searching for road signs. As they meandered through the one-way system of Edinburgh, she scanned frantically in all directions for the killer. She didn't see him but she had no doubt that he was out there somewhere, tailing her.

The famous Firth of Forth bridge was reserved for trains. Kate did not realize that there was a separate road bridge. It was a tall impressive suspension bridge. Through its massive network of cables, Kate looked down-river to view the three mighty steel skeletons that together spanned one and a half miles of the river and carried trains safely from the north into Edinburgh. Below, it seemed a long way down to the water.

Trying to cheer up the rather sombre mood in the car, her dad said, "I wonder if anyone's ever played Pooh-sticks between the bridges."

"At this height, you'd need logs just to be able to see them," her mum rejoined.

From the bridge, the dual-carriageway road evolved into the M90 and they surged north. They left the motorway at Kinross and took breakfast beside Loch Leven. While her parents tucked into a hearty meal, Kate took a few mouthfuls of a cereal and then waited outside the roadside café in the fresh Scottish air. After a while, she felt the chill of the early morning and so she went back into the café to get the car keys so that she could go and get her book.

"Be careful," her dad called after her.

She seemed to remember that they'd left the car in a bay next to the café but Kate could not spot it. Yet on the other side of the road, there was a shiny white Escort. Kate shrugged. "That must be it." Perplexed, she thought about it for a moment and then muttered, "That's right. It *was* on the other side."

She stepped up to the kerb. It was a quiet road. There was hardly likely to be any traffic. Even so, she glanced automatically one way and then the other. She saw nothing. It was safe to cross. She began to stroll across the quiet lane.

Unexpectedly, she thought that she heard a noise. A real noise. Sound that came in through her ears and not directly into her mind. She stopped in the middle of the road and looked around. Nothing moved. Yet she swore that she had caught the sound of a motor starting.

Just as she continued to cross the road, heading for the hire car, it happened again. She could not see anything but somewhere an engine had burst into life and was revving up. She was convinced. In that moment she realized that it was behind her. Near the café. She spun on the spot.

Beyond the building, a motor boat took off at speed from a small jetty. Its prow in the air, it wrote an ever expanding V on the surface of the water.

Kate smiled wryly and sighed. She had become far too jumpy. Walking round to the grass verge, she unlocked the car and took her book off the back seat.

She no longer felt like reading on her own in the back of a car that smelled of polish and other people. She dithered for a few seconds, then made up her mind. Suddenly resolute, she knew exactly what she wanted to do. She grabbed her coat and charged headlong back across the road, without looking.

She donned the heavy coat while she strode past the café. Ducking under a chain, she ignored the sign proclaiming that the jetty was private, and headed for the end. She had an urge to sit down on the last few wooden slats, swing her legs over the water and have a read.

In her haste and determination, though, she didn't heed the end of the pier. Not of her own volition, she marched its length and beyond. With a splash, she toppled into the dark, icy loch. Her heavy coat absorbed water straight away and its extra weight dragged her down.

In panic, she couldn't tell whether she was trying to swim to the surface or to the bottom. But she felt as if she were bursting. Water surrounded her, caressed her. Then her head broke the surface. She spluttered and gasped a mouthful of air and water. She choked. Her arms flailed for a moment before she dipped under again.

She coughed under water and tried not to breathe in. Her body burned and her skin froze. Kicking out with her legs, she came to the surface again. She thrashed about like a giant fish resisting the pull of a fisherman's line. Then her fingers felt something.

She tried to grip it but her numb fingers slipped off it. She went down again. Underwater, she felt a painful stab in the back. She rolled over and lunged at the weapon.

She had tenaciously grabbed a thin pole and submitted to its momentum. It dragged her slowly up and out into the air. In a moment, she found herself clinging to the edge of the jetty, coughing and spluttering till her whole body ached. Above her, a fisherman put down the rod that he'd used to land her, slipped his hands under her arms and lifted her on to the pier where she lay gasping like a stranded fish. Her book floated sadly, abandoned and forgotten, in the loch.

She was only vaguely aware of the next few minutes. Her parents trampled along the jetty. Someone carried her back into a warm private room in the café. Her mother stripped her and dried her with a big soft towel. Some fresh clothes appeared and she was wrapped in them. Her parents talked to someone about a doctor. She heard them saying that they were on their way to a doctor anyway.

When she had recovered sufficiently to stand on her own and murmur that she was all right, she was bundled back into the car. Without delay, they drove along the small twisting road to St Andrews. Anxiously, her mum glanced back every few minutes to check on her. She coughed occasionally but she really was OK. The rest in the car was working wonders. By the time that they found Dr Stead's surgery, she had regained her colour. She was composed but tired.

Waiting for Dr Stead, Kate did not know what to expect. She was not naive. She was not anticipating a witch-doctor who could snap his fingers or wave a wand and end her torture. She knew that nothing happened overnight. Besides, even if he could cure her, there was little he could do about the crazed killer who was stalking her.

If he had not come into the small waiting room and announced himself as Dr Terry Stead, Kate would not have taken him for a doctor. He had none of the seriousness and detached authority of doctors. He was short and tubby, with the smile of a concerned friend. He didn't even dress like a medical practitioner. He wore an old jumper with a hoop of white animals, possibly reindeer, for a pattern.

When Kate's parents began to describe their daughter's problem and her recent odd behaviour, Dr Stead put up both hands to stop them. "Whoa, whoa!" When he had their attention, he said, "Look. I don't mean to be rude, but I don't operate like that. Dr Thompson has told me all I need to know. I don't want further explanations, I just need time with your daughter." He looked into her face and asked, "Is that all right? We talk in my surgery for … as long as it takes, then we decide if there's anything I can do."

Kate nodded.

The doctor walked up to her and put his plump white hands on her shoulders. He had a gentle touch. Moving his warm right hand on to her neck and then to the back of her head, he deduced, "You're tired. Tense. And ... frightened. Are you scared of me?"

"No," she mumbled. "It's not you."

He released her. "OK. Let's go." Asking her parents to wait, he led the way to his surgery.

It was a surgery like no other that she had seen. Apart from a bed, an apparatus for measuring blood pressure, and a stethoscope, there was none of the paraphernalia of a medical practice. In the hub of the room there were two easy chairs and Dr Stead invited Kate to sit on one while he took up his position in the other. He did not speak immediately yet his silence made her feel calm rather than uncomfortable. Doctors normally put her on edge but there was something immensely relaxing about Dr Stead.

"Usually," he said, "I check out a patient first. A physical examination to find out if someone's missed something obvious, but not in your case. Dr Thompson's already examined you and she doesn't miss anything. From her letter, she seemed satisfied that somehow you're picking up the ... babble of everyday life."

"Yes."

"Do *you* think she's right?"

Kate murmured, "Yes."

"Do you mind if I try a little test?"

She would have trusted Dr Stead with her life. "No. I don't mind. I'm used to tests."

"OK. Just sit for a moment and, when I knock on that door, tell me what comes into your mind." He walked to another internal door and then looked back at Kate. "Ready?" he asked. Seeing her nod, he tapped twice.

There was no hesitation. She did not really hear the word "dog" and she could not see the image of a dog in her mind, but the characteristics of a dog formed in her head. A creature kept on a lead. Dependable. Faithful. Keen eyes. And a name of... Kate concentrated, then surprised herself by announcing, "Chips the dog. He's got good eyes."

Dr Stead shook his head in awe. "Remarkable," he uttered.

He opened the door and said, "Meet my friend, Mark, and his dog, Chips."

Kate's mouth opened. A young man with dark glasses made his way carefully into the surgery, led by a labrador.

"Mark's been blind since birth," Dr Stead informed her. "He's had to rely on other senses..."

"And Chips," Mark interjected. He held out his hand in Kate's direction.

Kate stood up, walked to him and shook it. He held her hand for longer than normal, as if he were extracting information about her from it. His behaviour did not make Kate feel uneasy. Quite the

85

opposite. He was about twenty, handsome, and his smile was kind, yet his sun-glasses distanced him from her.

Dr Stead explained, "Mark's telepathic. The only definite telepath I know. Think about something else, Mark."

Kate giggled happily.

Dr Stead asked, "Well? What's the joke?"

"He's ... complimenting me," Kate admitted. "He thinks my hand felt nice. Is that right?" she asked Mark without embarrassment.

"Yes," Mark declared. More sombrely, he added, "And I hope Terry can get rid of your fear and worry."

Kate nodded. For the first time she felt that she was among friends who understood and acknowledged her condition. It came as a huge relief to her.

Dr Stead opened the door for Mark and Chips, saying, "Can I rely on you for the next few days? Can you help us sort this thing out?"

Mark smiled as if he'd been asked an unnecessary question. "Of course."

Dr Stead tried to spell it out to Kate's parents. "I'm absolutely convinced. Kate is highly receptive – telepathically. She 'hears' the feelings of everyone around her. No wonder she has problems. It must be like living in an asylum where all the inmates scream their private torments constantly. No one could thrive like that."

Still astonished by the diagnosis, her parents

accepted it as if they were clutching at a straw. "Can you cure it?"

Dr Stead sighed. "This isn't a disease. There's no cure in the normal sense. But I can help. It's more a matter of training the mind than curing."

"Can you do it? At this visit? How long does it take?"

Dr Stead nodded. "No time like the present. Besides, Kate needs help right now. It'll be three or four days, I guess."

Her parents looked at each other, then agreed. "It's more than we expected but we're booked into a bed-and-breakfast place that'll have us for as long as we like. We'll stay – if you think it'll sort her out."

"We'll do our best," the doctor replied.

In the afternoon, Kate returned to the surgery. In Dr Stead's office, she unwound and listened to his reassuring voice. "You know sometimes you can be reading a book and you get to the bottom of a page and realize that you haven't taken in a single word? It might be because you're tired or simply because your brain switches off or drifts – diverts to some-thing else. It can happen when you're watching telly as well. All of a sudden you find that you're not with the plot at all. It's like waking up, but you haven't been asleep. Well," Dr Stead proclaimed, "we've got to educate your brain to divert attention from your noises. Just like that drifting feeling or switching off. Let the noises drift into the distance. That's all.

Control over your own brain. It's not easy but you can do it. You need to reclaim your own mind."

"How?" To Kate, it sounded impossible. The sounds in her head were so persistent that it would take more than idle thought to shift them.

"It's called many things. Religious chanting, transcendental meditation, incantations. That sort of thing. I'm going to teach you to calm everything down. To push away the world. Not by becoming a recluse but in your mind. All right?"

Kate shrugged. "I think so. I'll try anything."

"OK," said Dr Stead. "Whatever you've heard, the method isn't mystic or magic, it's just using the brain's natural capabilities. It's based on relaxation, shutting down, and a little internal chanting to occupy the brain. Bet you've come across science fiction where the goodies defeat the nasty out-of-control computer by getting it to work on an unending sum or confuse it with an impossible dilemma." He laughed. "Well, it's not such a daft idea. I'm going to show you how to do something similar to yourself."

For the next two days, with infinite patience, Dr Stead taught Kate how to be calm, to loosen her muscles one by one, to focus her brain on a single sound that she generated herself and repeated in her mind till the real world simply faded away.

On the third day of training, it happened. The method clicked into place as if it were the most natural and easy thing in the world. She was sitting, hands on her lap, fingertips touching, eyes closed, in an office in St Andrews but she could have been anywhere. On a desert island, floating in the middle of an ocean, or on the moon.

When she opened her eyes, feeling so serene that she could be the last person on earth, Dr Stead beamed at her and said, "You've done it. You blocked out everything, didn't you? Utterly."

Kate grinned widely. "I think so. In fact, yes, I know I did."

"I know as well. While you relaxed Mark came in and projected enough thoughts at you to wake the dead. You didn't even know!" Dr Stead was clearly delighted with her success.

Kate was staggered and overjoyed. It reminded her of learning to ride a bike years ago. Then, she could hardly believe it when her father had let go of the saddle and she really was riding independently. Now, she could hardly believe that she had taken control of herself. But deep down she knew that she had. She could cope with life. It was as exhilarating as rebirth. Even more, it was rebirth into an idyllic world – as if someone had held up a hand and silenced everything for her benefit. "It was tremendous," she sighed.

The next day was a time for consolidation, joy and confidences. Again, Mark tested her, yet, thankfully, she found that even his strongest thoughts could not intrude on her composure. When she emerged refreshed from her session, he celebrated with her

as well. Dr Stead told her that she could use brief
periods of meditation as she sat in a car, at school, in
a dentist's waiting room, anywhere, to top up her
new found ability to push away the hubbub.
Gradually, she would become oblivious to it all of the
time as her subconscious took control of the method
and used it while she got on with her life.

On impulse, she flung her arms first round Dr
Stead, then round Mark. She was free.

Later, after Mark had gone and she was seeing Dr
Stead for the last time, she confided in him. Like a
friendly priest, it was easy to make a confession to
him. She told him about the gaunt man, the
politician, the incidents on the train and the jetty.

Dr Stead listened to her in silence, a concerned
frown on his face. Kate knew that, at long last,
someone was taking her story seriously.

When she finished, he remarked, "You don't really
need me to tell you what's going on. You know
yourself."

Kate nodded slowly. "I guess so. He's telepathic,
that tall thin man, isn't he? And he can plant an
idea in someone's brain. A bit like those horrible
hypnotists on telly who get someone in the audience
to act like a chicken or whatever. They look normal
but they don't know what they're doing. This man
can do the same at a distance. And it doesn't have to
be dramatic. Just a slightly offbeat idea can put
someone in danger, can't it? Take a closer look at the
posters. The jetty's longer than you think. The

toilet's behind the outside door."

"So it seems," Dr Stead replied. "He's an assassin. And it's a simple, elegant method of killing. No weapons. Death by distraction. It leaves no clues and the victims die apparently in accidents." Horrified, he shivered. "The ultimate assassin. He must be able to guide his thoughts to one person – the victim. In the Underground, he targeted the MP but, because you're so much more receptive than anyone else, you picked it up as well. A bit like a torch beam, he focuses on one spot but there's a bit of scattered light that only the most sensitive eyes can detect."

"And that's me – sensitive," Kate murmured regretfully. "He's after me because I saw it. He tried to kill me because I'm a sort of witness."

Dr Stead nodded. "I'm afraid it looks like it. But now," he continued in a more optimistic tone, "you can protect yourself from him. If Mark couldn't penetrate your block, this assassin won't be able to."

Kate looked into the doctor's eyes. He meant it. He wasn't trying to give her unwarranted confidence. He had taught her how to deal with the unbearable babble of ordinary life and, at the same time, equipped her with a shield against the man who had followed her all the way to Scotland. "Yeah," she said. "You're right." She could smile again. "I'm safe from him." Her body tingled with an immeasurable sense of deliverance.

"That's right," Dr Stead assured her. "You've got nothing to worry about any more."

Kate owed Dr Stead a huge debt. It was infinitely greater than the amount that her father had written on a cheque. She probably owed him her life. She did not tell her parents that he had given her more than a remedy because she did not want to worry them about a threat that had already been countered. Besides, she was still not sure that they would believe her.

While her parents packed and settled the bill at the guest-house, Kate walked through the remains of the cathedral and down to the old harbour wall. She was enjoying the air but, more importantly, it was her act of defiance. She was certain that the killer was watching her. She was also sure that he could no longer pierce her mind. She stopped on the stone arm that reached out into the sea and looked over the edge to where the grey waves thudded against the stone. She knew that somewhere the gaunt man was willing her to take another step, but she had diverted her mind. She turned her head and saw a figure in the distance beside the magnificent arch of the ruined cathedral. It was him, she was sure, and he was projecting his malevolent message like a beacon. But he would not have her and neither would the sea. She lingered at the edge, a little nervous but still intent on demonstrating her immunity. And it was not just the assassin that she could cast aside. She felt at peace with the world rather than repulsed by it. The conflict had disappeared for ever. When she retraced her steps, the man by the arch had gone.

In the back of the car, heading south on the M90, Kate felt cheerful. She sat calmly practising Dr Stead's technique for excluding the hue and cry of Edinburgh. It would be her first test in a big city and she expected to pass with flying colours.

Her parents were looking forward to an easier life, seeing their daughter progress at school and acquire friends like any normal girl. Having stayed longer than planned in St Andrews, her dad had given up on the idea of sight-seeing in Edinburgh. He was eager to return home and so he was driving over the speed limit. They talked happily as they raced towards Waverley station and the midday train to London. They would be home shortly after nightfall.

Still incredulous, Kate's mum twisted in her seat and asked, "And you really think he's helped you, love?"

"Yes, Mum. Definitely."

"Thank goodness." Five years of worry had slipped from her face.

Kate's dad looked like a man just released from prison. "No more noises?"

"I can let them in if I want to," Kate commented. "But I can get rid of them when I want to as well."

"That's grand," he said, gazing at her in the rear-view mirror. "It was worth the time and money, then."

Kate smiled and nodded. "It was worth everything."

In the front, her parents glanced contentedly at each other, their eyes sparkling.

"Look," her father added. "Coming up to the bridge again. Tremendous, isn't it?"

The tower of the Forth Road Bridge loomed impressively in front of them.

"Sure is," her mother responded.

Kate's dad glanced at his watch and said, "Won't be long." There wasn't much traffic so he put his foot down a bit more.

Kate felt something. It was like a gale against a bedroom window. She knew that it could batter on the glass as much as it liked but she was safe within. A mere breeze might make its way through a crack in the frame and ruffle the curtain but the wind would be stripped of its strength. In her brain she felt the breeze but Dr Stead's barrier held firm.

With a sudden sense of terror, Kate understood. She sat bolt upright. The car was still accelerating. Her mum looked petrified. "Steady, love," she mumbled to her husband. In the mirror, Kate noticed that her father's eyes stared vacantly into the distance. He was seeing a way ahead that had been manufactured in his mind. She screeched, "Dad! No! It's not real. He's making you see it!" She clutched his shoulders and shook him.

But she could not reach him. He was in the grip of the assassin. It might as well have been the gaunt man himself in the driver's seat. Kate did not have the power to dislodge him.

Both Kate and her mum screamed as they veered off the road just before reaching the bridge. The car was travelling so fast that it smashed through the safety barrier and then the fence at the edge of the precipice.

On the mound beside the road, the gaunt man stood, surveying his handiwork. Below him, the car leapt off the headland, leaving behind it scattered splinters of the fence drifting in the air. After the noise of the crash, the car plummeted in total, awful silence. In an elegant slow-motion dive, it dipped its nose till it was falling vertically. Squawking, several seagulls dispersed from the hillside. On the first impact, the front end of the car crumpled with a hideous thud. The engine was pushed violently back into the car. The cries of the passengers were inaudible. The car bounced like a carelessly abandoned child's toy.

It somersaulted and next thumped into the embankment on its roof. For a moment it looked like a dying insect, writhing on its back. The roof buckled and collapsed, crushing the occupants. Then there was an explosion. The car burst into flame. Fire roared ferociously and thick black smoke rose from the spot. The barely recognizable vehicle began to gambol down the steep slope as a twisted tangle of metal, flame and smoke. Glass shattered. A burning wheel came adrift and raced down the hillside on its own. The blistered bonnet sprang into the air and lodged in a bush. The back bumper flew off. In a series of ghastly impacts with the bank, the remains of the car tumbled downwards. The land, intent on tossing the wreck into the river, would not allow it to rest. It cartwheeled twice more and then plunged with a splash and a hiss into the Firth of Forth. The flames were extinguished and the unearthly silence returned.

On the ridge, towering above the black pall, the gaunt unremarkable man smiled to himself as if all his wishes had just come true. He was tired but pleased. In disposing of the girl, he'd learned something about himself. He'd been able to lock on to his victim, her father, as soon as their car had come into view. It meant that as long as he could see his target, even a moving target, he could begin to weave his spell. The extent of his ability could still surprise and delight him. Having used it to take care of the loose end, the world had opened to him. He could ply his trade in safety, free from detection. The police would not even suspect that crimes were being committed. Word of his prowess would soon spread. It would start with the Minister who had paid for that first assassination. Before long, his efficiency and reliability would become legendary. His power over life would be ultimate.

THE RATTAN COLLAR

Garry Kilworth

David and Ruth Hammond were astonished when their uncle, Jack Hammond, arrived on the doorstep of the farm holding a battered suitcase in one hand and grasping the end of a piece of rope in the other.

Attached to the rope was a live pot-bellied pig, wearing a scruffy collar.

The dusty-dark creature was like no pig they had ever seen before. Its stomach touched the ground. There were rolls and ridges of fat around its neck and down its back. Its squashed-looking face seemed to scowl belligerently. A nasty twisted tail corkscrewed from its bottom. It stared back at them with intelligent and calculating little eyes.

"Aren't you going to ask me in, then?" said Jack, cheerfully. "I've come all the way from Borneo."

"What, *today*?" asked Ruth.

"No," replied Jack, stepping into the house. "I've been staying with a friend in London while Tippo here was going through his quarantine. They wouldn't let me keep him at my pal's smart Knightsbridge flat, so I've come down here to stay with your father and mother until I decide what to do next. Where is my brother, anyway?"

"Mum and Dad are out shopping," said David, unable to take his eyes off Tippo, who was sniffing and snorting around the kitchen furniture, quivering from head to tail when he found a smell he liked. "I'm not sure they'll like your pig either, Jack."

From the moment that Jack brought his pig inside, a cold atmosphere crept into the house. It seemed to come from the thick stone walls, as if the presence of someone, or some*thing,* were drawing it out. Ruth, the more sensitive of the two, shivered not with the low temperature, but because she sensed something *within* the cold, using it as a cloak.

"It's warm in here, isn't it?" said Jack, inexplicably.

Jack, one of the most untidy dressers they had ever seen, with his old trilby hat, his shapeless coats and baggy trousers, his seedy-looking shirts, began to shed some layers of clothing. He took off his jacket and a tie that was now almost as thin as a piece of dirty string. Then he removed what were surely the grubbiest track shoes on the face of the earth, to reveal socks with holes in the toes and heels.

Tippo sniffed around the track shoes, as if contemplating a flavoursome and aromatic meal. Jack removed the collar by pulling it over the pig's head, making it squeal when it bent back the animal's ears.

"That collar looks pretty flimsy," said David.

"Actually," replied Jack, "it's very strong – it's

made of rattan – coconut fibre. Tippo likes it because it smells of home, don't you, Tippo? He misses the jungle, you know. The rattan collar is impregnated with all the odours of the Borneo jungle."

David didn't doubt it. The filthy collar looked as if it had half the jungle floor in its matted fibres.

"Why shouldn't your mum and dad like Tippo?" argued Jack, accepting a cup of tea from David. "This is a farm, isn't it? You have animals here."

Outside the house, the sunshine dimmed as a dark cloud crossed the sun.

"This is a Yorkshire *sheep* farm. And anyway, animals are not allowed into the house – not even old Skip, the border collie," replied David, a little primly.

"But Tippo's a pet," said Jack, looking put out. "He's completely house trained."

They both stared at the pig, whose tummy brushed the floor with a sound like sandpaper rubbing wood. Covered in coarse dark hair, the creature blundered snorting around the room, knocking against chairs and tables, leaving dusty marks on the door jamb. David was full of doubts as to whether Tippo was clean around the home. Ruth expected the animal to do its business at any time, where it stood.

Every so often Tippo would stop dead, look up into Ruth's face with its eyes glinting, as if to say, "I've got your measure – you just watch it."

Ruth trembled involuntarily and went to the window to watch for her parents, Harry and Gwen

Hammond. The instant she looked out, a spray of
rooks flew up suddenly from a nearby clutch of
crags, as if something sinister had disturbed them.
It seemed to Ruth that the world had changed
within the last few minutes, though she kept telling
herself it was all in her imagination, that she was
being stupid.

When Harry and Gwen came home they were
indeed dismayed to find their kitchen full of pot-
bellied pig. Tippo was not an enormous creature, but
he was never still, always on the move sniffing and
snorting, searching for titbits of food. When an
object was in his way, like stool or a bucket, he preferred to barge through it rather than go round it. If
the bucket was full of water, Tippo did not even
evince surprise, but continued his never-ending
quest for grub – searching, searching.

"Out in the barn," ordered Harry. "I don't want
him in here."

"Isn't that a bit cruel?" protested Jack. "I mean,
he's used to a warm climate."

"The barn," Harry cried, unyielding. "The barn's
warm enough for the dog, it should be warm enough
for a pig. If I had a sty it would go in *that*, believe
me, cold or no cold."

Jack grumbled but agreed that Tippo would go
into the barn.

Skip didn't like sharing his barn much, especially
with a strange animal from Borneo, but his complaints went unheeded. He satisfied himself with

growling in the back of his throat, whenever Tippo came near him.

Not that Tippo took any notice of Skip's warnings, and even stole out of Skip's dinner dish when the collie wasn't around.

Ruth and David were glad when Tippo was banned from the house. David was happier simply because he did not like the pot-bellied animal; Ruth because she felt more secure with the creature under lock and key. The coldness she had felt when Jack had brought Tippo into the house remained to trouble her. She found herself shivering for no accountable reason when alone in a room. There was a new presence on the farm: a strange unaccountable presence which used the dark corners.

From the moment Tippo arrived at the farm, things began to go seriously wrong.

On the second evening, one of Harry's men reported that several sheep were lost somewhere amongst the Yorkshire crags. Everyone was called out to help search, even David and Jack, leaving only Ruth to watch over the farm.

When they had all left Ruth sat by the fire, listening to the wind wailing around the eaves. Even above this noise she could hear the pig, grumbling away in high-pitched tones in the barn. After a while the pig fell silent and the wind had a beguiling note. She found her eyes closing. Before very long she had fallen fast asleep in the chair.

* * *

Ruth awoke with a start, crying, "What is it?" Then she remembered she was alone in the house. It was now dark in the room. The note of the wind had changed and she decided this must have been what had disturbed her sleep.

Yet there was something else.

Ruth shivered, staring around her.

The fire had died right down and only the glow from the few small flaming embers lit the room. The dancing light was casting strange shadows on the walls and ceiling. At that moment they appeared to be the dark shapes of trees, with vines and leafy tangles, woven together. Amongst this forest of shadows a particular shadowy shape was moving, like a beast might move through the jungle, cautiously creeping forwards, its camouflage allowing only a shimmer here, or a flickering shade there, to give its movements away to any observer. Shadows sliding into shadows, nothing more.

There was a candle above the mantelpiece and she quickly took it down and lit it from the coals. A sudden movement near her arm, a light brush with pain, then the shadows rushed into the corners of the room, becoming furniture and fittings. Ruth's heart was beating fast. She could have sworn that, just as she had lit the candle, the strange dark shape leapt at her, out of the entwined darknesses. She looked down at her arm and thought she saw faint scratches on the skin which disappeared even as she stared at them. .

When she turned on the light she heard voices out in the yard and was thankful to realize the family had returned.

When she told David of her experience he laughed, saying, "You've got too much imagination."

"Did you find the sheep?" she asked him.

He frowned. "Yes, but they were miles away."

"Something scared them far away from here," Ruth said. "Then it came back for me."

"Oh, don't be so dramatic," said David.

Ruth saw it was useless to argue with her brother and left it at that for the time being.

More things began to go wrong at the farm. Important fields of grass began to turn brown and die for no apparent reason. There was ample rain to water the pastures within the drystone walls. Such a thing had only happened before during terrible droughts in the region.

There were lots of small incidents and accidents too, like the smashing of treasured pieces of china, scissors that snapped in two pieces, letters that ended up wet and unreadable on the mat, unexplained smells around the house, strange cold draughts that would not go away, the fridge and other devices inexplicably breaking down, and leaks in the roof that could not be found.

Even Misty the cat left home for no reason, going out into the moors one day and never returning.

Harry began to get very worried. It was not as if he could do anything to protect his farm against such mysterious occurrences. They seemed to be complete accidents, freaks of nature, which had singled out *their* farm alone. No other farmers in the area were suffering such catastrophes. Harry blamed bad luck, but Ruth believed that something far more sinister was lurking around the farm, waiting for an opportunity to strike.

"Things just seem to be getting worse and worse," she said to David. "It's as if there's a kind of strange force loose around the farm, which is out to cause havoc."

David cried, "Don't talk daft, Ruth."

However, several days after Jack had arrived, David began to change his mind. He had been to the orchard on his own, after sunset, to fetch a bucket which had been left there. On the way back he became convinced something was following him, tracking him, through the darkening green, using the shadows of the apple trees. He ran all the way back to the house, his heart jumping in his chest, terrified out of his wits.

That evening Jack told them a story about his travels in Borneo which underlined David's experience in the orchard.

Jack was an anthropologist, and often travelled to places like Borneo to study primitive tribespeople.

"These days they're not so primitive, of course," he explained, "as they earn money from tourists who pay to see the Hornbill Dance. The tourists want to watch them shoot with a blowpipe or fight imaginary foes with their swords, so the local people keep many of their old ways to entertain outsiders.

"They still live deep inside remote jungles and have little real contact with the outside world. They're served by rivers like the Rajang and Skrang, only reached by canoe. They have radios and televisions in the longhouses, of course, and they receive medical attention and some education."

"Longhouses?" repeated Ruth.

"Yes," said Jack. "The whole tribe live in one single house – a longhouse – split into separate rooms for each family. The tribesmen there used to be head-hunters and still have bunches of ancient skulls hanging in the rafters of their longhouses.

"They used to chase out demons too, with the chicken ceremony, but not any more. I had to pay them some money to see how it was done."

David said slowly, not *really* wanting to know, "What's the 'chicken ceremony'?"

"Well," said Jack, lighting up a foul-smelling pipe and causing Gwen to wrinkle her nose and frown a warning at her brother-in-law, "you know. If a demon was bothering a village, causing a lot of trouble, the shaman – that's a kind of witchdoctor – would perform a ceremony with a live chicken. Borneo demons always have to have a living creature to inhabit. They usually choose domestic animals, like goats or dogs. Goats and dogs are valuable creatures, so they know the tribesmen won't kill them. During the ceremony the shaman would persuade the demon to leave the goat or dog and go into a chicken – the shaman would use a hypnotizing dance to make this happen – then he would slaughter the bird, thus sending the demon back to the place from which it had first come – back to its own particular hell."

Jack puffed on the noxious tobacco he had brought with him, until he noticed Gwen's expression, then he hastily knocked out the pipe bowl on the edge of his plate. The dirty grey ash went into the remains of his dinner. Ruth and David thought their mother would explode, but she seemed to manage to keep her temper while she cleared the plates from the table.

"What would happen," asked David, "if the shaman killed the chicken *before* the demon went into it?"

Jack raised his great, shaggy eyebrows. "Well, I suppose it would go into some other creature, wouldn't it? Some other poor animal standing close to the shaman."

"That sounds terrifying," said Ruth. "Were you on your own, Jack?"

"Yes, I think I was. It was at full moon, in the middle of the forest, with the deep silence all around us. I had Tippo with me of course – I never go anywhere without my pet. Those sort of occasions don't bother a pot-bellied pig."

Ruth gave David a significant look.

Harry said laughing, "I think that's enough of that

kind of talk, Jack – you'll be giving us all nightmares."

"Oh, surely not," smiled Jack. "You don't believe in that stuff any more than I do. It's just an interesting piece of lost culture, that's all. Even the tribesmen don't believe in such things these days…"

That evening David and Ruth crept out of the house and went to the barn. They opened the stable door at the top, so they could stare inside at Tippo without him escaping. The pig heard them coming and rushed snorting up to the door, its tummy leaving a trail in the dust. It stared up at the two of them as they peered down at it. Tippo's eyes seemed to glow with malevolence in the moonlight streaming through the open doorway. The pig's mouth was half-open, as if it were grinning at them with evil humour. The sight of him sent chills through both of them. They instinctively reached out and held hands, something they had not done since they were very young.

"*Now* do you believe me?" whispered Ruth.

David glanced down again at what he was sure was the cause of all their recent troubles. Now he was convinced that there was a terrible demon inside the pot-bellied pig: a demon which was leaving the pig's soul during the safe night hours, and creating mayhem around and beyond the farm. David realized they would not be safe, any of them, while the demon was at large, especially now it knew they were aware of its presence. It seemed to need to get them when they were on their own, before it could

stalk and hunt them down. Gwen and Harry were
rarely apart. Jack, as Tippo's keeper, seemed to be
immune. That left David and Ruth, who of course
slept in different rooms.

"Will it try to kill us in our beds?" whispered David
to Ruth.

Tippo gave out a loud snuffle, like a barking
sneeze, which might have been an impatient request
for a windfall apple, but was more likely to be an
ugly threat to the lives of the brother and sister.
They knew which one *they* thought it was and they
backed away from the barn with fear rippling
through their bodies. They knew the demon inside
was saying, *"You shouldn't have found out – you
shouldn't have meddled – now you must pay."*

Ruth and David both went to bed fearfully, carefully locking the windows and doors of their rooms.
At just after midnight by her bedside clock, after a
fitful sleep, Ruth sensed an insistent buffeting at
the door as if something was trying to get in. She lay
in her bed stiff with terror, telling herself it could be
a strong draught, but not believing it. After a while
the sound stopped, but then the window panes
began to rattle gently. She buried herself under her
blankets. When she emerged an hour later, and
listened hard, all she could hear was the swishing of
a nearby pine tree in the wind.

The next morning David told her he too had been
visited by something in the night. They stood in the
yard staring at the barn. It was almost dawn. Out in

the surrounding hills the light was struggling to overcome the darkness. The rest of the house was asleep. David wanted to *do* something.

He said, "We – we have to kill a chicken. We have to get the demon inside one of the hens – and – and kill it."

"I don't want to," said Ruth in a very quiet voice. "I can't do it. I don't think you can do it either, David."

Tippo rushed to the stable door as they were backing away. The heavy pot-bellied pig went up on his hind legs. His trotters clattered and crashed against the closed bottom door, as he fought to stay upright. He almost rattled it off its hinges. Tippo stared out through the open top part, into the dawn, his eyes shimmering, his wet snout gleaming.

He grunted loudly at them.

At that moment he appeared to be almost human in appearance.

The pair ran back into the house.

Over the next few days things went from bad to worse. Horrible incidents and accidents continued, costing Harry and Gwen money to put them right, draining the farm's bank account.

David and Ruth felt besieged. In the daylight hours they were more secure, but once the sun went down they felt under threat and remained in each other's company until forced apart by having to go to bed. In their own rooms they secured the windows and doors and kept the lights on the whole night.

Eventually Harry was called into town to see the bank manager, who was worried about a growing debt. Miserably, Harry set off with Gwen in the family car, saying they would be home by nightfall. Jack said he would look after the place, but Gwen knew he was unreliable and asked David and Ruth to keep an eye on their uncle, instead.

"You know he usually goes for a nap around two in the afternoon," Gwen said. "Make sure he doesn't fall asleep with that rotten pipe still alight – he'll set fire to the house one of these days. Which reminds me," she said especially to David, "clean up that paraffin you spilt in the tractor shed when you were filling the hurricane lamps yesterday – it's all over the floor and it smells. And it's dangerous to leave paraffin lying loose."

"OK," said David, promptly forgetting about it in his concern over more important matters.

While their parents were away David was determined to do something about the demon pig. When Jack went up for his nap, David found his uncle's suitcase in which were still the books he always took on his travels to Borneo. Amongst those books David had noticed one about ancient native ceremonies, and he took it out and began reading it on the kitchen table.

"Listen to this," he told Ruth, after a while. *"All demons are afraid of fire. If you take something belonging to the creature which the demon inhabits, and burn this item, the demon will be wafted back from whence it came.*"

Ruth nodded thoughtfully, but said, "If it's that easy, why doesn't the shaman do that – instead of killing a chicken?"

"Because," replied David earnestly, "the shaman doesn't know which creature the demon is inside. That's why he has to go through a more complicated ceremony. *We do.* We know where the demon is – inside Tippo. All we've got to do is burn something belonging to Tippo and the demon will be gone."

"But," said the more practical Ruth, "Tippo doesn't *own* anything."

The truth of this struck the eager David like a slap across the face. Ruth was right. Pigs didn't have possessions.

David groaned and put his head in his hands.

"We're lost," he said, despairingly.

Suddenly Ruth jumped out of her chair. "Wait a minute!" she cried. "What about the collar? What about the rattan collar that Jack used to lead Tippo to the farm? That's Tippo's, surely? Who else does it belong to?"

David leaped out of his chair and rooted around amongst the suitcase contents, triumphantly coming out with the collar.

"To the yard!" he cried.

They rushed outside. They ran half-way to the barn. There they made a small fire of straw and twigs. David lit the fire. His fingers trembled as he fumbled with the match.

113

"The wind!" cried Ruth.

A wind had sprung up, out of nowhere.

The flames blew out.

"Here, let me," Ruth said, snatching the matchbox.

As she struck the match with a sharp *crack* and a flare, a dark cloud moved over the crags and hills. It settled above their farm. It was as though night had moved into day. It chased out the light with gloomy shadow. Cold draughts rose from cracks in the earth at their feet.

"Quickly, quickly," cried David. "Look, it's gone out again!"

But the straw fire had caught the join in the collar where the fibres were frayed.

Ruth snatched the circle of rattan and whirled it around her head. A tiny flare spurted from the smouldering ring.

Inside the barn the pot-bellied pig rushed from wall to wall. He was squealing madly. Skip the dog was barking.

"We have to do something more!" cried Ruth, as the wind shrieked, and the darkness thickened. "Another way."

"I know," David yelled. "Paraffin!"

David snatched the rattan collar. He ran with it towards the tractor shed. There was a pool of paraffin on the floor. With the wind screaming around the farm, the darkness rushing in to smother him, David tried to cross the yard.

When he was half-way over a hideous shape came

streaking out of the shadows. It was a kind of dark
blur: a beast ill-formed in the bowels of unknown
jungles. It filled the air with the stink of evil. Thorns
spiked from its limbs.

"David!" screamed Ruth.

With terror chilling her Ruth dashed out between
the onrushing shape and her brother.

The ugly shadow ignored her, slipped around her,
heading straight for David.

David turned his head, saw the danger, stumbled
in fear. Just as it reached him, he tossed the collar
like a quoit in a curving arc.

"Catch!" he cried.

Ruth watched it fly through the gloom. She caught
it on the run, snatched the fibre ring out of the air,
and continued on towards the shed. A shout from
David almost made her hesitate. She tripped, fell to
her knees. The puddle of paraffin gleamed just an
arm's reach away. She held the collar over the pool.

"Now!" she heard David shriek. "Let it go!"

Ruth was about to drop the rattan loop into the
paraffin when someone grasped her other wrist with
a rough-skinned hand. The grip was as cold and as
firm as moor granite. She turned her head to see a
grisly old man, the *shape* of an old man, his mouth
open and cavernous, his eyes wide and staring. Rags
hung from his form, trailing in tatters, torn shadows.
His features were distorted, as if he were trying to
look pathetic, as if he were begging for sympathy.

He reached for the collar, groping wildly in the air.

115

"*Help me,*" he breathed in her ear, his voice strangely urgent and captivating. "*Help me. Help me. Help me.*"

All the while he spoke, his voice like the wind soughing through rocks and trees, his face changed shape, contorting. It was as if he were made of smoke, though his clutch was as tight on Ruth's wrist as the grip of a real man. Below the wispy body his dark legs fluttered like flimsy, ragged banners.

"*Help me.*"

"Drop the collar!" she heard her brother yell, the fear almost choking off his voice.

"*Help me. Help me.*"

Ruth tore her gaze from the old man's face and let the rattan ring fall towards the paraffin.

There was a *whumpff* as the smouldering collar landed in the pool, immediately setting fire to the paraffin fumes. A high-pitched scream, as if a creature was in terrible pain, came from somewhere on the farm. The dry fibres burned instantly, fanned by the unnatural wind that was meant to snuff its flame. It was an incandescent flare that twisted and curled many times, while some unhallowed thing desperately tried to put it out.

The grip was gone from her wrist.

Thick black smoke coiled out of the fire, writhing and squirming like a spirit in agony. Flame and smoke entwined to become one, blazing hotly until there was nothing but a dark stain on the earth.

David arrived, breathless, to witness the last

thread of the rattan fizzling away to black smoke in the small inferno of blazing paraffin.

There was a shout from the house.

Ruth and David turned to see Jack stagger out of doors, his face as ashen as a Yorkshire grey dawn, his eyes staring, his whole body shaking violently. He looked around him for a while, at the light which was now filtering back through the swiftly scattering cloud, at the grasses which had been flailing around in the wind but were now only waving gently, and seemed slowly to gather in strength again. After a while he walked over to where the pair were standing.

"Sorry if I frightened you," he told them in a faraway voice. "I was asleep, you know, having my usual nap. I had a terrible dream, but it's gone now. I feel much – much better." He sniffed the clearing air, as if scenting the alpine flowers of the Yorkshire hills for the first time. "It's as if I'd been ill, but everything's all right now, everything's fine."

Jack went back into the house.

"What does it all mean?" David asked of his sister. "I don't understand."

"I do," Ruth nodded, her face grim. "The demon wasn't in Tippo after all – we just thought that because Tippo is a rather ugly-looking pig. In fact Tippo is quite harmless. The demon was in *Jack* – humans are animals too, you know. The collar belonged to Jack really, didn't it? Not Tippo. Pigs don't own things – only humans have *possessions*."

"Heck," muttered David, "that was close – right object, wrong owner."

"*Right* owner, as it happens."

"Only through sheer good luck."

They walked back to the barn together, now that the world around the farm had returned to normal. They looked over the stable door at Tippo, who was as usual rooting around in the corners of the barn, endlessly snorting and snuffling his way across the dirt floor, ever seeking scraps of food for his seemingly bottomless stomach.

He was simply a gluttonous old pig locked in an energetic, eternal quest for grub.

When Harry and Gwen returned from the bank, their faces were covered in smiles. It seemed the computer had made a mistake and their bank balance was not in the red after all. In fact their account was surprisingly healthy.

Surprising, of course, to everyone but David and Ruth.

That evening Misty the cat came home.

BOOMERANG

David Belbin

KATE MCKENDRICK STEPPED OFF THE TRAIN AND SIGHED. Nothing had changed. The small town looked the same and, to a casual observer, so did she. Three years at university had transformed her inwardly, not outwardly. At job interviews, they'd say, "Almost twenty-two? You look more like seventeen!" as though it were a compliment. Really, it was an excuse for not offering her the job.

Two minutes later, she was in the car with Mum and Dad: small town, small talk. Kate barely listened, only pretending interest when they reached the new house: an anonymous, identikit, boring bungalow.

"What do you think?" Mum asked.

"It's ... very practical," Kate managed.

"I'm so glad you like it. Your father and I love the place." This was Mum and Dad's retirement home, bought two months earlier. Kate never expected to live in it with them. But now she was. The moment Kate walked into the hall, her worst fears were confirmed. The decor looked like it hadn't been changed since the house was built, back in the nineteen fifties.

"Of course, it needs a lick of paint," Mum was

saying, "and I've got a few wallpaper ideas. But the carpets are really quite nice, and look what they've done to the kitchen…"

Kate pretended to admire the ugly units and built-in microwave. The only good thing about the bungalow, she decided, was that it was detached. When Mum and Dad were out, she'd be able to play her music as loudly as she wanted.

"And this is your room, for as long as you're here."

Kate looked into the room without stepping into it. Her room in the old house was four metres by four of friendly chaos. This cramped space was clearly meant as a "guest bedroom". There was a single bed and a built-in wardrobe with one of those naff mirrored fronts. That was all. The room was so cramped you could barely see the ugly mauve carpet. There was no room for her hi-fi and TV…

"There's plenty of storage under the bed," Mum told her. "Everything else you left behind is under there. And you can fit the television we bought you in the wardrobe for now. After all, we've got a much bigger set in the lounge. Why don't I leave you to unpack? I'll go and make us all a nice cup of tea."

There was no phone point in the room, Kate realized, as she dragged her bags on to the lumpy bed. Getting her own phone had been a major victory, finally won on her fourteenth birthday. Now it was lost.

Back in the kitchen, Kate ate sickly slices of shop-bought cake and gulped down tea while Dad asked blunt questions about her career prospects. Kate faked bland optimism.

"I always said electrical engineering was no career for a girl," Dad pronounced. "If you'd listened to me and gone into personnel, you'd have a job by now."

"Daddy, I've got an Upper Second degree and lots of skills which won't go out of date. I'll get a job eventually. It's nothing to do with my being a ... woman. Carl hasn't got a job yet either, and he's fourteen stone and six foot three."

"You're still seeing that Carl, are you?" Mum asked, changing the subject with her usual lack of subtlety.

"Yes. I said I'd ring him when I got here. Where's the phone?"

"In the hall, dear. But can't it wait until after six, when it's the cheap rate?"

"I suppose so."

Kate looked at her watch. Five past four. Dinner would be at six precisely, so she'd be lucky to talk to Carl before seven. Already, she could see this place driving her crazy.

"About money..." Dad said.

"I'll sign on tomorrow," Kate assured him.

"As long as you know," Dad lectured, "we're on a fixed income now, and this house needs a fair amount spending on it: decoration, rewiring, curtains ... they don't come cheap. You'll have to pay for your keep, not expect handouts."

"Yes, Dad. I think I'll go to my room now, finish unpacking."

Kate hurried out of the dining room before Dad quizzed her about the size of her overdraft and student loan, which were none of his business. Between the two, she owed nearly four thousand pounds, an impossible sum. But most of her friends were in the same boat. It wasn't Kate's fault. She'd get a job soon, and begin repaying it.

Kate sat on the bed of her childhood and burst into tears. Already, she hated being here. The McKendricks were not a close family. Her parents might as well have been orphans, for the amount Kate saw of her grandparents while growing up. On leaving university, she'd intended to get a job, set up house with Carl, and visit them maybe once a year. Instead, she was living at home again. So was Carl.

The media had a phrase for people like her and Carl: *the boomerang generation*. Just when you thought they'd left home for good, your kids came hurtling back, in debt, unemployed and unemployable. There were more graduates than ever before, but fewer jobs. Some people ended up living with their parents for years and years.

Kate rang Carl at twenty to seven, but he'd already gone out for the evening. He had lots of friends in Sheffield. Kate envied him. It was time for her to renew her friendships. She got out her address book and began ringing round. First Evelyn.

"Eve's not come home since finishing uni," Evelyn's mum said. "She's in Greece, with her boyfriend. Then she starts her civil service training in London as soon as she gets back. But I'll tell her you called, Kate. I'm sure she'll send you a post-card."

Next, Ruth.

"Didn't she tell you? Ruth's gone to Kenya, doing VSO."

Maybe Karen...

"Karen's stayed in Glasgow, she liked it there so much. She's applied to do a Ph.D., but she's working in a museum for now."

Evelyn, Ruth and Karen were the friends who Kate always saw when she came home during vacations. It was no surprise that they had found ways to avoid returning at the end of their courses. Given half a chance, Kate would have done the same. Her friends wouldn't be coming back here – to nowheresville – any more often than they could help it. Therefore, Kate was stuck with her other friends, the ones who'd never left in the first place. It was humiliating but she was trapped here until she got a job, or Carl did.

Petra.

"Didn't you hear, she got married at Easter? You don't know Darren, do you? I'll give you her number, Kate, but she's not too sociable at the moment. She's expecting a baby any day."

Clare.

"You can meet her in the Rose and Crown, if you want. But she'll be behind the bar. That's where she works. Only job she could get, after a year on the dole. Four 'A' levels she's got. I always told her she should go to university like you, Kate. I'll bet you've got something better than a bar job lined up..."

Judith.

"Kate? Kate who? Oh, it's you, Kate. I didn't think you'd be back, not after your parents moved. Where are they now...? Still in town? You mean, you're back living with them? *Gross*. Yeah, a drink, why not? But it can't be tonight. I've got to wash my hair, prepare for an interview tomorrow ... senior cosmetics consultant at Boots. All right, the Rose and Crown. Eight tomorrow. See you then."

In the morning, Kate asked Dad if she could borrow the car to go into town and sign on.

"I'm sorry, Kate. We didn't think you'd be back, so we took you off the insurance."

"Couldn't you put me back on again?"

"But then we'd lose our over-fifties discount. It costs an awful lot to insure drivers under twenty-five."

Kate checked the timetable. The bus stop was a ten minute walk and there was only one bus an hour. If she wanted to get home from the pub tonight, she would have to leave an hour before closing.

When she eventually got into town, the girl behind the counter at the DSS told Kate that her grant was meant to last her until the end of the month. She wouldn't get any money until the middle of August. In desperation, Kate showed the girl her bank statement. It made no difference.

"You're lucky you can live with your parents, aren't you?" The girl said, with a chirpy, irritating smile.

Suddenly, Kate recognized her. It was Trudy, from her year, who'd left school at the end of the fifth form. *I've got a job and you haven't*, her sick smile seemed to say. Kate wanted to punch her.

The bus fare into town was treble what it had been from the old house. Four journeys in a day left Kate with little money for drinks. In the Rose and Crown, Judith insisted on buying fizzy wine. She'd got the job. As the evening wore on, they switched to cider and spritzers. Drink made Kate depressed. She had nothing to say to Judith, or anyone.

When ten came, Kate was glad for the excuse to catch the last bus home. She would not have to pretend interest in conversations about make-up and Club Med holidays. Nor would she have to buy another round of expensive drinks. The journey home took a long time, though, and the dark, lonely walk from the bus stop was frightening. When she got to the bungalow, it was in darkness. Kate let herself in and watched the end of *Newsnight*. After a few minutes, Mum came into the room in her blue nylon dressing gown.

"Can you turn that down, dear? You woke us both up when you came in and now the noise from the television is giving your father a headache. We're always asleep by ten these days."

Kate went to the spare bedroom and listened to music on her walkman until the batteries ran out.

Over the next two weeks, Kate applied for every job going, anywhere. The monotonous replies began to come back. Kate was over-qualified. The vacancy was taken. Most places didn't bother to reply at all. The only interview she got was for a job she could have done with her eyes shut: trainee electrician. The interviewer spent most of his time staring at her legs.

"We called you for interview to see if your application was a joke," the man said. "You're way too good for us. We couldn't pay you a quarter of what you're worth."

"I'll take it," Kate told him, earnestly. He frowned, then smiled sympathetically.

"Job's already taken. The boss's brother-in-law's son. But we'll keep you on our files. And a word of advice since you've come all this way – if you're applying for jobs you're over-qualified for – lie. By the way – fancy going out for a drink with me tonight?" The bloke was attractive and Kate could have used the company. But she was in love with Carl, so she said no.

*　　*　　*

The next morning, she got a letter from Carl. She'd written to him, saying how much she missed him, that she wanted to visit him in Sheffield. In fact, she'd almost decided, she would go there, move in with him – live *anywhere*: Carl said there were council flats to be had on some of the roughest estates. Anything was better than this dreary, braindead suburb, where everybody washed their cars on Sunday morning as though it were part of their religion.

Kate fingered the letter lovingly over breakfast. She wanted to savour the anticipation of this, her first letter from Carl. They'd never needed to write before. Carl was clever, but he was useless on the telephone, virtually monosyllabic. In person, he was the funniest guy she knew, but she hadn't seen him for seventeen days.

I've got a job, he wrote, *with a firm belonging to an old friend's father. It's not using my degree, but it's got prospects.*

Kate's heart leapt. She could go there and move in with him now. They could even get married...

Thing is, the letter went on, *my old friend, Helen ... Well, the truth is, she was more than a friend. I never told you about her before because I thought it was over. Then, when we met up the day after I got home, all the old feelings were there. What I'm trying to say is, I'll always care for you, but I need to give Helen and me another go. I hope you'll understand.*

Kate began to scream, banging her fists against

the walls of her prison, tearing out lumps of her hair and kicking the horrible, horrible bed. Her mother came to the door and knocked timidly.

"I wish I'd never been born!" Kate screamed. "Why did you have me? You didn't want me! No one wants me. I hate everyone. Go away!" She would have liked her mother to come in, comfort her, but Mum took the words at face value, and left.

Although Mum and Dad must have guessed the contents of the letter from Carl, they didn't mention it. Kate was far too humiliated to bring it up herself. All Mum said over lunch, as Kate read the rejections which had come in the second post, was:

"I wanted to get a dishwasher, but your father says that they're an extravagance. What do you think?"

"I think they waste water," Kate said.

"Then perhaps you wouldn't mind taking charge of the washing up in future, dear. Just a little contribution to the house." Kate was too dejected to argue. That morning, she'd had a stern letter from the bank. She was way over her overdraft limit.

After three and a half weeks, Kate still hadn't got any dole money. Dad cut her dead when she asked for a loan. His only gesture was to have the local evening paper delivered. Even so, he would complain about the expense and go over it himself when she'd finished, pedantically pointing out any job adverts he thought she'd missed.

These people were her parents. But Kate felt like

a stranger in their house. She wanted to leave, but there was nowhere she could go. She had no money, no credit card. If she went somewhere else, the Housing Benefit people would say that she was voluntarily homeless. It was here, or living on the street. She was a good honours graduate. She deserved better than this. Didn't she?

During the fourth week, over dinner, Mum made a new rule.

"We're not getting any younger, dear, and we need our sleep. So, if you don't mind, we'd like you in bed by ten thirty."

"*Ten thirty?* I'm twenty-two years old!"

"Your father wanted it to be ten, but I thought we ought to compromise. Still, you know how your banging about gets on his nerves. I think that ten thirty is quite generous."

"Generous?" Kate nearly screamed. "When have you ever been *generous*?" But she was silent, and all she got was a sullen stare, because she hadn't rushed to clear the plates away. Mum liked to see everything dry and gleaming within five minutes of their finishing dessert.

The curfew was the final straw. How could Kate's parents fail to see how desperate she was? It wasn't fair. Mum and Dad had enough money put away to pay off Kate's overdraft. Mum had a pension from the office where she used to work. Dad was on half his old salary and he'd had a lump sum too. Each of them was fully insured in case one of them died before the other. Why couldn't they give Kate some more of their money? She was their daughter, and she needed it.

Suddenly, it hit Kate, with the blinding clarity which must accompany a religious conversion: *she had to murder her parents*.

Once she'd had the idea, the reasons came easily. Her parents were old, past it. Their lives were boring. They had nothing left to live for. The only thing holding them together was the hatred they felt for their only daughter. Kate had guessed the truth long ago: she was a mistake, an accident. Why else would they have had a child when they were both practically forty?

If she killed them, and got away with it, she could sell the house, which was worth a tidy sum. Then there was the life insurance. Kate would have enough money to set up her own business, anywhere. She would be free, independent. She could even hire Carl, win him back.

The decision was made. The only question now was: how to do it?

In the dining-room, Mum was dusting the ornaments.

"Where are you going, dear?"

"The garden shed. I thought the lawn needed mowing."

Before getting out the lawnmower, Kate looked at some stuff which Dad used to put down rats. It was bound to contain arsenic. All she had to do was put a sufficient quantity into something strongly flavoured, so that Mum and Dad wouldn't recognize the taste. She'd have to avoid eating it herself, of course. And there would have to be some kind of rational explanation of how the poison got into the food, so that the police wouldn't suspect her. But it could work.

The next day, Kate volunteered to help Mum with the weekly supermarket shop.

"If I can't help pay the least I can do is help carry."

Dad stayed at home for once, and announced that he would clean his coin collection. Kate developed a sudden craving for strong curry.

"Your father's not keen," Mum said.

"Oh, let's have a medium one, at least," Kate said, as they roved through the prepacked vindaloos and kormas. "I'll tell you what: let me choose, and I'll cook."

"I don't suppose you can go wrong with a microwave meal and boiled rice," Mum conceded.

Kate bought two packets of "Special Beef Curry". She would lace one of them with arsenic and make sure that she ate from the other. It would be *special* all right. Before leaving the supermarket, she told Mum that she had to use the loo. Instead, she went to the payphone by the entrance, disguised her voice, and rang the supermarket's customer care line.

"I've just injected arsenic into one of your prepacked meals," she said. "That'll pay you back for not giving me a job." She hung up, and toyed with calling the police as a back up. But they tape recorded all their calls, and might trace her voice.

Dad complained when Kate said that they were having curry, but grudgingly agreed to eat it. Kate slipped as much rat poison into one of the plastic trays as she thought she could get away with. She had no idea what was a fatal dose, but she'd read in a thriller once that arsenic built up in the body. If it didn't work this time, she'd give them some more, later.

"Make sure you have the biggest portion, dear," Mum said. "I know how much you like it."

Carefully, Kate divided up the curry from the poisoned plastic tray, then gave herself most of the safe one. She put a little bit of the safe food on the edge of her parents' plates, so that they would eat that first, and not suspect. Then she put large glasses of coke out on the table. Hopefully, it would help to disguise the taste.

"Coke?" Dad said, in a sneer. "It stains my teeth."

"We always had curry and coke at college," Kate lied. "It's a tradition."

They began to eat. Kate didn't dare look at her parents. The curry was surprisingly good, a refreshing change after a month of her mother's bland cooking. Kate ploughed into it. When she looked up, nervously, she saw that Mum and Dad had barely started theirs.

"Here," said Dad, spooning some of his on to Kate's plate. "Have some more."

"Have some of mine, too," Mum said, before Kate could object. "I'll stick to the rice. This is too strong for me."

Kate broke into a sweat. Her parents stared at her. *They know*, she thought. *They're testing me.* She couldn't tell now which meat was poisoned and which wasn't. Reluctantly, she took a small forkful of beef and took it to her mouth. It tasted horrible and bitter. She spat it out.

"Gristle," she complained. "Cheap supermarket meat. Actually, I'm full up. Throw this away if you don't like it."

"You're looking pale, dear," Mum said.

"I think I'd better go to the bathroom."

Kate stumbled to the bathroom. She felt faint. Surely arsenic poisoning didn't work this quickly? She splashed water on to her face. Her cheeks seemed to be swelling. Kate felt dizzy. Then she realized. This wasn't arsenic, it was...

She reached into her sponge bag, where she kept the syringe she hadn't needed to use for years. Then, carefully, she injected herself.

"That curry," she asked when she returned to the dining room, ten minutes later. "Did it have nuts in it?"

"I thought you'd have checked the ingredients, dear."

Kate pulled one of the boxes out of the bin and

checked the contents. There was a tiny quantity of almonds in the sauce. But a small quantity was all it took with a nut allergy as serious as Kate's. She'd been so intent on murder that she'd neglected to do her usual thorough check of the ingredients list. She might have killed herself.

Next day, Mum and Dad were both in bed with bad stomach aches. Kate knew that she'd never get away with the arsenic again. Never mind. She was beginning to form a new plan.

"Kate. Aren't you up yet? Kate?"

It was an easy matter, increasing the amount of time she spent in bed from twelve hours a day to twenty-four. Kate did it in two hour blocks. It was boring, but not much more boring than her normal life. It took three days before Mum or Dad seemed to notice. That showed how little they cared. After a week, they called the doctor.

"Your mother tells me that you've been having some bad luck lately," the doctor said, when he'd finished.

"Nothing out of the ordinary," Kate assured him, but the doctor proceeded to ask her a string of embarrassingly personal questions. Kate gave the answers she'd rehearsed in her head. She didn't need to exaggerate much.

"You're clinically depressed," the doctor announced.

"Will I have to go into a ... mental hospital?" Kate asked.

"No, no," the doctor assured her. "Depression is very common. One in four people suffer from it at one time or another. Maybe more. I'll give you some pills and they'll make you feel better."

"Please," Kate begged, "don't tell my parents."

"Why not?"

"Just don't. They're old fashioned. They wouldn't understand." The doctor shook his head impatiently.

"You need your parents' support at a time like this. But you're the patient. It's up to you. I'll write out a prescription."

The next day, Kate got up, went to the chemist's, and picked up the capsules. She had no intention of taking a single one. The bottle warned not to take more than the prescribed dose and to avoid alcohol while using them. Good.

Every year, Mum and Dad went to the Conservative Club Dinner Dance. It was the one event for which Dad would fork out for a taxi both ways, as they were liable to get a bit squiffy. They would come home late, and tired. But before they went to bed, they would make themselves a hot mug of Ovaltine each, as they always did.

Kate rang Myra, the university friend who lived nearest to her. Kate's dole cheque had finally come. She'd given most of it to Mum, but could afford a train ticket to Grantham. Myra was glad to hear from her. She didn't have a job either, and sounded bored.

"Are you sure you only want to stay for one night?" she asked.

"I have to sign on the next day," Kate said, truthfully. "What I need is a good, old-fashioned girls' night out."

Mum and Dad were surprised that Kate was choosing to go away the one night when they would be out late themselves. She joined them in their nightly Ovaltine that week, making sure that there was only enough left in the tin for two mugs on the night of the dinner dance. In the morning, before leaving, Kate sneaked the tin into her room, then broke each of the thirty tranquillizer capsules open so that the powder fell into it. Finally, she added some extra fine castor sugar, to help disguise the taste. After a few drinks, they probably wouldn't notice, but it was best to be on the safe side.

Myra was delighted to see Kate, but the evening wasn't a success.

"You seem so tense," Myra said. "Is something on your mind?"

Kate pretended that it was Carl. Myra sympathized.

"I always thought that you two were made for each other," she said. "I can understand you being depressed."

Myra talked about how awful she found it living with her parents. There was a younger brother at home, but that only made it worse, because he had taken over her old room.

"I feel like a boomerang," Myra said. "They've thrown me out as hard as they could, but I've spun back and hit them on the head."

Kate sympathized, but found herself brooding rather than listening. Maybe the doctor had got it right: she was depressed. Killing Mum and Dad was wrong. Only a crazy person would contemplate it.

But it was too late now. Kate had no idea what time they would get in and no means of getting home. The only way to stop them dying would be to ring the police and confess.

"I find myself lying on applications," Myra was saying. "Do you do that? Anything to get an interview. Then, when you get there, if they like you, maybe they'll ignore the lies."

"We'll get something eventually," Kate said, unconvincingly. "It's only been two months."

By eleven, she was very tired. It was hard, explaining to Myra that she was usually asleep by this time. When the two parted the next morning, their promises to meet again were half-hearted. *Another friendship down the drain*, thought Kate. She got into town just in time to sign on, then caught the bus home, trembling all the way.

Would the police believe that her parents had killed themselves? What if the dose hadn't been enough? Mum and Dad might turn into vegetables, and Kate would have to spend the next twenty or thirty years caring for them. It would serve her right, ungrateful child that she was. Instead of poisoning her parents, Kate should have been taking those pills herself. They might have made her happier.

From the end of the street, Kate could see that the curtains were still drawn. The time was nearly midday. It had worked. When Kate put her key in the lock, her hand was shaking so much, it took her two minutes to get the door open. The house was deafeningly silent.

Kate picked up the letters from the floor, put the newspaper on the kitchen table, and began to hyperventilate. She had to go to their bedroom, but couldn't face it. She kept seeing her parents as vegetables: rubber faces, mouths drooling, eyes vacant. If only they could have stayed at the dance and spent the night in a hotel.

But there were the empty Ovaltine mugs by the sink, every drop drained. And there was the empty tin. Kate would need to clean it before she called the police. First, though, she had to go to their room. Breathing more normally now, she opened the door.

They were both in bed. Kate opened the curtains and looked at them. There they were: her parents, dead. It was a terrible thing she had done. She deserved to go to prison for the rest of her life. Her father's face in death was gentle. His usual spiteful expression had dissolved. As Kate leant over him, one of her teardrops fell on to his cold brow. He blinked, and rolled over. Kate fainted.

When she got up, they were both still sleeping soundly. Mum had even begun to snore. Kate left the room. Half an hour later, she'd collected herself enough to ring the Samaritans.

"I've taken an overdose," she said. "I want to know what's going to happen to me."

"What have you taken?" the kind voice at the other end asked. Kate told her.

"How many?"

"Fifteen or so."

The Samaritan consulted some kind of manual.

"Those are very mild. You'd have to take four times that number to have a chance of killing yourself. They're used for treating depressed people who might be suicidal. If you don't have your stomach pumped, you'll sleep for a long time and wake up with a headache."

"I've been drinking too."

"You'll have a worse hangover than usual, that's all. Would you like to talk about it? Are you unhappy? Is that why you took the overdose?"

Kate hung up. Two hours later, a pasty-faced Dad stumbled into the living-room.

"That's never happened before," he groaned. "I'm going to have to give up drinking. This is the worst hangover I've ever had. Kate? What's wrong with you? Kate? Why are you crying?"

She tried her best after that, she really did. She helped with the shopping, and handed over most of her fortnightly dole cheque, despite the bank's threats. She applied for every job going, exaggerating her experience and emphasizing her enthusiasm. It made no difference. Mum and Dad treated her with disdain. They made her feel like a spare part, an encumbrance.

"Why don't you make some use out of that degree you got?" Dad suggested, as Kate finished cleaning the oven one day. "The survey said that the house needs rewiring. Could you take a look?"

"Glad to," Kate said, between gritted teeth. Rewiring was a dirty, dusty job, and involved removing large sections of wallpaper and plaster.

Kate started in the cellar. The wiring was a mess. She tidied it up in places, but the system was so bad that a single fuse going could plunge the house into darkness – or worse.

In the space beneath the roof, Kate checked the wiring above her parents' bedroom. It was lethal, and needed fixing immediately. Suddenly, Kate realized that she'd been stupid. The murder weapon had been staring her in the face all the time: no need for suicide, or poisoning – only a simple accident, brought about by their own meanness. Kate jumped for joy and banged her head on the rafters.

"I've sorted out the wiring in the cellar for now," she told Dad. "But the house needs fully rewiring by a professional. You ought to have it done just before you're ready to decorate." Dad ummed and aahed, like she knew he would. He hated spending money, and would put off the job for as long as possible. Great.

In her bedroom after curfew, Kate checked and re-checked her calculations. This was her last chance. She couldn't afford to get it wrong. The electronics was easy. All she needed was a way to get herself out of the house the night she did it. There was no friend she could convincingly visit. What she really wanted was a job interview, somewhere a long way away.

Kate checked the paper the next day, and found a single job that she could go for. The ad made it clear that the firm wanted people with experience, not new graduates, so Kate lied about her age and pretended to have been working abroad. All she wanted was an interview, not the job itself. She needed to spend the night in Motherwell.

A week later, the reply came, as she knew it would. The interview was in ten days. They'd set it in the afternoon to allow her time to get there, and would even pay for an overnight hotel stay. Kate hoped the firm wouldn't change their mind about the hotel when they realized that they'd been conned. She'd stay on the street if necessary, just to be out of her parents' house that night.

Kate mugged up on electronics, pretending to be preparing for the interview. Really, she was checking and double checking her plan. This was her last chance. She couldn't *half* burn the house down and *half* kill her parents. The job had to be complete and untraceable.

While Mum and Dad were out shopping, Kate moved plenty of flammable rubbish in the loft to a place where it would burn to maximum effect. She meddled with the wires so that a sudden surge would overload the system and cause a small explosion. Then she removed the battery from the smoke alarm. Finally, and crucially, she meddled with the timer for the storage heaters, which was above the immersion tank in the bathroom. Mum and Dad were on Economy Seven – they got cheap power by having their storage heaters and water tank heat up over night. The timer in the bathroom switched the power on at one. That wasn't all it would switch on...

Elsie McKendrick sat in the lounge, reading the Sunday papers, while her daughter was out for a walk.

"I can't take much more of this, Ted. I really can't."

Ted McKendrick, never any good at expressing affection to his wife or daughter, continued reading the business section.

"She's driving me up the wall. If she doesn't get this job on Tuesday..."

"She won't get the job," her husband insisted. "I saw her application. It was full of lies. Said she was twenty-five and had been working in the States for three years."

Elsie sighed.

"I know she's our daughter, but she's under our

feet all the time, and always whinging. It gets on my nerves so…"

Ted agreed.

"I told you she'd resent it when you imposed that curfew."

Ted didn't know that Elsie had said the curfew was his idea. Elsie had always used her husband as a stick to beat her daughter with. But she had never been able to control Kate completely. Ted, on the other hand, Elsie could twist around her little finger.

"There's something in the paper," she told him. "Listen:

DEATH BY CHOCOLATE – DEADLY BAR WITHDRAWN

Manufacturers are withdrawing all bars of 'Tosca', a high calorie bar which is being trialled in various parts of the Midlands. The bar contains a high proportion of ground peanuts, a fact which is missing from the product information on the packet. So far, there have been five cases of people with peanut allergies being hospitalized after eating the bar.

The two with the severest nut allergies died within minutes."

"There we are," Ted said, taking the paper from her and reading the item again. "All we have to do is find one of these bars, get Kate to eat it, then – chances are – we'll have her off our hands."

He laughed awkwardly, to emphasize that it was a joke. Ted never made jokes. Elsie replied in the same light tone as he'd used.

"We could sue the manufacturers for the loss of our daughter!"

"We'd make a fortune!" Her husband agreed, a bit too earnestly. The couple looked at each other over the coffee table. Their eyes met, and narrowed.

"Hide the newspaper before she gets back," Elsie ordered.

Next day, the McKendricks drove to several towns before they found a back street newsagent's with one bar of "Tosca" in stock. On the journey home, they planned how to use it.

"If she were to eat the bar while she was somewhere else, no one would know that she had a peanut allergy."

"We'd have to make sure that we couldn't be contacted," Ted said. "So the hospital wouldn't know what was wrong with her."

"She wouldn't get to hospital," Elsie said. "Not with so many nuts in the bar. She might not get to her syringe, but to be on the safe side, we'd better take it out of her bag after she's packed."

"Good luck!" Ted said to Kate, after driving her to the station. Elsie was in the car with them. She and Ted were using the early start to beat the traffic and have a day out in the Peak district.

"I'll need it," Kate told them, thanking her mother

again for the packed lunch she'd provided to save Kate wasting money on British Rail catering. "Have a nice day."

"You too, dear," Elsie said, giving her daughter a rare kiss. Kate might as well have a nice day. It was the last one she would spend alive.

The McKendricks went out for the day. They got home at nine, half expecting there to be a note from the police waiting for them in the hall. There wasn't.

"She may not have eaten it yet," Ted said. "But she will. Kate loves her chocolate."

"Suppose she's read about the nuts in the bar?"

"The only bit of the paper Kate ever reads is 'Situations Vacant', and then only when I nag her to. Now, I'm going to switch off the ringer on the phone. That way, if anyone calls to find out what's wrong with Kate, they'll think we're out."

They finished their Ovaltine, washed the mugs and went to bed.

"She *is* our daughter," Ted said, as they snuggled down beneath the sheets.

"She was an accident," Elsie insisted, "a selfish, whinging waste of space. And it's too late to do anything about her tonight. From now on, we've got the house to ourselves."

"Home Sweet Home," Ted murmured. "G'night, dear."

"Good night."

Soon, he was snoring. Elsie worried that the noise

would keep her awake. But it had been a long day. Before midnight, she was soundly asleep.

Kate couldn't believe her luck. They'd known she wasn't twenty-five the moment she walked in through the door, but they interviewed her anyway. She admitted that her application was a pack of lies, explaining that she was desperate. The Chairman said that he admired Kate's cheek, then asked a bunch of difficult questions which she somehow knew the answers to. It came as a shock to remember that she was good at her subject. By the end of the interview, she was confident enough to say:

"Of course, if you're willing to give me a chance in this job, I wouldn't expect the full salary mentioned in the paper – yet – not until I had the requisite experience."

"That's decent of you," said James, the attractive young man who would be her immediate boss if she got the job. "We'll bear it in mind when we make the appointment."

"When will I hear?"

"In the next day or two."

But it had taken less than a day. James showed up at the hotel at seven. He took her for a drink and told her that he'd persuaded the old man to give her a chance: six months' probation. She'd move on to full salary and a permanent contract if she passed.

"And I'm sure that you *will* pass," he added. "Because I'll be the person making the decision."

148

They shared another drink before he left, reluctantly.

"I think that we're going to get on very well indeed," he told her, with a twinkle in his eye which had nothing to do with work.

Kate was tired, and hungry. She'd been too nervous to eat much all day, and the hotel restaurant had closed by the time James left. She kept ringing up her parents. She wanted to tell them that she'd got the job. They would be *so* happy. The last four months couldn't have been easy for them, either. When they'd finished congratulating her, she would mention that they ought to unplug the timer in the bathroom. She'd been thinking about it on the train journey to Scotland, she would say. Potentially – she'd realized – it was very dangerous indeed.

Ten to twelve. Where were they? Suppose they'd decided to stay somewhere overnight and they came back to find the house burnt down? And burn it certainly would. The way Kate had set it up, once that timer went off, there would be a small bang followed by a big fire. By two minutes past one, the McKendrick bungalow would be the biggest bonfire their small town had ever seen.

Kate made herself a coffee with the kettle by her bed. She would keep ringing until she was sure that they were safe. Kate shuddered. She'd come so close to doing something so terrible, so wrong...

Her stomach rumbled as she sipped the hot coffee. Kate remembered the packed lunch her mother had made her. She'd been too tense to eat much of it earlier. She looked in the plastic box: a stale ham sandwich. Not very tempting. But there was something else: a chunky chocolate bar. *"Tosca"*. Kate hadn't come across one of these before. It must be new. What a treat. The energy from the sugar would keep her going until she got through to her parents.

Kate dialled the number again, then opened her chocolate bar while the telephone rang. The first bite tasted delicious.

THE
DELINQUENT

Maresa Morgan

IF I HAVE TO STAY IN THIS PLACE MUCH LONGER, I'LL GO MAD...

Tara Prince sat slightly apart from the screaming bunch of jeering, cat-calling girls, and wiped the handful of thick porridge from the back of her neck. She didn't know which of the girls were responsible for this morning's little episode, but it didn't really matter. They were all nameless, faceless. And they all hated her, envied her. She knew that. She could feel it in the air, emanating from them in vile waves. One hundred spiteful teenage delinquents. Brash. Tough. Hard-bitten. And now she was one of them.

The noise level increased as the inmates started to bang their spoons, beating a tattoo on the Formica-topped table, baying for some sort of retaliation. Tara stood abruptly, knocking over her chair, which crashed to the floor. She ran to the double swing doors and slammed her body against them. They gave way and she ran, away from the cacophony of sound, feeling the sticky mess clinging to her hair and sliding down the back of her neck in a clammy, soggy mass.

The rubber soles of her trainers slapped against the tiled floor and echoed down the empty corridor. The floor was cold and hard on the bones if you fell. Or were pushed, as she knew only too well. Pushed and held down and kicked by a group of girls while another tangled cruel fingers in your hair... She'd had all their little tricks over the past six months: drawing pins hidden in her trainers, well-placed ankles to trip her up. The seemingly harmless pranks were affecting her. Badly. Day after day of watchfulness, like a stalked animal; she was sick of it. *If I have to stay in this place much longer...*

She pulled open the bathroom door and made her way to the nearest sink. Hot water filled the porcelain bowl as she watched the mirror slowly mist over. She stared unblinkingly at her haughty reflection until it disappeared. Tara was shaking. But not with fear. With white-hot rage.

As a child, Tara Prince had been a spoilt, selfish brat. But more than that, she had seemed to be almost eaten up with vicious, spiteful temper. At an age when her contemporaries were playing with dolls, Tara was more interested in inflicting pain. She threw sharp, flinty stones at the family pets and laughed when she drew blood. She put maggots in the more timid of her classmates' lunch packs, spiders in their satchels, drawing pins on their chairs. Any retaliation she paid back ten-fold. One brave little girl, pushed to the limit by the hurtful

154

pranks, dared to fight back one rainy lunchtime – an unwise decision on her part. A bare thirty minutes later, an ambulance sped away from the school with the little girl inside, her leg broken. Tara was crafty. A nasty fall down the stairs, and no witnesses. But no matter; she was expelled from the school the same day.

If she had been unpleasant during her early years, since the death of her wealthy parents in an airline disaster when she was twelve years old, Tara had been uncontrollable. Any grief she might have felt at the loss of her parents was soon replaced by deep resentment. She hadn't really known them – they were nothing more to her than polite strangers with far more important things to do than worry about the upbringing of their only child. Especially when they felt that child wasn't quite … right.

The years passed. At sixteen, Tara was caught red-handed, breaking into a small convenience store on the outskirts of town. It wasn't for the money – as the sole heir to her father's fortune she had everything she could possibly want. No, it was for more than that. The sheer *destruction* of the shop, the smashing of bottles, the wrecking of the fittings gave her a "high" like nothing else and made her feel as if the fury inside her was slowly being released. It was unfortunate indeed that the sixty-two-year-old shopkeeper, who had worked all her life to build up her small business, heard the noise and crept down from her upstairs flat on pink-slippered feet to investigate. The old lady was in hospital after suffering a heart attack; the little shop was wrecked.

The court case was a bitter, humiliating experience. Row upon row of gormless onlookers sat practically drooling as each case was presented, daring to give their worthless opinions in hushed undertones. Tara's lip curled – one day she would give them all something to talk about. The summing-up took only minutes – Tara deserved everything she got. The old judge used a few well-chosen words to let her know exactly what he thought of her before passing a two-year sentence. (*Dried up old fool, what does he know about the REAL world?* she thought.) Even the family solicitor, a life-long friend of her father, turned his back on her, disgusted, in the juvenile court. The family money couldn't save her now and he, for one, didn't care. He closed his briefcase with an air of finality and walked away, leaving her to the dubious mercies of the ugly, uniformed wardens. This was retribution.

Retribution. The mist cleared and Tara stared at her reflection, blonde hair now clean and damp. Her eyes, blue and cold like splinters of icy fire in her pale face, *burned* with a rage so intense it should have frightened her. But it didn't. Faint laughter, no less cruel for being distant, reached her from the far-off dining-room. *If I have to stay in this place much longer...*

It rained all day. And the next day. And the day

after that. Tara stood on tiptoe and peered through the high, barred window in her bare little room. The sky was low over the high fences, the surly grey cloud pressing down on to the twisted wire barricades surrounding the Detention Centre, threatening to burst. She crept from her cell. She wouldn't go to the recreation room, that was asking for trouble. She had almost met her match here – this place was literally seething with the damaged offspring of a sick society – but not quite. She just had to bide her time, and then she would get her revenge. She would make them all pay, if only she could get out of here. She frowned. The fences loomed high around the grey building, and every window was heavily barred. Maximum Security. No one had ever successfully escaped from here. This was where the Dangers To Society were locked away. The resident psychiatrist was here to make sure there was no chance of her being released if she didn't show a marked improvement in attitude. The provocation of the other girls was even harder to bear as she knew any retaliation would earn her a black mark ... and she might never get out. She was intelligent enough to know that she was unstable, and unstable enough to hide it from herself. The whole world was out to get her. And two years in here was a life sentence. There was no way out of a place like this, she thought grimly. Except in a box.

She moved silently down the long corridors, listening to the distant shrieks of the other inmates as they played pool or table tennis in the recreation room. She knew she would find Mason in the caretaker's office.

Mason was a small, faded black man, world-weary, his crinkled hair greyed with age. His tired eyes, deep and dark, looked as if they had seen all that was bad in the world and had been left unutterably sad. He was the Centre's "Man Friday" and the only person with a kind word for her. She felt he understood her. As she reached the open door the phone rang shrilly at the far end of his office, and she paused outside while he answered it. From what Tara could make out he was talking to the Matron. She moved closer to the open door and strained to hear better. Was he making arrangements for a doctor to visit the Centre? Was someone ill? Her mind, constantly alive to opportunities which might come her way, groped at possibilities ... a doctor from the Outside would arrive in a car which wouldn't be searched or maybe – even better – an ambulance? If so, it might leave the grounds with a patient on board... She bit her lip. No, no, that sounded too easy, surely that had been tried before? She pressed back against the wall, out of sight and closed her eyes for a moment, thinking. Surely it was just a matter of getting some sort of vehicle, something from the Outside, into the Centre grounds? And then, more importantly, getting the vehicle out with her safely inside... *Think! Think! There must be a way... Something from the Outside...*

Mason finished his call and replaced the receiver. Then he looked up at the blonde girl as she sauntered into the room. Contrary to what Tara thought, he didn't particularly like her, but he felt immeasurable sorrow for her. That one would come to a bad end...

"What's wrong, Mason? You look worried," she asked casually, walking towards him.

"You could say that, Miss," the old man replied, rubbing his forehead. "Seems like there's a virus going round. Two girls gone down with it last night, one more this morning. It's serious. It looks to be a strain of the measles and the doctor reckons these girls haven't any immunity against it." He shook his grey head, worried. "Said it's no use moving them to a hospital, too dangerous by the sound of things." Tara cursed inwardly, but Mason carried on, oblivious to her frustrated plans. "He don't think they'll last for long. Matron asked me to get in touch with the undertaker, if needs be." He sighed deeply. "Reckon we'll lose them by the end of the week." He turned away.

Good riddance, Tara thought viciously. *But damn the doctor! This is too good an opportunity to miss! There must be another way...* "Where will they be buried, then?" she asked baldly. "I mean, if they die, that is."

"Well," the old man scratched his head, "there's a graveyard out on the moor about half a mile away, just beyond the bounds of the fences. The ones that ain't got no family to claim 'em will be buried there."

Something from the Outside... Astonishing how quickly the human mind works in desperate circumstances. *Something from the Outside...* Tara thought quickly. She'd had the measles as a child, therefore was surely immune to this sort of virus? Her mind raced ahead. It was a risk she'd have to take...

She glanced up craftily. How to play this one? Better to be blunt. "Mason," she said slowly. "You know I'm rich, don't you?" The old man nodded, his eyes unreadable. She paused. This was the biggest risk of all, and she took a deep breath, trying to gauge how best to play her cards. She spoke quickly, quietly.

"I'll inherit a fortune, Mason, when I'm eighteen. That's in just over a year's time. But it's no good to me in here. If the psychiatrist says I'm not safe to be let out, then that money just sits there. Such a terrible waste." She moved towards him.

"Now, that's no good to anyone, is it? And there's no one else to inherit it; it's all mine." She paused. It was probably more in her interest to be nice to the old man, at least until she had got what she wanted. She smiled, and moved even closer to him, whispering, "Think of what a man like you could do with half a million pounds, Mason. You could buy a big house, a nice car, go on holiday. You could leave this poxy job, for a start. Retire, live a little." She paused to allow the words to sink in. "I mean, what sort of life is this, anyway? You're surrounded by nutters... and that's just the staff." She giggled, a shrill, slightly unbalanced sound. "Think what that sort of money could do for you. It's more money than you've ever seen in your lifetime, or anyone else in this hell-hole." Her lip curled. "And all *you* would have to do is show a little human kindness." She searched his face for a sign of what he was thinking, but it was unreadable. He gazed at her placidly, silently. She felt her slender hold on her temper, her sanity, begin to slip.

"Well, say something, you stupid old man!" she hissed. "I'm offering you a fortune and you haven't even said thank you! What's wrong? Isn't half a mil enough for you?" she sneered. The calm black face was like a mask. "Or don't you believe I'm worth that sort of money?"

The old man looked at her for a few moments.

"I know how much you're worth," he said quietly, and with dignity, "but I'm not interested in money." Tara's jaw dropped in disbelief. What was he? Some sort of Born Again Christian? She'd blown it. He was bound to tell the psychiatrist that she was offering bribes and she'd be punished. Worse still, an offence like that would add months to her sentence. Stupid, stupid idea! She tried one last shot.

"If I don't get out of here soon," she said, trying not to lose her temper, her voice unnaturally calm, "then I'll kill myself." And she spun round and ran out to the corridor, looking both ways before heading for the stairs. She moved quickly, too quickly to see the taut wire stretched across the top of the stairs. Her

161

cry caught in her throat as the wire bit deeply into the soft flesh of her ankle and snagged the tongue of her trainers, checking the speed with which she fell as she was flung towards the shiny white wall at the bottom of the stairs. She threw her up her hands to shield her face and rolled over as she landed, jarring her back against the sharp bottom step and feeling the breath knocked from her body. Pain shot through her, making her feel dizzy, nauseous. She could hear sniggers and running footsteps echoing on the stairs below. She rolled painfully on to one side and tried to sit up, dragging oxygen into her burning lungs. With a feeling of dread she heard footsteps above her too, making their way down the stairs towards her. The footsteps paused and she tried to roll away; she was in no condition to fight back. Mason's quiet voice stopped her.

"I'll help you, Tara, but not for money." She turned back, surprised as much as anything by the use of her name. It was a long time since anyone had called her by her name, and kindly, too. She looked warily up at the old man.

"I don't know what's eating you," he continued slowly, "but you got too much anger in you for one person. That much rage turns on a person and destroys him. I seen it happen before. I'll help you, but only 'cos I think it would be crueller *not* to help you, and I ain't having that on my conscience." He helped her to her feet, giving her a tissue to wipe away her tears.

Tara stared at him uncomprehendingly for a few seconds. And then she smiled, dazzlingly.

The lights of the Detention Centre had been out for an hour, and the only sounds coming from each locked room were the steady snoring or occasional whimper from the occupant, trapped in a nightmare even worse than the reality of the day. Tara lay awake, listening. She had a key curled tightly in her palm, given to her by Mason last week. The cold metal cut into her flesh as she lay there, but she felt no pain. Her mind raced. The old fool talked a lot of rubbish about saving souls; if she'd known he was a closet bible-basher, she'd never have asked for his help. Her teeth gleamed white in the darkness. Who was she kidding? It was his religious beliefs that had made him such a soft touch – he felt he was saving her from herself, the old fool. It was almost too good to be true. She'd had enough of his ramblings over the past week to last her a lifetime. She giggled softly; the old nutter was definitely not the full shilling. But so what? Soon, she would be free.

Stealthily, she rose from the metal-framed bed and crept to the door. The key made a slight grating sound in the lock, even though it had been recently oiled, and she froze, listening. Nothing. She pulled the door softly open and slid through the gap into the darkened corridor. Her rubber-soled shoes made no sound as she crept down to the Infirmary. The unlit room seemed as vast as a cavern as she stole towards two dark shapes on the table. The moon came out from behind a cloud and filtered through the high, barred windows, just for a moment. Two identical coffins lay side by side, glowing eerily in the moonlight, their lids closed but not, she hoped, sealed. She sprang lightly on to the table as the moon sailed behind another cloud.

Darkness. She felt around the lid and smiled as she felt it move. She sensed, rather than saw, the body of her fellow inmate before sliding into the coffin. As Mason had promised, the coffin was large enough for two, but it was still a tight fit, in spite of his altered measurements. Never mind, it was sufficient for the next hour or so. She lay back and waited.

She didn't have to wait long. Fifteen minutes later, as she had expected, four men from the funeral parlour came to collect their charges. When Tara had asked why everything was done at night-time, Mason had explained that the Detention Centre was a local embarrassment. Property prices had slumped during the building of the Centre and the locals wanted nothing to do with it. If they discovered a contagious illness within the walls, there would be a public outcry. Therefore, the Governors had agreed this was the best way. Ironically, this was exactly what made the whole plan possible. Tara had had no symptoms of illness herself, so must be immune, as she had suspected. She felt satisfyingly smug.

Tara listened to the voices of the men as they dis-
cussed football results, the new barmaid at the local
pub, an argument one had had with his wife after
coming home drunk the night before, and she shook
silently with mirth. These pathetic creatures had no
idea about life, about the sort of life she would live
when she was free. She lay still, hardly breathing,
as they tightened the screws in the lid, and then she
felt herself moving as the coffin was lifted and
carried out of the building. She felt her bones jar a
few minutes later as the coffin landed on a hard
surface, probably the floor of a van. She knew that
the Governors weren't likely to allow the expense of
a hearse. She heard the sound of an engine as the
truck moved off and bumped down a gravel track
until it reached the road. A few minutes of driving
on smooth tarmac, then more bumpy gravel and the
van stopped.

The sound of the men's voices came nearer and the
van's doors swung open, then she felt herself being
lifted again and carried for no more than thirty
seconds. Then a long drop. Her eyes flew open and
her teeth rattled in her head. The idiots hadn't even
bothered with a rope! She'd just been heaved into
the grave like a ton of bricks! She swore under her
breath, and steadied her breathing. She'd soon be
out, so it didn't really matter. A dull thud, followed
by another, alarmed her for a split second until she
remembered that the men were supposed to fill in
the grave; it was part of the plan. Mason was

prepared for this, and had told her that he would be there, within ten minutes of the men leaving, to dig her out. She giggled unsteadily; if she wasn't careful, she'd really start to lose her head. She thought instead about all the things she would do as soon as she was free. The first thing would be to have a hot, steamy bath in sweet-smelling oils to wash the stench of the Centre from her skin. Then she would go shopping for some decent clothes, not this junk the Government doled out – ugly, grey, regulation wear. And the food! She would have wonderful food again, not the slop they dished up and expected you to eat. And she would get her own back on everyone who had ever hurt her, and a few others besides. Just for good measure. All those girls in the Centre would experience her wrath. Revenge would be sweet. She smiled into the darkness at the prospect of her new life. Quite how she was going to accomplish all this, Tara was unsure. Her first priority was getting out and away from this god-forsaken place. After that, well, she would deal with each problem as it came. Her mind wandered.

Soon, there were no noises at all. Just a deep, heavy silence. She lay quietly for a while, waiting for the sound of a spade on the coffin lid to tell her the old man was here. Minutes passed. The touch of silk next to her cheek left her feeling strangely chilled and when she placed her palms against the coffin lid, she realized fully just how close it was to her face, how little space she had. Lucky she wasn't claustrophobic, she thought. A few more minutes passed. Still nothing. She frowned uneasily. The silence was beginning to grate on her nerves. Her breathing sounded very loud in the enclosed space. Still nothing. She chewed a nail, doubts beginning to assail her mind. Had Mason double-crossed her? A few more minutes. Silence. The only sound was her breathing, which seemed to be getting louder. *Don't be stupid*, she told herself. *It's just your imagination*. She listened. Her breathing was definitely getting louder, wasn't it? Then with a flash of understanding she realized that her breathing wasn't getting *louder*, but it *was* getting heavier, as she struggled for oxygen. And it was definitely getting warmer in the box. *Don't panic*, she thought. *Keep calm. He'll be here any minute now*. She strained to hear anything, the slightest sound which would herald freedom. Nothing.

Panic set in and with it, fear. She started breathing more quickly in the enclosed space, muttering to herself.

"If he's let me down on purpose... I'll make him pay for this if he's leaving me to sweat. Who does he think he is? Does he get some sort of kick out of this? How dare he? I'll make him pay for this. He'll wish he'd never been born."

Venomous threats spewed from her lips as she muttered to herself. It was becoming more difficult to breathe. Anger flared and she raised her voice, shouting threats at nothing. She fumbled in the darkness for the box of matches, given to her by Mason last week as part of her "freedom provisions", which also included a ball of twine and money in small denomination notes.

"Freedom provisions! Don't make me laugh! A ball of string is really going to help me in here, isn't it?" she snarled. She paused in her rantings for a moment to listen to the silence once more and then struck the match. There had to be a way out of here while she was waiting for help to arrive. The smell of sulphur assailed her nostrils as the flame gulped greedily at the precious oxygen. She blinked in the sudden glare and twisted her head slightly in the tiny, cramped space, away from the flickering light ...

... towards the body lying next to her...

... the flame illuminated the still, waxy features of the corpse ...

... the dark face and the grey crinkled hair...

Tara screamed.

THE
GHOST
TRAP

Lisa Tuttle

Antonia Warburton loved ghosts – in fiction, at least, for she'd never met one. She passed the whole of the journey from Brighton to Lincolnshire reading a book of ghost stories, ignoring the scenery and her sister's attempts to make conversation until she heard a magic word.

"Gargoyles," said Laura. "Would you look at that!"

Antonia caught a glimpse through the car window, of two leering, hideous creatures perched on gate-posts, and then they were gone.

"Hey, what was that?"

"Somebody's house, I guess. On the gate it said 'Teind House'."

Antonia had a sense of entering a dream. "Say that again. Spell it."

Laura did. "What does it mean?"

Antonia looked at the book in her hand, and paged back to find the story called "The Ghost Trap" by Mark Eglinton. She half-expected it would have changed, would no longer be about a haunted house with gargoyles on the gate-posts ... but it was as she remembered.

"What does it mean?" Laura asked again.

"It says here it's an old word meaning tithe, or tax, and the house was called that because it took something from people who lived there."

Frowning, Laura reached for the book. "I thought this was fiction?"

"So did I."

The car was slowing. "Here we are," said their father. "Second entrance on the right. Our home for the next two weeks. Doesn't look too bad, does it?"

Antonia made politely enthusiastic noises to chime in with her mother and sister, but she scarcely saw the little white bungalow for the vision of Teind House looming in her mind.

Marcus Geary loved ghosts, so he was delighted when Teind House, widely rumoured to be haunted, came on the market. He stretched his finances to the limit to buy it, and it did not let him down.

Ghosts walked the corridors and drifted through the well-proportioned, high-ceilinged rooms of Teind House, and he saw them every night. He became obsessed with ghosts, almost to the exclusion of living company. They were mysterious, fascinating, undemanding company. He wondered why there should be so many in this one house, and not in other places he had lived. Who were the ghosts of Teind House? He became obsessed with finding the answer.

"It's fiction," said Laura. "That means it's not true;

172

somebody made it up."

"The house is real – you saw it yourself."

"I saw *a* house. The name could be a coincidence."

"And the gargoyles? Pretty big coincidence."

"So maybe the author saw it when he was on holiday, just like us, and got inspired to make up a story about it."

"But listen to what it says about the author!" Antonia, cross-legged on her bed, flipped to the author's biography at the back and read aloud: "Mark Eglinton lives in a haunted house in Lincolnshire."

"Teind House?"

"It must be. Oh, I'm so excited! Imagine seeing a real ghost!" Antonia flung herself backwards on the bed, clutching herself with excitement.

Her sister made a rude noise. "You'd have to imagine seeing one. I don't believe in ghosts."

"Well, the world doesn't run on what you believe. Lots of people have seen ghosts."

"People have seen Elvis shopping in Safeway – that doesn't mean it happened."

"You'd like this story," Antonia said suddenly. "You ought to read it – it gives a scientific explanation for ghosts."

"Yeah, it's called mental breakdown."

"No, come on. If ghosts are restless spirits, why don't we see them everywhere? Why should just a few, isolated places be haunted? And why do places like that tend to have more than one ghost? Mark Eglinton's theory is that certain places function as 'ghost traps' – it's to do with ley lines, and electro-magnetic forces connected with underground water and stuff like that. It's like corn circles. The atmosphere creates something like a photographic plate, and the ghost's an impression left by strong emotion – sometimes connected with violent death, but not always. It could be made by feelings of guilt, or hate, or fear, or even love."

"That doesn't make sense."

"Yes it does! If you read the story, it does – I'm just not explaining it very well. In the story, at first he thinks the ghosts must be from people who died in the house, but he can't find any historical evidence for that. And then one day, he's fallen in love with this girl, and he invites her to the house, to tell her how he feels, and it turns out she doesn't fancy him at all, in fact she finds him repulsive, and when he tries to kiss her she pulls away and looks at him with complete *horror* on her face, horror and disgust, and then of course she leaves. Later—"

"I don't care what happens; I don't like ghost stories."

"Later," she continued firmly, "he sees her in the same room, standing in the same spot, staring at him with that same look of horror until she fades away... The room is now haunted by her, as if it had taken a picture of her, preserving that moment for ever. That's when he realizes that his house is haunted by ghosts of the living as well as the dead; the house is like a psychic camera, triggered by strong emotion."

Laura shrugged.

"Don't you think that's interesting? Wouldn't you like to know if it's true?"

"Of course it's not true."

"It might be, at least partly. It says in the back he lives in a haunted house…"

"They probably just put that in to make him sound interesting. Honestly, Tone, I don't know how you can be so gullible!"

"I'm not gullible!"

"If you believe in ghosts—"

"I never said I believed. I'm interested, that's all. I don't pretend I know. I'd like to find out the truth for myself. It's called keeping an open mind." Antonia found everything to do with the supernatural so compelling she suspected her sister of shamming indifference, just to tease. "And this is the perfect opportunity, with Teind House just down the road – we can't pass it up."

"What do you mean? We can't just go knocking on a stranger's door and ask to see his ghosts!"

"Why not? If he minded, he wouldn't have used the real name of the house."

"I don't care."

"Then I'll go by myself."

"No, you won't."

"What are you worried about? I thought you didn't believe in ghosts?"

"It's not ghosts that worry me, but you're going to

bother a strange man."

"He's a writer, Laura! He probably gets visits from his fans all the time!"

"What fans? Mark Eglinton? Not exactly Stephen King, is he?"

"Then he'll be all the more pleased to see me."

Laura wore the pained expression of someone torn between two equally unpleasant positions. "If I told Mum…"

"You wouldn't!"

"All right. If it's so important, I'll go with you. Keep you out of trouble."

Antonia bounced on her bed with excitement and, when Laura made a disgusted face, began singing "Ghostbusters".

But several days of their holiday passed without a visit to Teind House. There was too much else to do – family outings in the car to Skegness, Tattershall Castle, a local arts and crafts fair; and the one fine evening when Laura and Antonia went out bicycling on their own, they didn't go anywhere near Teind House.

Laura might have forgotten, of course. But Antonia, who had reread "The Ghost Trap" twice more, was beginning to feel haunted by the house. She decided that rather than wait for her sister's grudging accompaniment, she'd go by herself.

So, one rainy morning she begged off the family visit to a stately home, saying she'd rather stay in and read. "I might go out on the bike if it clears up," she added.

"It's supposed to be like this all day; sure you don't mind being stuck inside?" asked her mother. "All right, then. We should be back in time for lunch."

As soon as the family car had passed out of hearing, Antonia put on her waterproof and set off on one of the bicycles, head down against the rain. Although the waterproof kept her upper body reasonably dry, a fair amount of rain got under her hood and her jeans were soon soaking wet. She felt, and looked, sodden and bedraggled by the time she reached the gates of Teind House. She blinked up at the hideous gargoyles, who seemed to leer down at her. All of a sudden she wasn't sure this was such a brilliant idea. It occurred to her that it would have been more sensible to announce her intended visit with a phone call or a letter ... but she'd come too far to turn back now. She walked up the gravelled path and knocked at the front door.

It opened immediately, almost as if the man who now stood smiling at her had been expecting her. He was rather nondescript, not very tall, with a youngish, cleanshaven face and thinning, mouse-brown hair. "Hello," he said eagerly. "Won't you come in?"

Thinking he must have mistaken her for someone else, some expected visitor, she stayed where she was, explaining, "I'm Antonia Warburton. I'm staying with my family in a holiday house just outside the village. I hope I'm not intruding, but – are you Mark Eglinton?"

His smile broadened. "Yes, I am. And you must be one of my readers."

"Oh! How did you – of course, I guess you must get visits from readers all the time."

"Not as often as I'd like. In fact, you're the first. But I knew, as soon as I saw you, who you must be. Please, come in. You came to see the house, didn't you?"

His eyes were fixed on hers, which made her uncomfortable, yet she could not break the contact. He stepped back, into the house, and beckoned her forward. It took an unexpectedly strong act of will not to follow him.

"I – I'm not sure I..."

"But you're not going to go away without seeing what you came for? And you're soaking wet – you'll catch a chill. At least come in and dry off a bit." When she still didn't move, he cocked his head and gave her a speculative look. "You're not afraid?"

No, decided Antonia, she wasn't afraid of this unintimidating little man ... yet she felt a reluctance to go inside. Stalling, she asked, "Is the house really haunted?"

"Yes, it is. Are you going to come in?"

Antonia knew she'd never forgive herself if she ran away now. "I can't stay long. I told my parents I'd be back for lunch."

"You told them where you were going?"

"Yes, of course," she said, stepping across the threshold after him.

"I don't suppose they believe in ghosts."

"No. But I'm not sure I do, either. You don't have to believe in ghosts to like ghost stories."

"I didn't believe in ghosts until I came to Teind House." Sidling around her, still keeping his eyes fixed on hers, he shut the front door. The solid, heavy, final sound of it closing made her stomach lurch. "But once I'd seen it, I had to buy it. I had to come and live here."

"Like your story?"

"I had to write that story. Once I came to live here, I had to write it."

"So it's true?"

A flicker of annoyance crossed his face. "No, of course not. It's a story, I made it up."

She remembered that Marcus Geary had been described as an unattractive, socially inept character drawn to ghosts because of his failure to relate to the living, and felt embarrassed. "Of course, I know that, I didn't mean... I only meant, about the ghosts. Is it true about certain places being so charged with natural energy that the presence of strong emotions triggers a kind of psychic photograph, which is what we think of as a ghost?"

"It's a theory," he said, shrugging. "I didn't just make it up; I read something like it in a book by Colin Wilson, I think. Anyway, it makes a certain amount of sense. If there wasn't something special about haunted places we'd see ghosts everywhere there'd been a violent death."

"And do they have to die, to become ghosts?"

Something happened to his gaze that made her uncomfortable again. "You'll know more about that than me."

"Me? Why me?"

"I don't know. But as soon as I opened the door, I recognized you. I'm sorry if my staring makes you uncomfortable, but I really can't help myself. Because, you see, there's a ghost in the house that looks exactly like you."

She clenched her teeth against a sudden, deep chill.

"Maybe you should leave now," he said, very softly. "I wouldn't blame you for being frightened. It might be best for you to go away."

But if she was frightened, she was also excited, curious and skeptical. "She really looks like me?"

He nodded.

"I wish I could see for myself."

He let out a sigh that sounded as if he'd been holding his breath. "Come on. I'll show you the room where I've seen her."

Antonia felt disorientated, almost dizzy, as he turned away, breaking eye contact for the first time since they'd met. The corridor she followed him down seemed to waver, as if the walls were expanding or contracting around them – but she supposed it must be a trick of the light, which was very dim in the windowless space.

The room he led her to was at the back of the house, empty except for a plain wooden chair and a mirror hanging on one wall. The window was un-curtained, and the floor uncarpeted.

"As you can see, I don't use this room for anything. It didn't seem right, somehow, after I'd seen you here."

"It's not me – how could it be me?"

"You're still alive, of course, but I explained that."

"Yes, but I've never been here before."

"Are you sure?"

She felt a strange, swirling sense of *déjà vu*. His voice was too close, insinuating. She moved away, abruptly. He didn't try to follow. "I've never been to this part of the country before. It was my parents' idea to come. There's no family connection with Lincolnshire, that I know of; I suppose it could be an ancestress, or just somebody else who looks like me."

"She wears modern clothes. Jeans, an anorak … it's your ghost. The more I look at you, the more sure I am."

She wondered if he was lying to her. She wondered if he was mad. She began to edge towards the door, but he was there before her.

"Why don't I just leave you here for a little while," he said. "Maybe she'll show herself. Or maybe if you just sit quietly, you'll sense something."

All she wanted to do now was get out, but perhaps it would be best to humour him. At least he was going to leave her alone, and if she had to, she could climb out of the window and escape that way, she thought, looking out through glass at the steady fall of rain and moist greenery everywhere. But first she would sit down, just for a minute, sit quietly on one of the chairs, that did seem like a good idea, just for a minute...

"Any luck?"

The sound of his voice came as a shock, and she stared uncomprehendingly at the man standing in the doorway, wondering what had happened. She felt as if she'd been asleep.

"Did you see her?" he asked, entering the room.

She shook her head groggily, wondering how much time had passed. What on earth had she been thinking?

"You must come back later," he said. "You mustn't stay now – your parents are expecting you. Come back tonight – don't tell anyone. Wait until it's dark, and then come here." His eyes probed for hers, but this time she evaded them. What a creep, she thought. Her normal alertness was returning, and she was up and past him out the door before he could do anything about it.

He followed her down the hall. "I'll see you later," he said.

"I'll think about it," she said evasively. She opened the heavy front door and stepped outside with a tremendous sense of relief. It was all right; she'd escaped.

Behind her, he laughed. Startled, she turned back.
"Oh, I'll see you later, whatever you think," he
said, grinning.

"You mean you'll see the ghost?"

"I'll see the ghost, and I'll see you. You'll be back."

Some chance, she thought, but didn't say it. "Goodbye," she called over her shoulder, running down the
path to reclaim the bicycle and her freedom.

That night Antonia went back to Teind House.

She found herself in the small, unfurnished back
room again. She wanted to leave, but for some
reason couldn't. When the door began to open she
was pleased, at first, until she saw the man who
entered, and understood that there were worse
things than being trapped in a room; that there was
much, much worse to come.

She woke with a strangled scream, and practically
wept with relief at finding herself in the narrow bed
that was hers for the holiday, the sound of her
sister's breathing close by. She soon fell asleep, only
to find herself back in Teind House.

After the third time she decided to keep herself
awake, switched on the bedside lamp and reached
for something to read. For once she regretted her
preference for horror fiction, and raided Laura's
stash of romantic novels for something to settle her
mind.

The next day, worn out, she fell asleep in the car,
and again dreamed herself back in that unfurnished

room in Teind House, trapped and terrified. And that night was just as bad.

She was caught in a trap. Whenever she slept, she dreamed about Teind House, and fear woke her. She was all right as long as she stayed awake, but she couldn't do without sleep for ever. She couldn't believe it would continue, but whenever she fell asleep, day or night, she found herself back in the same, terrifying, incomprehensible situation. After three nights of it she found it impossible to concentrate or even to think for very long about anything but Teind House. It occurred to her that maybe this, her apparent waking life with Laura and her parents, was the dream, and that in reality she was confined by a madman in his house, perhaps drugged into this confusion. She began to weep.

"Toni, what's wrong?"

She looked up, surprised to find herself in the kitchen with Laura. She noticed she was holding a tea towel, and then saw that her sister had nearly finished the washing-up: stacks of crockery waited by the side of the sink to be dried. "Oh, sorry—"

"Forget that. Sit down. I want to talk to you." Laura pushed her into a chair and pulled another one close. "Now tell me what's going on. Mum and Dad think it's just some adolescent phase, but I know better. Something's happened. What is it?"

Antonia looked at her sister and shook her head foggily.

"Look, this is your sister speaking. You can tell me.

Whatever it is. I won't tell anyone, unless you agree. I'll do whatever I can to help. And you obviously need help. Now, what is it?"

She opened her mouth but no words came out. Her mind was a blank.

"I mean, I know you're not sleeping, you're having some kind of horrid nightmare when you do sleep, and it's wrecking you – but I don't know why."

"I don't know why either."

Laura frowned. "It started that day we left you alone. You went out, didn't you? You went somewhere. Where? What happened? Where did you go?"

Just two words, but she could not voice them. She stared helplessly at Laura, begging her to under-stand – and by some miracle, she did.

"Was it that haunted house? Did you go there?"

She sighed hugely, and nodded, feeling released.

"What happened? Did you meet the bloke who lives there? What did he do?"

"Nothing. No, really. I biked over there in the rain, and knocked on the door, and he invited me in, and he told me—" She told Laura everything she could remember of her visit to Teind House. "But ever since then I keep dreaming about it. Every time I fall asleep I'm back in that empty room by myself, and then the door opens and he comes in and – I don't know what's going to happen, but I get really scared and I wake up. And it happens all over again every time I fall asleep, so I can't sleep properly."

"You're leaving something out."

"No, I'm not."

"You must be. Something must have happened, something more than you've said."

"No. Except—" she frowned and rubbed her eyes and yawned. "Sorry. There was one weird thing. When I got back here it was well after twelve. So I must have been out for more than two and a half hours. But it didn't feel like that. I mean, it's maybe fifteen minutes there, fifteen minutes back on the bike, and then I was in the house for, I don't know, I would have said fifteen minutes, half an hour at most. I can't think where another hour and a half went unless … well, unless it was a lot later than I thought when I first left here, or … or I fell asleep in that room."

"And now your ghost is haunting it."

"What?" she stared at her sister in horror. "What are you saying – that I'm dead and I don't know it?"

"Of course not. In the story living people become ghosts – you told me that."

"But there has to be a reason, a strong emotion—"

"Maybe that man did something, or tried to—"

"I'd remember. There wasn't anything like that."

"Maybe you can't remember because the part of you that remembers is still in the house."

"Could that happen?"

Laura made a face. "I shouldn't think so, but I don't know, do I? *Something* happened to you, and it happened in that house."

"And I have to go back there," said Antonia. The prospect frightened her, but she knew, as soon as she spoke, and her heart leaped, that she had also, ever since she left, been longing to return.

"We'll go tonight," said Laura. "Of course I'm going with you! It was going alone that got you in trouble in the first place!"

The sky was clear and the August moon nearly full. Laura had brought a torch, but it seemed unlikely they would need it. They set off without a plan, which made Laura, in particular, uneasy, but they couldn't anticipate what might happen. Mark Eglinton's story, although it proposed the idea of ghosts of the living, had not suggested that the living originals might feel the loss of their image, any more than they'd feel the loss when a photograph was taken.

"But didn't people used to think that if you took a photograph you took a part of their soul?" said Antonia.

"Sure, and then they'd get the witchdoctor to get it back. Know any witchdoctors?"

The night was quiet and seemingly empty. They saw no one. No cars passed them. They stashed the bikes in some bushes and then walked through the front gates with an apprehensive glance or two upwards, at the motionless gargoyles. Teind House was in darkness; at least, no lights showed from any of the front windows.

"Let's scout round the back," whispered Antonia. "That's where the haunted room is."

As they rounded the house they saw, through the uncurtained window of the bare room, that it had an occupant.

They both saw her: a girl wearing jeans and a mac, sitting on a chair against the wall, her arms folded. She was not solid; she wavered slightly, and seemed made of light. You could just about see the chair and the wall through her. And she looked exactly like Antonia.

Laura's hand came up hard against her sister's mouth, stifling her cry, and then she hugged her tightly.

That's me, thought Antonia dazedly. My ghost, in there... It was true, then. She was trapped inside Teind House, just as in her dream. And now, although she felt deeply frightened by the prospect, she felt she had no choice but to enter her dream, to go inside the house and rejoin herself.

The window, she saw, was open. Her heart was pounding. She looked at Laura but did not speak; saw her sister bite her lip, and nod. This was what they had come for, after all; they both knew whatever they did must be done quickly.

Laura gave her a leg up, and Antonia slithered in through the open window, hoping that the noises she made (which seemed, like her own breathing, very loud) would not carry to other parts of the house; hoping Mark Eglinton was deeply asleep, and that this was not a night he would choose to visit the haunted room.

Arms open in a tentative embrace, she walked towards her own ghost. An unexpected light glared out of the mirror and momentarily dazzled her. She was aware of spots of colour dappling her skin. She stumbled against the chair.

The ghost was gone. She was alone in the room.

What now? She couldn't believe that her mere return would end the nightmare; it couldn't be as simple as that; and, as she gazed around the dark, empty room she felt, again with a sense of *déjà vu*, a sort of mental paralysis creeping over her, an inability to move or even to think. Dimly, she recognized that this was dangerous, that something like this had happened to her on her last visit to the house; that she must escape before it was too late—

And then it *was* too late. The door to the room opened, and there he was.

"It worked," he said, simple wonder in his voice. "The house brought you back." He took a step into the room, towards her, and she saw that he was holding a knife.

Recognition of danger cut through the strange paralysis which held her, and she made a dash for the window. But he caught her there and hauled her back over the sill. Although not a big man, he was stronger than she was. "Oh, no. You won't get away a second time," he murmured, his breath hot against her ear. Then she felt the cold blade of his knife against her throat, and stopped struggling.

Laura's voice brought a note of hope into the nightmare: "You let her go! Or I'm calling the police!"

"Two," he whispered. Then, aloud, answering Laura: "Go ahead. She'll be dead before they get here."

"But they'll get you. You won't escape."

He gave a short laugh. "The police don't scare me."

"I think they do. You don't want to get caught. That's why you let Toni go the first time, without hurting her – because her family knew where she'd gone. Let her go now and you're still safe. We won't say a word to anyone. Let her go."

He said nothing. He didn't even move. Antonia wished she knew what he was thinking. Although she was terrified of moving, even of talking with a knife at her throat, she couldn't just wait passively for someone else to decide her fate. She thought about the character in the story he had written, a man obsessed with ghosts, trapped in a haunted house. Surely the story was autobiographical.

"Look," she said, trying to sound brisk and practical. "You know you don't have to kill me to get my ghost. You've proved that Teind House can trap the ghosts of living people. You have my ghost already, so..."

"That was a trick." The pressure of the knife against her throat lessened slightly. "Couldn't you

190

figure that out? Didn't you wonder why I'd hung a mirror in an empty room? It was to hide a hole in the wall – with a camera on the other side. After I left you alone in here I went through and filmed you. Then I made a film-loop, and projected the film against the wall. Instant ghost – at least to the suggestible mind! And yours, prepared by my story, and worked on by the house, was very suggestible indeed."

"What do you mean?"

"This house wants to be haunted. There's something here, a power – you've felt it, you know what I'm talking about."

She could feel it even now, Antonia realized, although her fear of this man had nearly blocked it out. There was an *atmosphere* – she couldn't think of a better word for it – which on her earlier visit had muddled her thinking, made her passive and slow, had got into her head in the form of her dream, and worked to draw her back here. "Yes, but—"

"But it's not the kind of geo-magnetic force I wrote about in my story. It's nothing like so passive as that. It's much, much stronger – and it's evil. It takes something out of you, part of your soul. And the longer you stay here, the more it takes." He raised his voice suddenly. "Hey, you – big sister – are you still there?"

There was no reply. Antonia felt her heart sink, knowing she was alone, yet she clung to the knowledge that this meant Laura at least was safe. "She's gone for the police. It's not too late – if you let me go I'll pretend it was all a mistake, that we were trespassing and you never meant any harm—"

"But it *is* too late. I wasn't a bad man before I came here, but Teind House took part of my soul, and now it's going to have all of yours."

"You don't have to do what the house wants," she said desperately.

"Oh, no," he said, and laughed. "That's not it – it lets me do what *I* want, as long as I give something back. I get your body; Teind House gets your soul."

Just then the door to the room opened, and she saw Laura. She'd been bluffing about the police; she hadn't been able to abandon her sister – and now Teind House had her, too. Antonia could see by the way her sister swayed in the doorway, by the blank look on her face, that there was no hope for either of them. There would be two new ghosts in Teind House after tonight, and two dead bodies.

CLOSE CUT

Philip Gross

CROAK... THERE WAS ALWAYS A TIME-LAG – THREE seconds, Mark counted, between pressing the bell-push and that dead sound in the upstairs flat. Downstairs, deaf Mrs Prawle's TV wittered on in the back room, regardless. Mark rang again – short-long, the secret sign. He had grown out of spy games years ago, but still... This was Mr Krasnik.

The upstairs curtains twitched; in the crack you might just glimpse a long greyish face. By the time Mr Krasnik got down to the door, and that could be several minutes, with his gammy leg, it would be: "Ah, my boy. So good to see you!" But the face in the curtains was watchful and pale, as if *they* might still come knocking for him any day.

Who *they* were, no one said, but Mark's dad explained about the War: how thousands like Mr Krasnik fled from Poland; how they lost their homes, friends, family, everything... True, that was fifty years ago, but Mr K was an old man now, old and alone; if he behaved a little oddly sometimes, you could *understand*.

Understanding was what Mark's mum and dad

did best. When a couple of joyriders overturned a stolen BMW in the street at 4a.m., after bouncing it off the family's new Escort, the first thing his dad said was: "Of course, the background these kids have, you've got to understand..." Mr Truscott, the Neighbourhood Watch man from three doors down, would have got up a lynch mob, though the kids had rolled out of the wreck and run off down the alley laughing. And Mr K? His curtains parted, just a crack, then fell shut. *They* had not come, not yet.

Mark gave the bell another jab. He didn't have all day.

Neighbours liked Mr K. So many old people got to be pathetic. Not him: he was proud. You could tell from the way he stood – chest out, back straight – that he had been a military man. A Captain, he said; and that *meant* something, even fifty years later, to have served in the Polish cavalry. His heels clicked, out of instinct, as he said it. Even Adolf Truscott, with his "healthy distrust of foreigners", would greet the old man on the doorstep. "Morning, Captain," he would say, and Mr K would nod back slowly, like an officer.

You could understand that. Just sometimes Mark wished his dad and mum would be a bit less under-standing. Running errands at ten is one thing, but at fourteen...? His friends would be down in the precinct now, crowding round for a look at the latest Judge Dredd or Batman. He would have been there too, if his mum hadn't breezed in: "I just saw Mr K.

He said he's got a special job for you."

Today the old time-lag was longer than usual. Mark ran a hand across his hair, still bristly from the new cut. He glanced in the downstairs window. The Mark who looked back was a new Mark. This one was sharp. He had style.

Mark's hand dropped from his hair. He had a sudden feeling that the old man might be there, inside the door, watching him through the spy-hole. He grinned awkwardly at the small glass eye. Nothing happened. Mark buzzed again. Inside, a voice said "Ach, have patience!" on the stairs.

Clunk. The door opened on its chain and half a face peered out. One deeply-creased cheek, one white moustache that drooped at the end like an icicle. "Thank you," said Mr Krasnik as he hustled Mark inside.

It was always half-light in the hall, like evening. Everything about the house sighed *old, old, old...* It was all brownish-grey, like the stains in a tea cup. Only the bit of coloured glass above the front door left a carmine puddle on the mat. Mr Krasnik did not smile today. He pulled himself upright until he almost looked Mark in the eye. In the back room, the 2.15 from Newmarket rose to a frenzy, but in the stairwell everything was very still. "Thank you," he said again solemnly. "You have come. It is good, at last." Then, before Mark could speak, he was hitching his stiff leg – clunk, creak, wheeze – up step by step by step.

"Sit down." The armchair had a teacloth arranged to cover where the stuffing leaked out by the head. Old people's flats smell of oldness, every child knows that, but there are different flavours. Mrs Prawle's downstairs was boiled sweets and Guinness; Mr Krasnik's was boot polish and ... something else, sharp, metallic, that Mark had never been able to place.

Mr Krasnik slid the bolt, then glanced out through the curtains. The usual routine. Then he looked at Mark – a long look, as if he had never seen him before. Or not for a very long time. "Your hair... It is right."

"Oh, my friends have had theirs like this for ages..." Mark trailed off. Mr K did not seem to be listening. Suddenly the old man clapped his hands. "Coffee!"

"I'd rather have a Coke ... if you've got one."

"Today, no Coke." The grey plastic kettle was already steaming. "No child's drink. Today you take coffee." He thrust out a mug half full of something very black. Mark took a sip and winced.

"One moment..." The old man was unscrewing a bottle. "Slivovic! No, no refusing. Today you drink with me, like brothers, man to man." He dashed some clear spirit in each mug. "Prosit."

"Wh—" Mark began, but the first glug stopped his breath. The taste was foul, but the feeling creeping through his stomach was OK.

Mr Krasnik downed his at one swig. "You still read

your hero comics?" he said, out of the blue.

Mark blushed. "They're just a bit of fun. I read proper books too."

"No apology." Mr K smiled. "I know about heroes and avengers. When I was in the 18th Lancers..." Not now, Mark thought, not the memoirs, please... Suddenly the old man was leaning forward. "Do not believe," he whispered urgently, "when people tell you there are no heroes any more. Not so. Anyone may be called to be so, any time. Come!"

The last door on the landing should have been a cupboard. "Hey," said Mark, when he saw the bare wooden steps leading steeply upwards. "It's a secret attic. Like Anne Frank. We did her at school." For a moment Mr Krasnik turned and Mark felt he had said something wrong. But the old man nodded, slowly. "Yes," he breathed. "The Jew girl, yes, of course." Then he was climbing, painfully. His heavy boots gleamed as he hauled them up to eye level with Mark, then out of sight. At last he called down, "Come."

There was a grimy skylight high up in the attic. At first that was all Mark could see. He could hear Mr Krasnik beside him in the darkness, with a little rattle in his breath. Then he felt, no, he sensed, no, he *knew* that there was something waiting for them, something large and dark and heavy, something hanging, in the room.

As Mark's eyes adapted, he thought of the butcher's, and the stiff pigs you see dangling on a hook. Then Mr Krasnik chuckled. He stepped up to the thing and thumped it. A small puff of dust rose in the slant of light. "A punchbag?" Mark said. The moment of chill had passed – silly of him. He grinned, trying to imagine the old man doing southpaw round it in his secret room.

"We keep in practice..." Mr Krasnik clicked the light switch, and the question "We...?" stuck on Mark's lips as a bare bulb lit the corner of the attic, where another figure faced them in its riding boots and spurs and khaki uniform.

Where Mr Krasnik got the tailor's dummy Mark could not imagine. Maybe Mrs Prawle had been a seamstress in her better days. Above a collar trimmed with zigzag silver braid was a stiff-peaked cap, with a white metal eagle. In between was nothing, where there should have been a face.

"This," said Mr Krasnik softly, "is the better part of me." There were gloves tucked in the leather belt, but no hands. Between the cavalry breeches and the boots were no legs. "This I wore when General Pilsudski reviewed the 18th Lancers in the spring of '39..."

His voice faded out. There was a long pause. Downstairs, crowds cheered faintly, over and over. In the action replay of some past game, strikers scored and scored.

"Uh, what was the job you wanted doing?" Mark said, a little too fast. His heart felt too high up: in the way of his breathing. "Only ... only I told Mum

I'd be back soon..."

Sssst! With a glittering swish, Mr Krasnik's arm seemed to stretch two, three feet longer, in a smooth sweep from the scabbard at the dummy's side. Then he held it upright: a long curving blade. Mark swallowed: "That ... that's real."

"Of course." With a couple of strides the old man faced the punchbag, and with a quick double slash, left-right, sent a thin shred of sacking drifting through the air. "With this," he said, "we faced the German Wehrmacht, in their tanks and armoured cars. We raised our sabres – so! – and charged."

"On horseback? But that's crazy."

"No matter. We were heroes." With a movement faster than Mark's flinch, he thrust the sword out to him, handle first. "Take it. Feel."

The grip was warm though the bronze guard was cold. The blade was not light but it had balance. Mark moved his wrist; the tip quivered. In his mind's eye, Mark could see how it might play. "No," he said. "I can't."

Mr K leaned closer. "No? I think you wish to, really." He stepped back from the punchbag. "You are not afraid? Then try."

OK, thought Mark, why not? Humour the old man. Show him. There! He gave the bag a poke.

"No, no! It is a sabre. *Slash.*" Mr Krasnik lifted the sword from his hand, cut a silvery figure-of-eight in the air and in a single movement pressed it back in Mark's palm. "Again!" This time Mark let the blade sweep and the air sang. "Good!" the old man cried. "Now, strike..." The bag was hard, but it gave, like when you chop a cabbage with a carving knife. He's made it like that, Mark thought, so it feels like ... like it really would. He knows.

"Never stop. Slash. This is the art of it. Each cut *flows*..."

This stroke bit deep, and the blade stuck. The bag shuddered as he jerked it free. "No, no!" the old man crowed. "Not *hack*! Not like a farmer with a billhook. You must glide, like skates on ice." Mark slashed; a clean cut opened in the sacking. "Yes! Now, dance!" the old man almost sang.

When Mark stepped back he was smiling. "That was good," he said. "But what's the job?"

"My friend, *this* is."

The warmth of the slivovic slid off Mark's mind like a duvet on a cold night. The old boy had flipped. All these years, skulking at cracks in curtains, double-locking doors, waiting for *them* to arrive...

"Uh-oh," said Mark. "Not me..."

"You are the one. You do not know it, but you are."

Mark glanced at the door. He backed towards it, breath by breath. "They're expecting me home."

"I swear: you will come to no harm. Not if you are brave."

"You've got the wrong bloke." Mark's voice came out too high, as if it was still breaking. "Go ask Mr Truscott. He'd just love to start a private army..."

"No!" Mr K shook his head, almost sadly. "It is

you." He held out his hands, palms upwards. "Those heroes in your books. They take lives…"

"Those are *stories*. There are bad guys."

"You think there are no bad guys?"

"Well… It's more complicated, isn't it, in real life?"

"And if a bad guy says: yes, I have done things so bad I should die?"

"I'd say … no. No one is just *bad*. There are always reasons. You've just got to *understand*."

"And if the bad guy said…" He paused. "I spit on your *understanding*. I wish to die like a man."

There was a hollow pause. Beneath their feet, Mrs Prawle's TV hit a commercial break. "*It's the Real Thing*," it sang.

"The bad guy," said Mr K slowly, "stands before you." He unbuttoned his shirt collar, down to the frayed thermal vest, and leaned his head back so the stringy tendons of the neck went taut. "Strike," he said. "One swift slash, here. Then you may go."

Mark's back was pressed against the door. His left hand found the plastic handle, and with a swift tug he turned to run. The door did not budge. Locked. No key. Mark dropped the sabre, grabbed the handle with both hands and heaved. With a rip, the screws came out of the wood. Mark held on to the handle, foolishly, as he turned back to face the old man who slowly, gravely, shook his head.

"Stop right there," said Mark. "I mean, unlock the door, or I'll…"

"You will what? Kill me? Take up your sabre, like a man."

"You need to talk to someone." Mark's voice was not behaving, but he did not care. His foot was on the blade but that was shaking too, as if the thing might wriggle out from under. "Mum could help you. She's a social worker." Mr Krasnik spat.

"A world of cowards," he said. "You will not look evil in the face."

"What ... *evil*?"

"I shall tell you. Then surely you will want to strike the blow." Shoulder to shoulder with the dummy in its uniform, Mr Krasnik slid a hand round behind its waist. He could have been about to waltz with it. "I know what you are thinking," he said. "Maybe you rush the old fool, take his keys...? You try, one of us dies for certain. Better that you listen."

Talk. Get him talking, Mark thought. That's what they do with nutters. That's what Mum does all the time. "Go on," he said.

"Good... See this in your mind and see it good. We are retreating – no shame in that, our line is shattered by their Panzer tanks. What is left of my unit, we make for the border, and the Germans follow fast. Those who they catch they cut down from behind. There, not far off, is a village, and I know what to do. We turn our horses that way. I know that when the Germans come upon it, they might pause a little, for it is a village of the Jews."

The old man paused, looking hard into Mark's eyes, letting the cold scorn of the last word hang between them.

"By the time we gallop in, they are already swarming in the street. Like insects, they are, in the dirt of their filthy village. You look shocked? Oh, it was not for them we fought the Germans, oh no. But these old Jew women rush out of their hovels and there are children and chickens everywhere beneath our horses' hooves. My plan is only that we ride through and make for the forest, but suddenly there comes one of them, in the narrow road, blocking my way. A boy, it is. A boy of your age. With a face, a build, like you. With hair cut short, just so.

"He has warning. But he jumps up, with his arms out, shouting in his ugly language. *Stop!* he cries. *Save us from the Germans!* And he grabs my bridle, so the horse begins to rear up, with the others pulling up behind. Then I lash out with my boot, but he will not let go, so I raise my sabre and I shout and curse him, *Let go, Jew, or...*" His voice dropped to a whisper. "The others, they all scattered, they all ran. Only he, he looked me in the eye. All the time, even when I brought the blade down, still he looked me in the eye as if to say: *I will meet you again...* And now you come."

In the back of Mark's head was a feeling like falling, as if the time-lag, just a few seconds at the front door, had opened up beneath him and he was falling backwards into somewhere deep and cold.

"Look," he said hoarsely. "I don't know anything about this. I don't want to. It's nothing to do with me."

"But it is. You are sent. I have watched you growing, all these years. At first I was not certain, but this week – now, with your hair so – now I know." The old man stiffened his back. "My friend, I am a murderer. A war criminal. I killed Jews."

"Then ... then go to the police or someone."

"Fool! There is no time. Don't you see, I am dying? Maybe weeks, maybe days. Then I have to meet him, with this debt not paid." His voice broke. "Help me. I must die by the sword. You have his hands..." He slipped his arm out from behind the dummy, with an army pistol.

"That's not real..." Mark started. *Crack.* The punchbag shuddered, and swung slowly. "No one will hear," said the old man. "For that we thank deaf Mrs Prawle."

"You wouldn't."

"Why not? The Jews have a saying that to take one life is like to kill a whole world. So can the blood of two boys be worth more than one?" He took a step towards Mark, with his head held high, his neck bared. He twitched the pistol. "Pick the sword up. Now!"

Time... Play for time, wasn't that what they said? Keep him talking... Mark picked up the sabre, very slowly, though his hands felt far away and numb. "Tell me about him," Mark said.

"No more words." The old man's voice was almost soothing. "I have pain – pain of body and soul. Be kind. Strike well..." The pistol quivered. "I do not want to hurt you, my friend. I *beg*. I feel him waiting. I can almost hear him speak."

That's it! In the swirl of cold mist in Mark's mind, there was a clearing. "Yes! I can hear him too." Mark forced his eyes away from the old man's gaze and looked up, to and fro among the rafters. "He's here. He's saying... Wait a minute, I can't quite make it out."

"What? What is he saying?"

"He's saying... He forgives you. It's OK."

The pistol point wavered only slightly. "Tell me," Mr Krasnik whispered. "Tell me *exactly* what he says."

"Just ... *I forgive you...*"

"Liar!" The old man's face blazed. In one step he was right up close, his breath like pickled gherkins on Mark's face. "The boy spoke Yiddish!" The pistol jabbed Mark's breastbone. Mr Krasnik's left hand brought the blade up slowly, till it rested on his jugular. "Just draw it sideways..." The cold mist had closed again, swirling, full of Playschool jingles and nursery rhymes from when he was small, mixed with football results from downstairs – Queen of the South 2, Kilmarnock 1 – and the meaningless words: *I'm going to die*.

"Now!"

Mark opened his mouth to say "No..." What fell

out from the jumble inside him was a string of
sounds he had never heard before. *"Du kenst fon
dem grieb nit heroys, alte mann."*

Mr Krasnik gasped. His face was purple for a
moment, and his eyes so wide that a rim of blood-red
showed right round them. *"Du kenst fon dem grieb
nit heroys,"* said Mark's voice – but not quite his
voice – again.

For a moment the space round Mark was still but
full of bodies running, stopped in mid-stride as if
frozen in ice. There was mud spattered up, and
chicken feathers drifting; there were hooves and
metal and a toddler wailing. And there was the
horse above him, plunging and rearing, yanking him
up as he held on to the bridle and came face to face,
looking straight in the young cavalry officer's
arrogant, frightened eyes. He said it again, in his
head, even as the sabre sliced down. Though he did
not have a word of Yiddish Mark knew what his
voice was saying: no escape, old man. *You can't get
out of the hole.* The grave, the pit.

With a slow thud and a clatter Mr Krasnik toppled
backwards. Mark blinked and he was in the attic; he
was Mark again. When he bent down to look, the
flush on the old man's face was darkening to grey.
Mark thumped on the floor and shouted till his head
spun. Then he leaned against the door and let some
unheroic tears come.

If this was a story he would use the pistol, shoot off
the door lock, something... He might even get an

ambulance in time, it might not be too late. Was that what the old boy would have wanted? Mr Krasnik. The bad guy. What was cruel? What was kind?

So what's justice? Mark asked Judge Dredd, Superman and Batman, but the heroes shrugged and turned away.

GRANDMA

Colin Greenland

"Now then, Robert," said his mother for the twentieth time, "are you *sure* you'll be all right?"

Rob, who was watching the cartoons out of sheer boredom, gave a loud sigh. He slumped down further in the armchair, scraping his heels through the deep-pile carpet.

His mother was trotting up and down the hall, accumulating shopping bags. "I don't like leaving you with her all day," she said, as if they hadn't been talking it over and over for weeks.

"Mum, I'll be all right!" All he had to do was give her her dinner and help her to the bathroom, and give her one of her tablets if she got "worked up", as Dad called it. It wouldn't be the first time he'd done those things for his grandma, even if he couldn't exactly say he liked doing them.

"But are you sure you can manage, poppet?" his mother went on. Rob hated it when she called him that.

"Dinners in the fridge," he recited, in a singsong voice, "Grandma's tablets in the bathroom, Grandma's fags in your room—"

"Cigarettes, Robert," said his mother, automatically. "Three minutes in the microwave on full power," she said. Rob supposed she was talking about their dinners now, rather than the cigarettes. "Three minutes *each*, remember, and make sure it's really hot before you eat it. I've put Grandma's tray out ready." She was looking in the hall mirror, checking her lipstick. "You *will* put the ironing board away for me, won't you, darling?" she said. "I wish you could come with us."

"Mum, it's the Ideal Home Exhibition," said Rob, reaching into the magazine rack beside his chair for the remote control.

"You used to like it," she said.

"I used to like being taken out in my pram to see the ducks," growled Rob, turning the sound up so she wouldn't hear him.

His mother came into the lounge in a great wave of perfume. "Don't watch that thing all day," she told him, "and whatever you do, Robert – Robert, are you listening? Whatever you do, don't—"

He chorused the line with her. "Don't let Grandma downstairs!"

Outside his dad started sounding the horn. Still flapping bags about and dispensing random advice and reminders, Rob's mother kissed the air at him and ran out of the house.

Rob stood by the window with his hands in his pockets as they drove away. Then he went and made a mug of coffee, and a mug of tea for his grandma.

214

He leaned on the ironing board while the kettle was boiling. When the tea was made, he carried the mug upstairs and stood it on the floor while he turned the key in Grandma's door.

Rob's grandma was sitting on her bed, in all her clothes. Her eiderdown was on the floor and she had managed to knock the radio off the bedside cabinet again. It was still playing, lying on its back somewhere among the ancient junk that Grandma kept piled up like a fort, around her bed, her boxes of clothes and stacks of old papers. A choir of children was singing happily about little flowers that open and little birds that sing. The room smelled bad, the way it always did, of old clothes and old slippers and old woman.

"Hello, Grandma," he said loudly. "I've made you a cup of tea."

Grandma moved her mouth about resentfully. She looked at Rob like a sentry with orders to shoot intruders on sight.

Rob locked the door and brought her the mug. "Here you are," he said. "Take it, then."

Rob's grandma's glasses were half an inch thick. She stared suspiciously into the mug. "What's this?" she demanded.

"Rat poison," said Rob.

"What?" said the old woman, screwing up her eyes and opening her mouth at him. The last hair on her head straggled over the wrinkled pink skin like strands of white cotton. "What? I can't hear you all the way you mumble."

215

"Tea, Grandma," said Rob, louder. "I've brought you a cup of tea."

Grandma took the mug, grudgingly. "I suppose we haven't got any cups and saucers," she said, sarcastically.

"It's got three sugars, Grandma," Rob said, "the way you like it."

She ignored that completely. She was looking past Rob as though she expected to see someone standing behind him.

"Where's your mother?"

Rob pulled a face. Between Mum saying everything fifty times and Grandma making you say everything fifty times, conversation was a bit limited in this house.

"Mum and Dad have gone out," he reminded her. He picked up her eiderdown and put it back over her thick old legs. Grandma's legs always made him think of the pale white fatty joints of meat piled in the freezer at the supermarket. "They'll be back soon," he lied. He knew better than to try to explain about the Ideal Home Exhibition. He wondered if the Ideal Home Exhibition would have something that could turn your grandma into an Ideal Home grandma, a smiley one with rosy cheeks who would sit in a rocking chair and suck humbugs and knit woolly hats for everybody instead of wandering around the house at all hours of the day and night, knocking over the ornaments. "Drink your tea," he told her.

"People today have got no respect," said the old woman.

Rob found the radio behind one of the boxes of old clothes Grandma would never wear again but would never allow anyone to throw out. He picked it up and stood it back in its place on the bedside cabinet, next to her magnifying glass and her indigestion tablets and her photo of Grandpa. The children had stopped singing; now there was somebody playing the organ.

Grandma glared at the radio with hatred. "I don't know what you want to put that on for," she said, as if it had been his idea. "I can't understand a word they say."

Rob switched the radio off. Grandma had started drinking her tea, making horrible slurping noises like an old dog.

The last time they had left her with the door unlocked she had come down in the middle of the night and started messing about in the kitchen, thinking she was cooking breakfast. If she hadn't dropped the teapot on the floor and smashed it they might never have woken up and caught her. She had turned the cooker on, all four burners and the oven, and the kitchen was full of gas.

Her room got stuffy with the door locked all the time. They couldn't even open the window, Rob's father had screwed it shut, just making sure. Rob looked out into the garden. Next door's cat was sitting on the roof of the shed, gazing down

217

at the sparrows on the ground as if it wanted to put a bet on one of them and was judging their performance.

"I'm going down to have my coffee," Rob told his grandma. "Are you going to have a little sleep before your dinner?" *Yes*, he wished at her. *Yes*. When Dad talked to Grandma he would keep nodding his head, trying to get her to imitate him, to make her agree to whatever it was. It never did any good.

"I want my cigarettes," said Grandma.

"You have your cigarette after your dinner," Rob said.

Grandma stuck out her teeth at him. "I want my cigarettes," she said.

"Later," Rob said. "You have your cigarette later."

Grandma put her head down. She looked as if she was going to spring off the bed and headbutt him. "Where's your mother?" she said. "Tell her I want my cigarettes."

Rob could hear the frantic cartoon music playing downstairs. "The doctor said you could have one cigarette after your dinner," he told her.

"I want to have them here," said Grandma implacably, "so you don't forget." She turned to her bedside cabinet and started to pull things out of it, as if she thought the cigarettes might be somewhere in there. She knocked her photo of Grandpa over. Rob made a dive and rescued the tea before that went everywhere too.

Grandma was pulling paper hankies out of the box

and dropping them on the floor. "I can't find them!" she said, her voice rising. "What have you done with them?"

"All right, all right," said Rob. He went out of the room, locking the door behind him. "Smoke yourself to death," he said aloud, as he fetched the packet from the shelf inside the door of his parents' room. "Government health warning, old people can cause fatal diseases."

He unlocked Grandma's door and went back in to her. She was sitting on the bed still, crushing the tissue box in her yellow hands. Her eiderdown was on the floor again. Rob leaned over to give her the fags. "Here you are, Grandma."

She looked at the little white packet as suspiciously as she had looked at her mug of tea, as if it really might be rat poison this time. "People have got no consideration," she said, snatching the packet from Rob and clutching it tight.

"Don't squash your cigarettes, Grandma," said Rob. He picked up the eiderdown and put it over her legs again.

With a look of triumph on her face, Grandma buried the packet of cigarettes away in her lap somewhere. As she did so she caught sight of her tea where Rob had put it, on a pile of faded old magazines, out of danger. She groped determinedly towards it, threatening to fall off the bed. "Give me my tea!" she shouted. "Give it to me!"

"Calm down!" Rob shouted back. He picked up the

tea and held it away from her. "Calm down! Grandma! Now then!"

"You don't know what I put up with," said the old woman, full of injury and indignation, clutching at the air in the direction of the mug.

"Sit back and you can have it!" It was more like looking after a baby than a grandmother.

"Not good enough for you, I suppose," she grumbled. "People these days."

She seemed to come to rest, to be still for an instant, so Rob gave her the mug. "Don't spill it, Grandma," he warned.

The old woman sat back, breathing through her mouth, slopping tea on her cardigan. She drank, her hands quivering with the effort. "I don't know why we can't even have the radio on," she said resentfully. "I suppose that's too much to ask now, is it?"

Rob wiped her cardigan with a tissue, trying not to notice the sour smell of her. He put the radio back on, tuning it to a rock station and turning it up extremely loud. Pealing guitars blasted out, over a cannonade of drums.

"Oh!" cried the old woman. "Oh! Oh! You—! You—!"

"All right, all right," said Rob. He twisted the dial at random, found some soft strings playing, turned the volume right down. His grandma glowered at him. "That's to put you to sleep," he told her. Funnily enough, it seemed to work. Very soon he could see her head begin to sway, her eyelids starting to close.

He took the mug out of her hand. She mumbled, barely protesting.

Rob hurried downstairs, quietly. He went and got his cooling coffee and took it in to the lounge. The cartoons had finished. Now there was an old western on, a musical. People riding around on horseback, singing. It looked really stupid. He tried the other channels. There was skiing, a gardening programme and a thing that reckoned it was a teen magazine, with teen pop videos and lots of people showing off on rollerskates. Rob went back and watched the musical. It was stupid, but there was nothing else to do till dinnertime except his boring homework, and that could wait.

Rob's heart nearly stopped when his grandma said: "I can't find my cigarette lighter."

He jerked his head round. She was standing in the doorway like a bulldog looking for somebody to bite. He must have forgotten to lock her bedroom door.

"It's upstairs, Grandma," he said immediately. They had taken Grandma's lighter away before they had even started locking her in. Thank goodness she hadn't actually gone and found it.

Rob got up and went towards the old woman, trying to herd her back towards the stairs. "Let's get you back to bed, then, and I'll fetch it for you."

Ignoring him, Grandma came lumbering into the lounge. She went to the little table beside his dad's armchair and picked up the big glass ashtray. "I don't know what you think you're playing at," she

221

said. "People today haven't got the sense to tie their own shoelaces."

Fortunately, there was nothing in the ashtray. Rob reached out and grabbed hold of it before she could drop it or smash something with it. Grandma hung on.

"That's right, Grandma," Rob said, thinking quickly. "Let's take the ashtray up. What a nice ashtray. That's what we need, isn't it? Come on, then. Shall I carry it for you?"

She stared at him belligerently over the ashtray, as though he was a thief trying to steal this trophy from her. Her eyes looked weird through her thick glasses, like something forgotten at the bottom of a bottle.

"Let me carry the ashtray, Grandma," Rob said.

"I need my lighter," she said very definitely, as if he was the one who was deaf and stupid.

"When you're back in bed I'll fetch it for you," he promised. He pulled on the ashtray, trying to tow her out of the room. "Come on, Grandma, back upstairs. It'll be dinnertime soon," he said.

She grunted and swayed her head about. It was like trying to lead a cow into a slaughterhouse. She would neither come nor let go of the ashtray.

Rob let it go. "Carry it yourself, then," he said.

Grandma lurched backwards, the heavy ashtray sliding from her grip. It fell with a thump, denting the thick carpet.

Grandma went red. "Now look what you made me do!" she scolded.

Rob stepped forward and kicked the ashtray under the sofa, out of reach.

"You pick that up, young man!" Grandma raged.

"Pick what up, Grandma?" asked Rob.

"That, that—" She was losing it already, forgetting the word, then forgetting what it was she was trying to find a word for. Bending forward, towards the vanished ashtray, she caught sight of the magazine rack. Purposefully she reached inside.

"Do you want something to read, Grandma?" said Rob. "You've got your papers upstairs," he reminded her.

She'd got hold of some catalogue of Mum's. She was pulling it clumsily out of the rack, holding it by the cover with the pages hanging down. The cover was starting to tear from the weight of them. He would have to hide that before Mum came home.

"You don't need that, Grandma."

"You've got no right," she said, standing up.

"Put it back," said Rob. "Come on, Grandma."

"Put what back?" she asked, aggrieved. "I don't know, ordering me about, I don't know what—"

"Put Mum's catalogue back where it goes," he said, patiently.

The old woman looked at the heavy publication hanging from her hand. She twisted her head at an angle, as if she was trying to read what it said on the cover without lifting the book up to her face.

"They have nice things in here," she said conversationally.

Rob gathered his forces. He put his hand on her arm. "Well, let's take it with us, then, Grandma, shall we, eh? You can look at it in bed."

But she turned away from him, pulling her arm free. She was moving towards the bookshelves now, catalogue in hand.

Rob dived to intervene, almost toppling the standard lamp that stood in the way. "I'll help you, Grandma!"

"Bookshelves are the place for books, young man," wheezed Grandma righteously. "Not on the floor for people to tread all over." She reached up shakily with the catalogue, trying to push it in between the books on the shelf. The books at the end of the row started to tilt.

"Careful, Grandma," said Rob. "Let me do it!"

He made a grab for the books. Some were already sliding off the end of the shelf. He threw up his hands, half to catch them, half to shield his face. He saw she was looking at him with a fixed, intent little smile like a malicious toddler. She started to push the row of books along the shelf on to his head.

"Grandma! No!"

She got hold of the shelf, lifting the end of it up off its bracket, and shoved it at him. As Rob threw himself to one side, the rest of the books, road atlases and DIY manuals and books of pictures by Constable and Canaletto, big hard books with sharp corners, slid down the shelf in a colourful avalanche and hit him on the shoulder, in the chest, on the side of the head.

His face stinging, his ear ringing, Rob skipped back, tripped over the flex of the standard lamp and fell back into Dad's chair. The lamp came crashing down, just missing his arm. The cream satin shade hit the wall and buckled and he heard the bulb break.

Wide-eyed, he stared at his grandma. "Grandma, be careful! You could hurt somebody!" He heard himself shouting. He sounded just like his dad.

The old woman stood in the middle of the room like a wrestler gloating over an overthrown opponent. "Look what you did," she told him. "You didn't ought to have done that."

Rob, breathing hard, was trying not to be angry. She was just a loony old woman. She didn't know what she was doing, half the time. He knew that. But that look he had seen in her eyes, that was an evil look. Like someone that really meant to do you harm. The glasses. It must have been her thick glasses, making her eyes look all twisted up like that.

Then five shots rang out. A horse whinnied shrilly in terror. Women started to scream.

Blinking, Grandma swung around on her heel, looking for the source of the noise.

"No, Grandma, that's just the TV." Rob ducked in front of her, shielding the set from her, groping around behind his back for the button and switching it off.

225

"I'll show them," Grandma said. "Frightening people like that." She seemed to be looking around for another weapon.

Rob scampered for the door, pulling at her sleeve. "Here, Grandma!" he called. "Here! Grandma, here!"

She swayed towards him, then back towards the silenced set. He had to get her out of the lounge and back upstairs before she really damaged something. A broken lightbulb was one thing, a broken television would certainly be another.

"I'm going to get your lighter," announced Rob. He walked out of the room importantly, stamping his feet down. He started off upstairs. If he could get her upstairs, perhaps he could get one of her tablets into her. Two, three, a whole bottle of tablets. That would calm her down. "I'm going to get your cigarette lighter, Grandma," he called.

He heard her following him. Then half-way up the stairs, he looked round and saw Grandma go stumping down the hall, into the kitchen.

He just made it in there as she collided with the ironing board. "This way, Grandma," he said, catching hold of it before it could fall.

She turned and looked at him as if she'd never seen him before. Casually, with one hand, she tipped the ironing board up on its hinge. The iron slid off and crashed to the floor, narrowly missing Rob's foot.

His heart was thumping. It was all getting out of control. Every instinct told him to lash out at her.

But this was like a fight in a nightmare. She was an old lady; she was his grandma. You couldn't fight your own grandma.

"Upstairs!" he said.

She cursed him.

"All right. All right, Grandma." Rob made himself act and speak calmly. "Look – let's put this all away, Grandma, shall we? Mum would like that, wouldn't she? She'll be pleased." More and more he sounded as if he was talking to a baby. Busily he wrapped the flex of the iron around its cleats, then folded up the board, swinging it into an upright position. "Grandma, could you pass me the ironing board cover, please?"

The cover for the ironing board was where Mum had put it, on top of the washing machine, folded up. Grandma located it, foggily, and picked it up in one fist. She held it up, squinting at it. It started to come unfolded, tapes flapping.

"Doesn't look very clean to me," she observed.

"Let me have it, Grandma," said Rob.

"It needs a good wash, this does." She went to the sink and turned the tap on, hard. Water splashed everywhere.

Rob pushed past her and turned it off. He took the ironing board cover out of her hand. "We'll put it in the machine," he said. "In the washing machine, look. That's what we'll do."

"We never had no washing machines," said Grandma, contemptuously. But she let him take the cover.

Rob crouched down and opened the door of the machine. "Here," said Grandma. "Here."

He sensed her above him, moving something across the draining board. He looked up just in time to pull away as she started pouring hot water over him. The water in the kettle was still hot, and she was pouring it over him.

"That's what we'll do!" cried Grandma. Now she was imitating him.

Spitting, Rob wiped his face with his sleeve. "Grandma! You could have scalded me!"

He couldn't take this any more. In a minute she would be turning on all the switches and pouring water into the sockets. Abandoning the struggle, he dashed for the stairs.

"Well, where are you going now?" Grandma shouted after him.

Just you come and see, he thought.

Grandma's bedroom door was open. Rob pushed it open wider. The key was still in the lock. He snatched it out, and ran into his parents' room. Then he looked around frantically. Where was the lighter? It wasn't on the shelf where they kept it, near the fags. Rob groaned. They must have put it away in a drawer or a cupboard somewhere, "just to be on the safe side" – it was one of his dad's favourite phrases these days. What had they done with it?

From downstairs came the complicated sound of two or three things going over together.

Rob grabbed his mother's lipstick from the dressing

table and ran back to the top of the stairs. He leaned out over the banister. Explosions and cries rose from the television, a burst of fiddle music. Something exciting was happening on the wild frontier.

He could see Grandma in the kitchen, wrenching the lead out of the kettle. He held the lipstick out where she could see it.

"Grandma! Grandma!" he called. "I've found it! Here's your lighter, Grandma, here it is!"

It started to work. Grandma dropped the kettle with a clatter and came along the hall. She stood there at the foot of the stairs, peering sideways at them as if they were some new kind of puzzle she hadn't encountered before.

"Well, what good is it up there?" she demanded, sarcastically.

Rob shook the lipstick at her. "Come and get it, Grandma..."

She put one heavy slippered foot on the bottom stair. "I don't know what you think you're doing," said Grandma wearily, "playing about like that."

"Come on, Grandma..."

Grandma came labouring upstairs, breathing hoarsely, working her whole body. She had shoulders like a road-digger's.

Rob danced backwards to the door of her room, holding the lipstick up in the air. "The first woman of a hundred and ninety-nine to attempt the south face of the Eiger without oxygen!" he cried, as Grandma mastered the final stairs.

She came trundling towards him, the kettle lead dangling from her fist. She was still complaining. "If your mother knew—"

Rob backed into Grandma's room. It was working. He was winning the battle. He felt exhilarated now.

Grandma came in after him, like a rhinoceros entering its house. Rob threw the lipstick on the bed, where he could see the cigarettes still lying; then he turned, took hold of the old woman and steered her in the same direction. She kept moving, dazedly, while he stepped neatly behind her back and locked the door, pulling out the key and sticking it in his pocket.

"You think I don't know what goes on down there," said Grandma in a loud voice; but on the contrary, she sounded baffled and confused.

The eiderdown was on the floor. Rob picked it up and dangled it in front of Grandma like a bull-fighter's cape.

Under cover of the eiderdown he chucked the cigarettes and his mother's lipstick in the bedside cabinet: out of sight, out of mind. Then he whisked the eiderdown away. "Olé!"

He started straightening her bed, tucking the blankets in, making a performance of pulling them tight. "Come on, now, Grandma, dinnertime," he told her. "Back on your bed now, and let's get you some nice dinner, shall we, eh?"

"Not right," Grandma pronounced. "People these

days." She set off to walk around the bed, banging awkwardly into the side of the chest of drawers.

"This way, Grandma!" shouted Rob. "Grandma!" He smacked the bed with his hand.

She wasn't taking any notice. She was coming round the foot of the bed. Her trunks and boxes were getting in her way.

"What do you think's for dinner, Grandma?" asked Rob wildly. "It might be shepherd's pie, Grandma! Your favourite! Mmm!"

She bore down on him, knocking a pile of papers over. He grabbed her arm, hauled her towards the bed.

She resisted him. "Trying to pull the wool over my eyes," she accused him.

"Pull a plastic bag over your head, in a minute!" said Rob, losing his temper.

She came at him with the kettle lead. The plug hit him on the head. She had the lead around his throat. She was throttling him.

Rob's hands went to the lead, pulling at it. He felt Grandma trying to put her hand in his pocket. She was after the key. He barged her with his shoulder, but she was like a rock. She was all on top of him suddenly. He got a purchase on the lead around his throat and inhaled, blindly, choking. His face was full of smelly cardigan. She trod on his toe, hit him in the chest.

He twisted away from her, jerking the lead from his throat. All her weight was on his back. He tried to push her over, on to the bed, but he couldn't shift her. They staggered together like an eight-limbed monster. Rob felt the key go from his pocket.

Gasping, he saw a gap and put his head up into clear air. He could see the key, in Grandma's hand. He made a desperate lunge for it.

"Oh no you don't!" she cried.

There was a smash and tinkle of breaking glass. Grandma had thrown the key straight through the window.

Rob pulled free. The old woman just stood there, swaying, nodding her head proudly. "What do you think of that?" she said.

Rob opened his mouth to tell her what he thought of that. Then he heard himself start to laugh.

"What do I think?" he echoed. "What do I think?" He went and tried the door. Of course it wouldn't open. He shook it. "You've done it now! We're both locked in now!" It was hilarious.

Grandma subsided, sitting down heavily on the bed. It squeaked hideously under her. "Throwing things out of the window," she said disgustedly, as if he'd been the one who had done it. "You just wait till your father comes home."

"Yes, well, we're both going to have to do that now," said Rob. He was exhausted. Green and pink lights were coming and going inside his head. His ear was still hurting where the books had hit it. "We'll both just have to wait for them to come home," he said. What they would say, Rob didn't know. At least he wouldn't ever have to look after her on his own again, though, that was for sure.

"I don't know what you're laughing at," said Grandma, some moments after he had stopped. She was trying to pull the eiderdown over her again. She wasn't getting very far. "Throw everything out of the window, why don't you."

Rob looked outside. Birds were flitting from tree to tree. A cool breeze was flapping the washing in the gardens, the same breeze that was now streaming in through the broken pane. Rob wondered where the key had landed. He didn't suppose he could see it anywhere. He stood on a chair and pressed his face to the glass.

Beneath Grandma's window was a narrow slope of slates that ended in a grey plastic gutter. Rob could see sodden dead leaves in the gutter, and unidentifiable bits of rotting furry black slime. Maybe the key had fallen in there.

He turned. There was a big straight-edged shape falling towards him. It hit him, hard.

Then he was on the floor, with part of the chair digging into him. There was something on top of it, on top of him. It was incredibly heavy. It was crushing him.

It was the wardrobe. He was pinned under Grandma's wardrobe. He heard a voice yelling out in shock and pain. It was him.

Grandma's face came round the wardrobe. It came very close up. It had skin like old wallpaper and cracks like ancient mud. There was a pair of thick glasses on it, from behind which big eyes were staring at him, like something in a case at the zoo.

A crêpy yellow hand held a lipstick in Rob's face.

"This isn't mine," said Grandma.

Rob jerked away from her. Pain grabbed at his hip, savagely. Everything went dark blue, with red round the edge.

Grandma was walking away from him. He was trapped under the wardrobe, and she was walking away.

Rob shoved at the wardrobe. Pain bit him in two. The wardrobe didn't budge.

"You think you're so clever, all you youngsters today," said Grandma. He couldn't see her any more. He heard the bedsprings clash and jangle. Grandma was climbing on to her bed. "You think you can do anything you please," she told him. The noise of the springs continued while she settled herself, puffing and blowing as she laboriously rearranged her pillows. "You've got no consideration."

Rob felt cold and clammy. He was sweating. He was going to be stuck under the wardrobe for hours, until Mum and Dad came home, until they could get the door open. He could feel his foot, turned the wrong way. It felt like somebody else's.

Grandma's voice continued, righteous and un- stoppable. "When I was your age I had to do what I was told. If you didn't like it, you had to go without! Some people have got no right, just barging about willy-nilly without so much as a by-your-leave. Now look at you."

She seemed to think it was his fault that the wardrobe was on top of him. It hurt. It hurt, it *hurt*: nothing had ever hurt so much, nothing could.

Rob heard the radio go on. It was the middle of the racing results. A man's voice was saying rapidly: "– *On the Nod, 5-2; second: Bright Day, 8-1; third: Hungarian Rhapsody, 5-1; eight ran.*"

"Now this is more like it," said Grandma.

Rob passed out.

He dreamed he was a racecourse. Hundreds of horses were galloping over him, pounding him with their hooves. Rob could see people walking about. He saw police in uniform; he saw some sailors, and a boy selling newspapers, and his mum and dad. He tried to shout out to them, to tell them he was under the ground, but when he opened his mouth, nothing came out.

Suddenly he was awake again. The radio was still playing, the same voice reading out the same meaningless names and numbers. Rob's head was at an angle, hard against the wall. He could see part of the ceiling, and the top of the wall opposite. He was dizzy. He thought he was going to be sick.

He could smell something. A sharp, pricking smell.

He tried to rock the wardrobe from side to side. It hurt, it hurt, it hurt – !

Something was floating across the ceiling, something thin and shapeless.

Smoke.

"Grandma?"

His voice sounded like a little boy's, somewhere else, in a different room, a different world.

Now he could hear a soft crackling noise. Smoke began spilling over the top edge of the wardrobe, white and grey, dribbling into his face.

Startled, he sucked in a lungful. He started coughing. The cough hurt. His leg hurt worse. He squirmed in pain and felt the broken chair shift. He tried to push his back up the wall, clutching at the side of the wardrobe, straining to see over it. He gained perhaps six inches. The pain made him scream.

When he stopped screaming, he looked at the scene before him. Then he screamed again.

The room was hazy. The smoke was everywhere now, everywhere Rob could see. At the centre of the smoke was Grandma's bed. The crumpled bedclothes were burning nicely, curling up in flames, throwing a cheerful, dancing, red and orange glow on to the possessions of the old woman's life that she kept piled round about. Her boxes and carrier bags full of musty, many-times-mended clothes, her hoarded heaps of magazines and newspapers, all were blazing merrily as rubbish on a bonfire. Heavy black fumes were pouring out from under the eiderdown that trailed across the rug. A wave of heat came drifting across to Rob, and a reek of burning feathers.

"Grandma!" croaked Rob, choking. "Grandma, no!"

But there she was, sitting up in the midst of the flames, puffing happily on six cigarettes at once and smirking like a mad Guy Fawkes.

She held her lighter up to show him. It glinted gold in the firelight.

"It was in my pocket all the time!" said Grandma, contentedly.

Vampire in Venice

John Gordon

GEMMA BATHED HER EYES. THE ITALIAN TRAIN GLIDED so smoothly along the rails and was so silent she could almost have been leaning over the wash basin of last night's hotel. The brightness of the day hurt her eyes. She splashed her face again. Florence was slipping away, further and further into the past, and in a few hours she and Jane would be in Venice. Gemma had to be in Venice; it was vital. Yet it was Florence that filled her mind, as it had from the moment she had opened her eyes that morning.

She had slept heavily, and when at last the first glimmer of daylight crept between her eyelids, Jane was already up and dressed and sitting at the desk between the two tall windows of their room. Jane was, as usual, writing postcards but she heard Gemma stir and, without looking away from her busy pen, she said, "I warned you."

Gemma yawned. "Warned me? What about?"

"Last night – I warned you how you would feel this morning."

"I feel fine."

"Then you'd better take a look at yourself in the mirror."

Gemma heaved herself upright. Jane had left the wardrobe door open so that the mirror was visible, and Gemma could see herself from across the room. It was true that her hair was tousled, but it was like that every morning, and she was pale, but no paler than usual – except that the blackness of her hair did seem to emphasize the whiteness of her cheeks.

"You look a fright," said Jane.

"Maybe," Gemma agreed, but she was not listening. She was looking at her reflection, and for a moment the mirror was the doorway to another room where some other girl crouched in a bed with the clothes pulled up to her chin so that only her head was visible. And the girl was very small and a long way from her, only a pale face and straggles of black hair resting on the mound of bedclothes. It was as if only the head existed. Gemma smiled, and the girl showed her teeth in reply.

Jane criticized her. "You have rings under your eyes."

"I know," said Gemma. "I always have. It's the way I'm made –" she threw off the bedclothes so that a complete girl appeared in the mirror, "– but it doesn't make me any less beautiful."

Jane was silent for a moment, waiting for Gemma to laugh or at least make a comment that was less conceited, but Gemma stood silently examining herself in the glass. "You really do believe you're beautiful!" Jane exclaimed. "Huh!"

"Some people think so."

Jane finished writing a very full postcard with a tiny signature in the corner before she spoke. "It's because of last night," she said. "It's gone to your head. And the rings under your eyes are *much* darker than usual. It's all that wine you drank."

"Now you're trying to make it sound like an orgy."

"Well, it very nearly was."

"Two girls having a meal in a trattoria – is that an orgy?"

"That restaurant," said Jane, who from the very first moment of their holiday had refused to use any Italian words, "was a nasty, poky little place in a back alley."

"All streets in Florence are back alleys."

"But not like that – plaster coming off the walls and you could practically touch both sides of the street at once!"

Gemma had advanced closer to the mirror. "You are right," she said, "I do have rings under my eyes." Not that she minded. Her eyes were large, and dark and sleepy, and they had succeeded, as she knew they would, when the waiter came to their table last night. If he truly was a waiter; this morning she had doubts. "I shall never forget Florence," she said.

"It was dark in that nasty little back room," said Jane, "and hot."

"Only because it was crowded," said Gemma. There had been no places in the front part of the restaurant so they had been shown to a tiny room in the back. It had made Jane very uncomfortable to lose sight of people passing in the street, and sounds from outside were muffled as if they were hearing the sea from within a cave. "I liked it." Gemma turned slowly in front of the mirror. "I felt I'd known it for a long time."

"It was smelly."

"Candles," said Gemma. "It was only the smell of the candles." Hot wax had drowsed the air, and the glow from the candles, instead of dissolving shadows, had deepened them. "I felt like a moth," said Gemma. Last night she would not have cared if she had singed her wings. Perhaps she had. "Last night I felt I could fly. Anything could have happened."

"You should never have ordered so much wine." Jane was scolding again. "A glass each would have been quite sufficient – enough for me, anyway."

Quite suddenly Gemma did not have the energy to argue. She sat on the edge of the bed, stretched her arms high and pushed her black hair behind her head with both hands, holding it like a rope. "Red," she said, "dark red."

"Red?" Jane glanced at her. "I hope you aren't referring to your lips ... because they're far from red this morning. They are so pale you don't look well."

"I meant the wine," said Gemma. "It was so red it was black."

"Black or not, I didn't like it." Jane examined another card and approved it. "Now that's quite nice

– I wonder who it's right for." She turned the card face down and began to write. "And I was glad to leave that place. I couldn't wait to get out."

"I could have stayed all night." Gemma twisted the rope of hair behind her head and tied it at the nape of her neck. She yawned.

"And when that man – that waiter – came into the room with such a rush it blew out the candle on our table I'd had quite enough of it." Jane raised both hands and flapped the air in front of her face. "More than enough."

"I could tell that," said Gemma. "You didn't make a secret of it."

Jane had quit the room in such haste that she had made all the other candles dip their flames as if they were waving her goodbye. But Gemma had hardly been aware she had gone. The waiter – he had to be a waiter because he was wearing black, as they all did – stooped over the table and blocked her view of Jane's departure. He said something as he leant further to pick up the wine carafe and top up her glass, but what his words were she could not now remember ... just the slight huskiness of his voice as the black wine surged into the glass.

"You were ages," said Jane. "I waited and waited at the cash desk wondering what on earth had happened to you."

"Nothing happened," said Gemma. It was hardly a lie, but neither was it the truth. All she knew was that the waiter had stood at her table where the candle had died, and there was so much shadow in the room that his face was shrouded in blackness. "Nothing happened," she repeated.

"Oh, no? Then how was it that when I got tired of waiting and came back he was sitting at your table?"

"Was he? I don't remember."

"Don't remember! He was sitting at the table leaning towards you."

"Really?" Gemma paused. "Well, maybe he was, now that you mention it." Her voice was listless. The man had spoken to her, but with words she could not recall; perhaps they had been in a language she could not understand. But the sound of his voice remained in her head. His husky murmur had been like the deadened rasp of pebbles under a sea wave or the slow movement of heavy stone on stone, and it had made her shudder with the beginning of fear that, as she listened, became a secret pleasure. She had been told something forbidden. She shuddered again. "I had to finish my drink," she said. "That's why I kept you waiting."

"He was kissing you!"

"Oh, no." Gemma shook her head slowly from side to side. This was something she could be definite about without lying. "He could not have been kissing me because I was drinking my wine. He had poured it for me." She recalled every detail: the paleness of his hand in contrast to the dark flood of the wine into her glass, and the slenderness of his long fingers. His hands had seemed too long and too thin, and she had drawn back, repelled by them, until his murmur had made her lean towards him to try to catch his words. "He watched me drink, that's all."

"He was too close to be watching!"

"Well, he couldn't have been doing what you said." The glass had been at her lips, and her chin had been raised as she drained it. She could still taste the slightly metallic tang of the dark liquid. "So why do you pretend he was kissing me?"

"He was trying, that's all I can say. And I could see you wouldn't have minded if he had succeeded. You leant right forward, even if you were drinking."

"I was only trying to hear what he said."

"And what was that?"

"He said I'd called him to the table."

"And had you?"

"No, of course I hadn't." Gemma's head swam, as it had done in the small, dark room. "I didn't call him." But that was a lie. She had used no words, but she had called him. Her mind, as she sat alone, had been drifting like a moth in the night, far away into the darkness, and he had detected her. The throaty rasp of his voice had told her so. And suddenly she recalled his words. "From far away," he had said, "you called me from far away."

Jane's voice broke in on her. "You were leaning towards each other," she said, "and then you threw back your head."

"To drink my wine."

"Drink nothing!" Jane snorted. "I've never seen

such an exhibition. It was so he could kiss your neck!"

"No!"

"Yes!" Jane was adamant. "He kissed your neck!"

Gemma shook her head, but her eyes could not hold Jane's. She felt again the touch of his breath on her neck, and at the same instant the wine had caught sharply in her throat. She remembered the sharp stab of pain that was almost a pleasure, and then the swooning dizziness that Jane, coming back into the room, had interrupted.

Jane's sharp voice cut in once more. "And do you have to stand there with nothing on? You look ridiculous." Gemma blinked. "What an idiotic expression. Now you look as stupid as you did last night when I came to fetch you."

"What happened to him?" Gemma asked. "I didn't see him go."

"I'm not surprised. He got out quick because he'd spilled wine on the collar of your dress. It's ruined." Jane sighed as if looking after Gemma was becoming far too much of a chore and she picked up the dress from the chair where Gemma had left it. "Quite ruined – look." The dress had a low-cut collar, and the white lace was spotted with rusty stains. "This was an expensive dress and you've spoilt it." There was satisfaction in her voice, but Gemma was stretching again, and smiling. "And you needn't smirk like that – the mark will never come out."

Gemma turned a yawn into a little growl. "It's an

improvement," she said. "I hate white."

"Get dressed," Jane ordered. "I've had enough of you in this mood."

Gemma made no response. Nothing Jane said could disturb her because she had remembered one more thing. It was the last word he had said to her – but Jane would never know what it was, because Jane preferred postcards to mysteries. "I never even saw his face," said Gemma.

"Too bad." Even when Jane was being cruel, as now, Gemma could not get angry with her. Jane was blonde, and pretty, and sensible – and knew nothing. "You never will see him now."

"Maybe."

"How can you? We are on our way to Venice this afternoon."

"Venezia," said Gemma.

"Venice," said Jane firmly.

"Just as you like." Gemma crossed the room to take a shower. She kept the blinds closed and did not switch on the light. She held her face up to the cool water and let it slide over her, a barrier to the heat of the day. By night-time they would be in Venice, and that was the last word the waiter had said to her. *Venezia.*

On the train, Gemma bathed her eyes. The journey was turning into an ordeal she had not anticipated. Her distress had begun at the station where the platforms, glaring in the sunshine, had made her head ache. There had been some relief when the train had snaked into the tunnels that had taken them through the hills around Florence, but now they were crossing flat fields where the baked earth sent up a dazzling shimmer that not even the blinds seemed capable of blotting out. She patted her eyes dry and went back to their compartment.

She was hungry and thirsty, but she would taste neither the food nor the drink that Jane had bought at the station. The pale bread of the sandwiches repelled her, and she shook her head at the can of drink that Jane held out to her.

"You'll make yourself ill," said Jane, "and that will be the last straw."

But Gemma was paying no attention. Two young men across the aisle had seen her grimace, and it amused them. They had been drinking from a bottle of wine, passing it from one to the other, and now one of them, wiping the neck of the bottle against the palm of his hand, lent across and offered it to her.

"*Signorina?*" He smiled, raising his eyebrows, urging her to drink.

"No!" The voice was Jane's, but she was too late. Gemma had grasped the bottle, and the red wine was already cool on her tongue. She drank deeply and the boys applauded while Jane, horrified, pulled on the tag of her drink can.

"*Grazie.*" Gemma handed the bottle back, but as she did so she heard Jane give a little shriek and turned her head to see that the tag of the drink can had cut Jane's finger.

The boys were instantly concerned and were offering help, but it was Gemma who knelt in front of Jane, examining the cut. It was deep, and the blood was welling out. Jane was reaching for a tissue to staunch the flow when she suddenly snatched her hand away from Gemma and cried out, "No, I'll take care of it!"

Gemma said, "I was only trying to help."

"I thought you were going to put it in your mouth!"

Gemma turned large, dark eyes on her and Jane immediately felt guilty. "Sorry," she said, "I didn't mean anything." She tried to bind her finger but she was clumsy and some drops of blood dripped on to the sandwich which had fallen into her lap. "Ugh!" she cried and she handed it to Gemma as she left to wash her hands.

The boys, making the most of this chance to get to know the two girls, were making a fuss and soon both of them were saying things to Gemma that she did not understand but it was plain that they admired her. She smiled and nodded, and glanced down at the sandwich in her hand. Jane had bled copiously, and one edge of the white bread was dark red while the rest was speckled. One of the boys leant over to take it from her, but Gemma shook her head and drew back. They saw her raise it to her mouth.

Gemma bit the bread. It had a metallic tang like

wine. She reddened her lips on the sandwich and licked them.

Gemma did not see the boys' expressions change, but when Jane returned they were sitting solemnly facing each other, no longer interested in the English girls, and Gemma was fast asleep.

It was dark when they reached Venice and it was confusing to leave the platform, walk just a few paces and suddenly find themselves on the edge of the Grand Canal. Lights glinting on the water stabbed at the darkness and all seemed to be turmoil as they stepped on to a little jetty where a water taxi was waiting. Their luggage went aboard and they sat alongside it as the engine was throttled up and they surged out into the night.

Jane was fussing about the passports they would need when they booked into their hotel, but Gemma breathed the cool night into her lungs and knew she was in the place where she had to be. "It's like coming home," she said.

"That's the stupidest thing you've said yet." Jane was indignant. "This is a terrible place. You'll have the strap of your handbag cut and you'll be robbed."

"I hope so," said Gemma. She narrowed her eyes like a cat. "I hope someone attacks me – he'll get a surprise."

"Why? What do you think you'll do?"

Gemma smiled. "I'll think of something," she said. She allowed the night to enfold her, and when they were in their hotel room she sat silently by the window long after Jane was asleep.

They were on the fifth floor, and their room was at the side of the hotel, set back from the broad sweep of the Grand Canal and overlooking a waterway so narrow there was barely enough space for two boats to pass. Earlier, by leaning out over the broad window ledge, she had seen the long shapes of gondolas tied to the mooring poles far below, but now the night had closed in so that a deep chasm of darkness separated the hotel from the wall of the building opposite.

Small sounds echoed from below: the lap of water against the stone foundations and occasionally, when a motorboat on the canal pushed a wave between the buildings, the sleeping gondolas nudged each other, complaining for a moment before they settled again.

The night air was still, and Gemma sat by the open window listening to Jane's quiet breathing from across the room. Outside, a wavelet lapped and chuckled and died. Gemma listened. The flooded alleyway held its silence. Then something scratched against stone. She held her breath. The sound echoed against the wall opposite and faded.

Gemma folded her hands in her lap. When the sound came again, it was louder: a shuffling slide like the rasp of heavy cloth dragged over stone.

Gemma got to her feet and, despite herself, took a step backwards. Like the smell of an ancient well the breath of the cold canal came in through the window, and with it came the furtive shuffle of something hauling itself up the wall.

Then came a pause. Whatever it was that was climbing in the darkness was clinging to the vertical stone in silence, listening. Gemma did not move. She too, listened. She slowed her breathing and stood like a shadow among the other shadows of the room. She could see the outline of the window, and there was sufficient starlight to show the broad ledge jutting out into the darkness. She widened her eyes and watched.

At first, nothing showed, but then, little by little, the line of the window ledge was broken by shadow as a hand, groping from below, hooked thin fingers over the stone. It was then that she tilted back her head and sighed.

Her breath caught in her throat and she mewed like a cat. The sound disturbed Jane and she stirred in her sleep. As Gemma turned towards her the thin light filtering into the room from outside was blotted out and a figure, crouching for a moment on the ledge, raised itself to its full height in the window.

Gemma faced it. "You found me in Venice," she murmured, and he stepped down to her.

She went to him. The fingers of his pale hands were cool against her flesh, and his breath, although as cold as a cellar, was as heady as wine and she breathed it in.

She was sinking towards him when Jane, in the

grip of a feverish dream, flung back the sheet that covered her.

Gemma had never seen his eyes, but she knew when his gaze left her. She turned to look where he looked. Jane lay on the bed, as pale and smooth as marble. Her shoulders were naked and her head was flung back on the pillow. From the foot of the bed they stood and gazed down on her.

Gemma was the first to move. She glided silently forward as though she herself was in a dream, and knelt at the bedside.

He allowed her to leave him, and then he too advanced and knelt on the other side. They leant forward together. Gemma bared her teeth and felt the throb of the vein in Jane's neck against her lips as she waited for him. His breath was exhaled in a long sigh as his head came forward and his lips drew back.

It was then that Gemma saw the dark pits of his eyes for the first time, and the pale hollows of his cheeks and the lank black strands of his hair. They gazed at each other face to face as their teeth punctured the soft skin of the neck that lay between them, and they snuffled as they drank together.

PICKING UP THE TAB

Stan Nicholls

ADAM TOOK ANOTHER HANDFUL OF TWENTY-POUND notes and threw them into the fire.

They disappeared in a cloud of oily smoke billowing from the old tin bath. He tossed the last of the petrol after them and it ignited with a *whoomp* that made him take an involuntary step backwards. Flurries of orange sparks drifted over the lawn.

He dipped into the stuffed hold-all for more bundles of money to feed the blaze. Inch-thick wads of fives, tens and fifties turned to brittle ash.

A useless gesture, but Adam felt better for it.

He wiped the back of a hand across his forehead and glanced at the house.

Police sirens wailed in the distance. It wouldn't be long now.

He emptied the rest of the bag into the fire. The wind caught a single fluttering note. Snatching it from the air, Adam crushed it in his fist and flung it at the inferno.

The sirens were louder.

Frightened as he was, there was no point in running.

Spellbound by the flames, he let the events of the recent past flow through his mind.

It had been just seven days since it began.

A week and a different world ago...

"Do me a *favour*, Wanda!"

"What?"

Adam shoved the compact disc at her. "You've got butter all over it."

"Oh, yeah. Sorry."

"Can't you be more careful? I haven't even played it yet."

"All *right!*" She used her sleeve to wipe off the butter. "There. That do?" With a jab of her palm the CD slid back across the table to him.

"Thanks," he said sarcastically. "*Very* thoughtful."

"If you don't get off my case—"

"Button it, you two." Their mother slammed down a tray. "Saturday's one of the few times we have a meal together as a family, and you always ruin it."

"It's Adam," Wanda complained, glaring at him, "looking for something to moan about as usual."

"Is it my fault I've got a sister with the habits of a pig?"

"*Just once*," their mother interjected sternly, "I'd like your father to enjoy his breakfast in peace. Let's have a truce, shall we?"

Wanda scowled and reached for the cereal box. A vigorous shake produced one small cornflake. She looked at the empty packet, then at Adam's overflowing bowl.

The door opened before she could renew hostilities.

"Hi, Dad," Adam greeted him.

"Morning," Wanda said.

"Uhmm."

Unshaven, and still in his dressing gown, their dad seated himself. Mum pushed forward a cup of coffee. He took a sip and sliced open a brown envelope from the morning post. The sheet of blue and white paper it contained restored his power of speech. "Look at this, Babs," he said, handing it to their mother.

"What is it, Dad?" Wanda asked.

"A telephone bill. A *large* one."

Adam and Wanda suddenly became very interested in their plates.

"It is a little on the high side," their mum agreed.

"More than a little," Dad grumbled. He eyed his daughter. "*Some* people might consider that the next time they're chattering to their friends." He turned his attention to his son. "Or using their computer madam for hours on end."

"I think you mean *modem*, Dad," Adam corrected him.

Wanda stifled a giggle.

"Whatever it's *called*, it costs money to operate. Remember that."

"We're not the only ones living here," Adam protested.

"You might just as well be! Every time I want to

use the phone there's either a sniggering teenager or a brainless machine on it."

Mum stepped in as peacekeeper. "If you think the amount's unreasonable, Mark, why don't you query it?"

"You know," he said, folding the bill and putting it in his pocket, "I might just do that. And while we're on the subject of cutting expenses—"

The doorbell rang.

Adam leapt up, glad of the interruption. "OK, it's for me."

"I'm off too," Wanda announced, stuffing a last piece of toast into her mouth and grabbing her coat.

They left their father muttering about them treating the place like a hotel.

The visitor on the doorstep was cleaning his sunglasses with a tissue. He wore a black leather jacket covered with patches. A red sports bag hung from his shoulder.

"Hi, Perry."

"Morning, Adam." He grinned. "Hello, Wanda."

"How many more times do I have to tell you, Warner?" she bridled. "It's pronounced *Van*da, not *Won*da. *Van*da, *Van*da ... *VAN*-da."

"As in vandal," her brother said.

She gave him a menacing look.

"Nah, can't be right," Perry replied innocently. "That's like calling me *Var*ner."

"I don't know why I bother," she sighed, elbowing aside the smirking pair.

" 'Bye, *Won*da," Perry called after her.

"If you keep winding her up like that she's gonna deck you," Adam laughed.

"I know. But I can't resist it." Despite the absence of sunlight he put on the shades. "Let's go."

In three hours, fourteen minutes and twenty-two seconds, Adam would stand in the shadow of death.

He didn't really like the gaming arcade. The place was seedy, as were some of the people it attracted, so he wasn't sorry when Perry eventually looked at his watch and said he had to leave.

"I've got to be at Cost Savers by one o'clock," he explained.

"Dressed like *that*?"

He patted the bag. "Change of gear."

As they made their way out, Adam said, "I don't know how you can stand working in that supermarket."

"It's just until I've saved enough to upgrade my PC, then I'm out of there. My folks say money's a bit tight at the moment."

"I know all about *that* one," Adam sympathized.

They emerged blinking into daylight and crowds of weekend shoppers. Perry spotted his bus.

"Call you later!"

"Right."

Adam decided to head for home.

Death was thirty-one minutes away.

He took the long route, but regretted it when

leaden clouds appeared overhead. A raindrop splashed on the back of his hand and a chill wind knifed at him. Flipping up his collar, he walked faster.

Catching a bus for the rest of the journey seemed a good idea. Turning into Terminus Road he walked up the incline leading to the station, where he noticed a man leaning against the waist-high wall of the railway bridge and looking down at the tracks. Nobody else was around.

Seven minutes and fifteen seconds would elapse before death put in an appearance.

As he drew level with the unmoving figure Adam dug in his pocket for change. Fingers numb with cold, he fumbled the coins and dropped them. They showered tinkling to the pavement.

The man swung around.

Adam was rooted by his terrified expression. Middle-aged and dishevelled, he wore an unkempt blue suit with a slept-in look. He clutched the wall with knuckles as white as his face. His eyes were wild.

The stranger's gaze flicked from Adam to the coins and back again. But he appeared to be more frightened than threatening.

Hoping that was true, Adam bent to pick up the change and said, "Sorry."

The man's look of fear softened. He mumbled something.

"Pardon?"

"Money ... talks." His voice was low, hesitant. "That's what they say, isn't it? Money talks."

For want of any better response, Adam nodded.

"All it ever said to me was *goodbye*." The man laughed. It lacked any humour.

Adam smiled politely. A weak smile for a weak joke.

"Now *I'm* saying goodbye to *it*," the man added. The laugh came again, just as hollow and cynical.

Adam thought he might have been drunk. But his speech wasn't slurred and there was no alcohol on his breath.

Deranged then? Mad, perhaps?

This was getting spooky. And it might just turn nasty. Adam decided it was best to break contact and began moving off.

The man seized his jacket.

"Hey!" Adam tried to twist free.

The man yanked him closer. His eyes blazed. "The root of all evil," he rasped. *"Evil."*

"Yeah, yeah." Alarmed, Adam made another unsuccessful attempt to pull away.

"They're here. Here, *now*. And they're going to get us."

"They?"

"They ... it ... who knows? They've always been here, always collected their dues."

"Look, I—"

"You tell 'em. Tell everybody!" The man was shaking him. "Money! Do you hear me? It's pure evil! You've got to *believe* that!"

Adam was near panic, and there was still no one in sight. The man's grip was unbreakable.

A high-pitched whistling noise cut the air.

The man glanced down at the tracks. A train was approaching. He seemed to forget about Adam and let go of his jacket.

As Adam made for the other side of the road, the train's whistle blasted again, louder and keener than before. He looked over his shoulder.

The man was standing on the wall. Arms straight out from his sides, he wobbled unsteadily like a tightrope walker. Metallic vibrations ran through the rails below as the locomotive came closer.

He stared at Adam and bellowed, *"The root of all evil!"*

Then turned and shuffled to the edge.

Adam opened his mouth to yell but nothing came out. He willed his legs to move but they wouldn't obey.

The racket from the approaching train was deafening. Its whistle screamed once more to add to the din.

And the man stepped off the bridge to keep his appointment with death.

Rain pounded against the barred window of the interview room.

Adam was still shaking and had to hold the mug of tea in both hands. The dark, syrupy liquid was too strong and too sweet, but he drank it anyway.

Detective Inspector Frank Ingram sat on the other side of the table going through Adam's statement. A short man with a neatly trimmed moustache, and dressed in an immaculate three-piece suit, Ingram's expression was permanently severe.

He cleared his throat. "Well, that all seems to be in order. Although what the late Mr Lambert said to you doesn't make a lot of sense."

"Was that his name?"

"You didn't know?"

"Of course not. How could I?"

Ingram laid a brown leather wallet on the table. "Craig Lambert, according to his ID. He worked for a firm of stockbrokers."

The Inspector studied Adam's face, as though expecting some kind of reaction.

"All you spoke about was money?" he continued.

"He did most of the talking. A lot of it seemed to be about money, but I didn't really understand what he meant. And, as I said, there was the stuff about somebody being out to get him."

"He didn't say who?"

"No. He just said 'they'."

"Hmmm. I see." He scribbled something in his notepad. "Is there anything else you'd like to tell me?"

"I don't think so. Except..."

"Go on."

"I suppose I feel bad about not stopping him."

Adam thought he saw disappointment on the

inspector's face. "People who commit suicide are unpredictable. You weren't to know."

"But *why* did he do it?"

"As far as we can tell, he lived a perfectly ordinary life, and there's no record of him trying this before. We may never find out why."

He pushed the statement and a pen across the desk. "I'd like you to sign this. But before you do, there's something that's been puzzling me."

"What?"

Ingram glanced at the wallet. "I mentioned that Lambert had ID on him. But that was all he had. There was no money. No cheque book or credit cards either. Doesn't that strike you as strange?"

"I don't know. Jumping off that bridge was pretty strange."

"True. Are you *sure* you don't want to add anything to your statement?"

"I'm sure."

Adam had the uneasy feeling he was being accused of something.

They sent him home in a police car.

"He was just a poor, disturbed man, Adam. He would have jumped whether you were there or not."

"I guess you're right, Dad."

"He is," Wanda assured him. "Try to forget about it."

Adam wanted to believe them, but couldn't shake off the unease that had troubled him for the last twenty-four hours.

They crossed to the High Street. There wasn't much in the way of traffic this early on a Sunday morning, and even fewer people. The air was cool enough to turn their breath into little huffing clouds of condensation. A sheen of frost covered the pavements.

"I'll get the papers and catch up with you," Wanda suggested when they reached the newsagent's. She held out her gloved hand. Their dad sighed and dropped some change into it. Wanda pushed open the shop's door and went inside.

"The thing is," Adam said as they resumed their walk, "I can't stop thinking about that weird conversation I had with Lambert."

"Don't dwell on it."

"It's OK; it doesn't upset me or anything. It was sort of fascinating in a funny kind of way. All that stuff about money and evil, and something out to get him. Out to get *all* of us. He looked really terrified, Dad."

"The man was unwell." He frowned. "I'm more concerned about that policeman... What was his name?"

"Detective Inspector Ingram."

"Yes, Ingram. I don't like him implying you knew something about Lambert not having any money."

"He didn't actually accuse me of anything. And it was a mystery, wasn't it?"

"Well, yes, I can see that," his father admitted.

"And I suppose if you're a policeman and always dealing with the dark side of human nature you become suspicious of everybody."

They arrived at the bank and Adam's dad fed his card into the cash dispenser.

"Quiet a minute," he said, concentrating on punching in his pin number. "I always have to think about this bit."

The screen above the keys flashed a red message: *Invalid.*

Dad groaned.

"Sure you did it properly?"

"I'm not *that* senile yet, Adam."

He tried again.

Two more messages appeared, alternating from one to the other.

Unauthorized withdrawal... Enquire at branch... Unauthorized withdrawal...

"*Unauthorized?* What's the matter with it?"

"Let me try." Adam pressed buttons at random. The message continued flashing.

"Forget it," his Dad said. "I'll go to another one."

A new message came up.

Card withheld... Enquire at branch... Card withheld... Enquire at branch...

"The blasted thing's eaten my card!" He thumped the machine in frustration. "And what good is it telling us to enquire anywhere on a Sunday? Now I've got to come back tomorrow and sort it out."

Wanda came along with a bundle of newspapers

under her arm. "Can I have that fiver you promised me, Dad?"

"*No you can't!* What am I, a money pit?"

They trudged back in frosty silence.

It was the end of Monday afternoon before Adam got a chance to talk with Perry. As they made their way along the school's bustling corridors, he filled him in on the tragedy. He tried explaining the bizarre things Lambert had said, but Perry was more interested in the gruesome details.

"I bet it was really gross, eh?" he persisted. "When he went under that train."

Adam shuddered at the memory. "What do *you* think, ghoul? It wasn't a movie or an arcade game; it was real."

"Sorry. It must have been rough."

"Funnily enough, that isn't what I remember. It's what he *said*. I keep thinking there was some kind of crazy sense in it, you know?"

"No, not really. And if you try to figure it out you'll wind up as mad as he was."

"Maybe." He changed the subject. "Going to Cost Saver?"

"Yeah. Three hour shift."

"Me and Dad are going there for some shopping. Stick around and we'll give you a lift."

"Great."

"Only I've got to see Miss Barrett first, in here." He indicated the common room door.

Perry leaned against the opposite wall and dropped his bag. "OK, I'll wait."

Adam knocked and went in.

Pamela Barrett was alone. She put down the file she was reading, took off her glasses and smiled.

"Hello, Adam. Take a seat."

He drew a chair from the large wooden table that dominated the room and sat facing her.

"How are you?" she said.

"Fine."

Adam had always been comfortable with the young teacher, maybe because she wasn't that much older than him. He could talk to her without feeling patronized the way he did with some of the other members of staff.

She swept aside a stray lock of blonde hair and put the glasses back on. "The police have been in touch about the ... incident at the weekend. It must have been a terrible shock."

"It wasn't that bad."

"But after seeing that man—"

"I didn't actually *see* him hit by the train. And I only took a quick peek over the bridge afterwards."

"How have you been since? Any nightmares, for instance? You can be honest, Adam, there's nothing to be ashamed of."

"No, it's not affected me that way."

"You're implying it's affected you in some other way?"

"I keep thinking about what the man, Lambert,

said before he jumped. You know he spoke to me?"

"Yes. Want to tell me about it?"

Adam recounted the conversation on the bridge. Miss Barrett made a few notes but didn't interrupt. When he finished, she said, "He was ill, Adam."

"That's what everybody tells me. But suppose he wasn't? Even if he was, why couldn't he have been telling the truth?"

"The truth about *what*? It all sounds very confused to me. He probably *imagined* that somebody was after him. You know, a persecution complex. I expect those references to money were part of his delusions as well. You mustn't get hung-up on what a sick person said to you."

"Everybody's been telling me that, too. But he seemed ... I don't know ... *genuine*. Sincere."

"Mentally ill people can be very convincing." She riffled through some papers in the file. "Would you like me to arrange for you to meet a counsellor, Adam?"

"Thanks, but I don't see the need, Miss Barrett."

She studied him thoughtfully for a few seconds then said, "OK, we'll put the counselling on hold for the time being."

Adam got up.

"There's, er, something else."

He noted her uncomfortable expression as he sat down again.

"The policeman in charge of the investigation," she began nervously, "Detective Inspector Ingram, said

273

he was ... puzzled ... that Lambert..."

"Didn't have any money on him?" Adam offered.

"Yes. He told you that, of course." Miss Barrett was practically squirming with embarrassment. "And, uhm, Mr Ingram wanted me to ask—"

"Whether I stole it?"

"Adam! He didn't say that at all."

"It's what he meant though, isn't it?"

"No. No, of course not. It's just that the people Lambert worked with said he always carried cash and credit cards. The inspector thought you might have remembered something that—"

"I don't know anything about the man not having any money, and that's the truth. If he thought money was evil, isn't it logical he wouldn't have any on him?"

"Hmmm, I suppose it would fit in with his psychosis... And I'm afraid the police do tend to see most teenagers in a negative light." She closed the file. "Sorry. But I hope you understand that I had to ask."

"I understand."

Miss Barrett looked relieved at having got the subject over with. As he was leaving she added, "I'm here if you need to talk."

Adam nodded and quietly closed the door behind him.

Perry stood and dusted himself off. "How'd it go?"

"OK."

His tone didn't encourage further questions.

They walked to the front gate. Adam's father was parked on the other side of the road, impatiently drumming the steering wheel with his fingers.

Once they were underway, Adam said, "Did you sort out the cash card, Dad?"

"No," he replied brusquely. "According to them I'm massively overdrawn on the account."

"That's not right!"

"I *know* it isn't. Some mix-up with their damned computer, I expect. They're hanging on to the card while they look into it."

They arrived at the supermarket and cruised the street looking for a parking meter. When they finally found one, Adam's father dug through his pocket for change and pushed coins into the slot.

The meter pinged and displayed the red *penalty* sign.

"I don't *believe* it," he groaned.

Perry said, "I really ought to be going, Mr Ferguson."

"Why don't I go on with Perry and start getting the shopping organized?" Adam suggested.

"Good idea. I'll look for somewhere else to park."

They left him glaring at the meter.

At the supermarket Perry went off to change while Adam equipped himself with a wire basket. But he couldn't concentrate fully for thinking about the odd things that had been happening lately.

Twenty-five minutes later his father turned up, flushed and sour-faced.

STAN NICHOLLS

"What took you so long, Dad?"

"You may well ask. I found another meter and *that* one did exactly the same thing. Soon as I put the coins in it went to penalty."

"Where's the car then?"

"Had to leave it on a yellow line. So let's not hang around."

Perry was operating one of the tills. The baggy white coat he wore was several sizes too large and he'd had to roll up the sleeves.

"They've promised me one that fits," he said defensively.

Adam tried not to laugh. "How long have they let you work on the checkout?"

"From this evening. You're my second customer."

"Can we get on with it, boys?" Adam's father said.

Perry took each item of shopping and ran it across the scanner that automatically registered its cost. The tiny oval screen next to the till displayed the prices in green numerals.

All went well until he pressed the total button.

A grinding noise came from the cash register. The screen flickered and showed *00.00*.

Perry looked mystified. "It's not supposed to do that," he said, stating the obvious.

He hit the button again.

The screen began flashing a series of random figures.

24.95 ... 112.16 ... 92.81 ... 303.38 ... 18.42 ... 77.23 ... 215.64 ... 11.09...

With a loud *ting* the cash drawer flew open. The printer clattered and started spewing an endless receipt covered in gibberish.

Other shoppers craned their necks to see what was going on. Beetroot red with embarrassment, Perry jabbed buttons in a futile attempt to control the situation. The ceaseless outpouring of receipt paper continued. Meaningless numbers flashed ever faster on the screen.

The semi-circle of onlookers parted for a stout man identified by a plastic name tag reading *Manager.* His face was as cheerful as an undertaker with a migraine.

"What's going on?" he barked.

"There's something wrong with the till, Mr Harvey," Perry replied sheepishly.

"I can see *that.* Stand aside."

He leaned across and punched buttons with a plump finger. It made no difference. Frowning, he reached below the till and wrenched out its plug. The machine instantly died.

Except for the screen, Adam noticed. For a fraction of a second it froze on *666.00* before fading to black.

The manager glared at Perry. "I think it would be better if you went back to shelf-filling for the time being."

"It wasn't his fault," Adam's father said.

The manager gave him a transparently false smile. "Sorry you've been inconvenienced. If you would care to take your purchases to another—"

"We're in a hurry. Is there any way to speed this up?"

"Of course." He produced a pocket calculator.

Once the bill was totalled, Adam's dad gave the manager his credit card and he took it away for processing.

When he came back, the synthetic smile had gone.

"It won't be possible to serve you," he announced.

"*What?*"

"I've just spoken to the credit card company and they say you no longer have a valid account."

"But—"

"Furthermore, I'm authorized to destroy the card in your presence."

"Just a minute! What gives you the right—"

"Take it up with the company, Mr Ferguson."

He slipped a pair of scissors from his pocket and cut the card in two. "Put those goods back on the shelves, Warner. Good day, sir."

In a state of shock, father and son left empty-handed. Neither found anything to say to each other, and Adam's insides were gripped by the cold, clammy hand of doubt and apprehension.

When they reached the car there was a parking ticket on its windscreen.

The next morning saw little joy in the Ferguson household.

Adam's mum came in with the post.

"This one's from the telephone company." She

passed Dad a brown envelope.

He ripped it open and took out two sheets of paper. The first was a letter.

"Is it about the bill you queried?" Wanda asked.

"Yes. Hang on." He scanned the sheet. "After the usual guff it says, 'We have reviewed the account and can confirm that the sum requested on your current bill is incorrect.'"

"See?" Mum said with a smile. "It was worth getting in touch with them."

"'An amended bill is enclosed,'" Dad continued, "'and we take this opportunity of reminding you that payment is due within fourteen days of the receipt of this letter.'"

He looked at the second sheet.

The colour drained from his face.

"What is it, Mark?" Mum said.

Speechless, he handed her the bill.

"'Total due,'" she read, "'eight...'" Her jaw dropped.

"Mum?" Adam prompted, a ripple of icy fear growing in his stomach.

"'Eighteen thousand, two hundred and forty-four pounds, twenty pence.'"

Wanda gasped, "*What?*"

Dad found his voice. "I don't know what the *heck's* going on here, but I'm going to get to the bottom of it!" He marched to the telephone and snatched the receiver.

"Don't bother," Mum told him, "it's too early."

He slammed the phone down. "First the cash card, then the credit card and now this!" His furious gaze turned on the children. "If you kids have been up to anything with that telephone, I'll—"

"Oh, *come on*, Dad!" Adam retorted indignantly.

"It's nothing to do with us!" Wanda complained.

Mother held up her hand. "Calm down! All of you. Mark, get on to the telephone people as soon as they open for business. Tell them you want an *itemized* bill right away."

He grunted, then strode out of the room, slamming the door behind him.

Adam wondered why he hadn't thought of consulting Cyrus Archer before.

The elderly academic had been his mathematics master for less than a year, but Adam had got on with him remarkably well, despite the great difference in their ages. Archer had one of the liveliest intellects Adam had ever encountered, and he thought of him as a kind of mentor. Their friendship had continued beyond his retirement.

He yanked the ancient bell-pull, setting off a discordant chime deep in the house's gloomy interior. A few minutes later the door creaked open.

Cadaverously thin, Archer wore his usual faded but once expensive tweed suit, and the thick bifocals that almost seemed a part of him. His unruly hair and goatee beard were a little whiter, but he was otherwise unchanged.

"Adam, how nice to see you; it's been far too long."

"Evening, Cyrus." He still felt slightly uncomfortable about Archer's insistence that he use his first name.

Once they settled into a pair of over-stuffed armchairs in the study, the old man got straight to the point. "Your telephone call was fascinating, and your encounter with the unfortunate Lambert was certainly bizarre. I found what he told you most intriguing."

Adam was pleased at having someone finally take him seriously. He glanced at the thousands of books surrounding them. "I thought you'd be interested, knowing your fascination for the more unusual side of human nature."

"And that I might be able to give you some insight into the workings of a disturbed mind."

"Well, yes, I suppose so. I've been trying to make sense of it all, and as you're well up on psychology—"

"I believe you've come to the right person," Archer interrupted, his expression serious, "but for the wrong reason." He indicated the overflowing bookshelves. "The answer may well lie in my other passion."

"Folklore and myth, you mean? The occult?"

"The word occult merely means 'hidden' or 'unseen'. The great scientist Thomas Alva Edison once said, 'We don't know a millionth of one per cent about anything,' and he was right. But I believe the study of paranormal phenomena could increase that percentage."

"I don't see the connection with Lambert."

"Your question is simple, the answer less so, I'm afraid. It's possible that he found out about..."

"About what?"

"I need to think this through, Adam. But it's possible that your experience touches upon a particular area of my research. Suffice it to say that the key is in that phrase the 'root of all evil'. The full quotation, of course, is, 'The love of money is the root of all evil'. However, I think the ... *intelligence* behind this is far from loveable."

"You're not making a lot of sense."

"I know. Be patient." His face darkened. "And be careful."

Adam tried to get him to say more, but he wouldn't be drawn.

"I feel a bit guilty about this, Mum."

"Don't be silly, Adam. You saved the money and you can do what you like with it. Let's go in."

The sports shop was filled with lunchtime shoppers. At the footwear section, Adam said, "Maybe I should leave this for now. I mean, considering the mess we're in—"

"You know we've *got* money, it's just that we can't get to it. Your dad'll sort it out, don't worry." She took three twenty-pound notes from her handbag and gave them to him. "But I'm glad I drew this from the bank last week, before all the trouble with the account."

"You can say that again." Adam selected the trainers he wanted.

At the sales desk the cashier held one of the crisp new notes up to the light and frowned. Her expression became harder as she examined the other two.

"Anything wrong?" Adam's mother asked.

"Just a second." One at a time, the cashier laid the notes on an illuminated plate. Eventually she said, "I'm afraid these aren't genuine."

"They *have* to be!"

"I can assure you they're fakes," the cashier insisted. "See? No metal strip. And there are other things wrong with them."

"I don't understand it."

"No, madam," the woman said coldly. "Perhaps you'd better talk to the manager." She pressed a button beside the till.

"You should be getting back to school," Adam's mum told him, her voice dreamy with shock.

"No. I'll stay and—"

"*Don't argue.* There must be some mistake. I'll see what the manager says."

Once more, Adam experienced the feeling of dread that had visited him regularly in the past few days; the sensation of reality slipping out of gear and turning the world into a hostile place.

Reluctantly, he made his way out of the shop, aware of every eye in the place burning into his back.

*　　*　　*

283

When he got home that evening, Adam saw two men come out of his house and drive away in a van.

The atmosphere indoors was tense.

"Who were they?" he asked, hoping it wasn't more bad news.

"Bailiffs," Wanda said.

"Bailiffs?"

"They had a court order," his mum explained. Her face was etched with worry. "It said we owe hundreds of pounds in unpaid parking tickets."

"Do we?"

"Of course not. All we've had this year was the one your father got outside the supermarket this week. Fortunately we managed to persuade the bailiffs to hold off for a couple of days. Dad's on the phone to the court now."

"And he isn't happy," Wanda added darkly.

Adam could see that for himself when his dad came in from the living room.

"It's like talking to a brick wall!"

Mum laid a hand on his arm. "Take it easy, Mark, and tell us what happened."

"I told them it had to be a mistake. *They* said it wasn't. When I pointed out that today was the first we'd heard of it, they obviously didn't believe me."

"That's crazy."

"It's on their computer, so it *has* to be right, doesn't it?" he said bitterly. "I'll have to get a lawyer to deal with this. More expense!"

Unwisely, Wanda said, "At least you can't blame us

this time."

"We'll have a little less of your lip! Particularly when you're trying to ruin us by sending for that junk!" He waved his hand at a pile of shrink-wrapped magazines on the table.

"I keep telling you, they're nothing to do with me!" she protested.

"What are they?" Adam said.

No one answered so he looked for himself. The dozen or so periodicals were addressed to Wanda. Adam flipped through them and was puzzled by the wide variety of subjects: *Surf-Boarding Monthly, Tropical Fish News, Classic Chess Problems, Golfing World, You and Your Pension*...

Dad brandished a handful of envelopes. "And these are the invoices for subscriptions to all of them. Nearly three hundred pounds' worth!"

"I didn't order them!" Wanda complained. "Why would I want any of that stuff?"

"Did you get a chance to ring about them today, Babs?" he asked their mother.

"Sorry, Mark, no. I was in the bank most of the afternoon trying to sort out those counterfeit notes."

"Any luck?"

"Not really. They denied it could have had anything to do with them."

"Of course." His voice dripped sarcasm. "How silly of me to expect something to go right for a change." He turned to Adam and snapped, "And why were you so late back from school?"

"Oh. Er, Perry and I dropped into the gaming arcade."

"You've got money to waste now, have you?"

"No. Actually, I only went to please Perry. He's still a bit ratty about what happened at the supermarket the other day. And ... we had a slight problem."

"What?"

"We got thrown out." He quickly added, "We weren't mucking about, honest. It's just that I put some money into one of the machines and it ... broke down."

"Why don't I find that surprising?" his father sighed.

The following day's mail brought another batch of magazines that sparked a further row between Wanda and her father. And the itemized telephone bill, running to eleven pages, contained scores of numbers no one recognized, many with foreign prefixes.

The two remaining letters were worse.

Dad, who looked as though he hadn't slept, gave them the gist of the first one. "The building society want to know why the mortgage hasn't been paid."

"But, Mark, it *has*," Mum said.

"I know." His anger had been replaced by weariness. He opened the last envelope. "And this is from my accountant." He related the contents like someone in a trance. "The Inland Revenue have found a discrepancy in my tax returns. They're demanding immediate payment of..."

"Yes?"

"Twenty thousand, near enough."

Mum gasped.

"That's not all. There's a problem with VAT, too. They want what the accountant calls a 'substantial' sum. He finishes by saying, 'I must remind you that as a self-employed person it is your responsibility to conduct your financial affairs in an open and honest manner.' And here's the kicker. 'It is my duty to inform you that failure to do so could result in a large fine or even imprisonment.' "

A knot of fear tightened in Adam's chest.

"You're not going to jail are you, Dad?" Wanda exclaimed.

" 'Course not, dear," her mother told her. "We're just having some bad luck at the moment. It can't last for ever."

"Can't it?" Dad said.

The telephone rang and mother answered it. "Adam, it's Cyrus Archer. Why don't you take it in the other room?"

When he got to the extension, Adam told the professor it wasn't the best time for a chat.

"I understand. And in fact it would be unwise for us to speak too freely on the telephone."

Adam was puzzled by that, but let it pass.

"Could you come and see me tomorrow evening?" his old teacher said. "It's very important."

"We've some family problems at the moment, but I think so."

"Are they of a financial nature?"

"How did you know?"

"I won't go into that now. But please be here tomorrow. It's *vital*."

Adam promised he would and hung up.

He spent the rest of the evening trying to rid himself of the thought that things were getting out of control.

At school, Perry greeted him with surprising news.

"Heard about Pamela Barrett?"

"No, what?"

"She's only won a bundle on a lottery ticket."

"Yeah? How much?"

"Two hundred and fifty grand! And they say she's never bought a ticket before. Talk about luck, eh?"

"Wow. I wonder what she'll do with it."

"Gonna travel the world, apparently."

"I'll have to congratulate her."

"You're too late. She's quit already. Came in early this morning, cleared her desk and left."

"That was a bit sudden, wasn't it?"

Perry shrugged. "Perhaps she likes acting on impulse."

Adam couldn't understand why he felt there was something unsettling about Miss Barrett's good fortune.

A storm was brewing.

Lightning flashed, briefly illuminating the shadowy recesses of Cyrus Archer's study. Distant thunder rolled.

As Adam finished relating his family's troubles the old man snapped on a table lamp. A pool of soft orange light embraced them, intensifying the surrounding gloom.

"I'm having some financial difficulty myself at present," Archer said.

"Really?" The nameless dread crept back.

"Yes. My private pension, usually paid into my bank like clockwork, has gone astray. It looks as though they're beginning to take an interest in me too. I'm surprised it took so long."

"I don't understand any of this."

"I shall endeavour to explain. But you may regard what I say as the ramblings of a deranged wrinkly."

Adam smiled. "I doubt it."

"Very well." He paused for a moment to gather his thoughts. "What would you say if I told you we have always unknowingly shared this world with another life form at least as intelligent as us? And I'm not talking about dolphins."

"I'd say tell me more."

"Then bear with me. Human history is littered with references to this ... *species*. In Biblical times, people believed in demons. And angels, of course. The Middle Ages abound with tales of vampires and werewolves. Sea serpents were reported as early as the second century, although sightings are much less

289

common now. Ghosts and spirits seem always to have been with us, and the nineteenth century saw the first recorded instances of poltergeists. Our own century has the Yeti and the Loch Ness monster, not to mention UFOs and their presumed alien occupants."

"I don't know where this is leading, Prof. But I'd be more convinced if anyone had ever caught one of these things."

"Suppose that's because they only take physical form when it suits them? Imagine an intelligence composed of pure thought that can become whatever it chooses."

"So all these different supernatural creatures and so on are—"

"A single, controlling intelligence that takes many guises. And don't you see, Adam? It adopts a new form for each age."

"Why?"

"To suit changing human beliefs. There can't be many people these days who take vampires or fairies seriously, but you'll find plenty of folk who accept the existence of, say, flying saucers."

"But what's the point of it? Why would this intelligence behave that way?"

"Because it's in its nature to sow discord, confusion ... and fear."

Lightning flooded the room and thunder boomed.

"Oh, yes," Archer continued, "there's a great deal of evidence indicating this thing is malevolent. The *real* history of the human race is of an unending war between the powers of Darkness and Light. We live side by side with an invisible empire. An empire of evil!"

"I still don't see how this all ties in with me and my family."

"*Think*, Adam. This life form is jealous of us, it resents our dominance of the planet. It may even be older than our race; it could have been here when our primitive ancestors heaved themselves from the swamp. Up to now, its battle with us has been a draw. But given its ability to assume any guise, and its ambition to replace us, what form do you think it might take now?"

"Monsters of some sort? Or—"

"There's no need! Our civilization has produced something that gives it the opportunity finally to conquer us."

"I don't see what that could be."

"*The financial system!*"

"You can't be serious!"

"It sounds insane, I know. But can you think of a more powerful force in the world today than money? Look how it rules our lives. You've seen yourself how difficult things get when the system breaks down. *Becoming* that system is the perfect way to manipulate and ultimately destroy us!"

"Why hasn't anybody realized this before?"

"I believe they have. But the life form guards itself jealously. It doesn't take any risks. Lambert, for example, who must have discovered the truth somehow, was driven to suicide."

"But how did he find out?"

"Perhaps by chance, like you. It hardly matters now."

Adam paled. "And he spoke to me before he killed himself."

"Exactly. You *know*. That's why you're being persecuted. This thing will get at you any way it can. Where it can't do it directly, it applies pressure to your family and friends. It has many weapons at its disposal. Take Pamela Barrett. There's a possibility she might have tried to help you, so she was, in effect, bribed to go away."

"What does this intelligence expect me to do?"

"I don't think it expects you to *do* anything. I think it wants to eliminate you."

"Just a minute, Cyrus. Don't take this the wrong way, but I'm far from buying your theory. Why try to get rid of me if I don't believe it?"

"As I said, it doesn't take any chances. If there's just a possibility of you believing, or passing on your story to someone who would, that's enough to have you ... *silenced*."

Adam thought how sad it was that the professor had allowed his imagination to run away with him.

But trying to be rational didn't stop a chill from tickling his spine.

He didn't tell his parents what Cyrus Archer said. They had enough to worry about.

The next morning, Saturday, they both went out

early to see the accountant. Mid-morning, the post arrived, and there was a package for Adam. It contained a note and a key.

The note read:

Dear Adam,

I am sending this in advance of our meeting tonight. If anything happens to me before then, use the key to let yourself into my house. You will find a letter addressed to you in the top drawer of my desk. It will tell you what I would have explained this evening.

Should anything happen to me after *our meeting, you will understand why. In that event, my library may provide a clue to defeating them.*

I have good reason to believe we are in danger. Take care.

C.A.

It made him realize how seriously the professor took his theory. Surely there couldn't have been any truth in his fanciful story?

Could there?

The doorbell broke Adam's reverie.

He heard Wanda answer it, and the clump of boots overlaid with unfamiliar voices in the hall. Adam stuffed the key into his pocket.

Detective Inspector Ingram came into the kitchen. Two uniformed officers stood behind him.

There were no pleasantries. "I need to talk to you,"

the policeman said. "I understand you're acquainted with a Mr Cyrus Archer."

"What about it?"

"He's been seriously injured."

"*No!* What happened?"

"There was a raid on a betting shop in Union Street. He got in their way outside and was shot."

"Shot?" Adam thought of the note. "Where *is* he? I have to go and—"

"I'm afraid not. He's in intensive care. And I'm only telling you because we found your name in his address book."

"Mine couldn't have been the only name in it. Why come to me?"

"I'm mentioning it because it seemed quite a co-incidence as we were coming here anyway."

Adam was baffled. "Why?"

"In connection with another of your friends. Perry Warner."

Wanda appeared at the doorway. "Is Perry OK?"

"He's under arrest on suspicion of stealing money from the supermarket where he works part-time."

"Never!" Adam said. "Perry's the most honest—"

"And we have reason to believe," the inspector interrupted, "that he had an accomplice."

Adam could see where this was going. "You mean *me*?"

"We understand you and your father tried to obtain goods under false pretences there the other day."

294

"It wasn't like that. We—"

"And there's a report of you and your *mother* attempting to pass counterfeit notes in a sports shop."

"But—"

"Add to that the little mystery of Craig Lambert's missing money and it begins to look like we're dealing with a criminal family here. I'm going to have to ask you to come down to the station."

Wanda said, "This is ridiculous!"

"Stay out of it, young lady," Ingram warned.

"You're not taking my brother!" Without warning, she flung herself at the inspector. The other two policemen moved in and struggled with her. "Run, Adam!" Wanda shouted. *"Run!"*

He hesitated for a second, unwilling to leave her.

Then fled through the back door.

Adam went to Cyrus Archer's house.

When he looked in the desk for the letter he found a hold-all crammed with bank notes. He knew it didn't belong to Archer. It was there to implicate him in something, to frame and discredit him.

Adam was a believer now. For all the good it did him.

And he knew real fear.

The least he could do for his elderly friend was get rid of the contents of the bag. He found an old galvanized bath and a can of petrol in the garden shed.

They made a perfect ... *funeral pyre*.

The shrieking police cars drew up as he gave the last of the notes to the flames. He didn't bother to run. Where would he go? He was up against something ruthless and all-pervading. And as Archer said, it took no chances.

It had isolated him, and left him with a story no one would believe.

"Destroying evidence, are we?"

He turned. Detective Inspector Ingram was walking toward him across the lawn.

Adam had no doubt that more "evidence" would be produced. It even occurred to him to wonder how much it took to bribe a policeman. Anything was possible.

Ingram took him by the arm. "Running away like that wasn't very smart. It makes you look guilty of something. What's the matter, cat got your tongue?"

"I don't think whatever I say is going to make much difference somehow."

The inspector smiled. It wasn't pleasant.

"You can put money on it," he said.

EVIDENCE OF ANGELS

Graham Masterton

BEFORE HE WAS BORN SHE LOVED HIM WITH A FIERCE and sisterly love and called him Alice. Her mother let her rest her head against her stomach and hear his heart beating inside her, and sometimes she felt the strong fleshy ripple of his kicking. With some of the money that her parents had given her for her thirteenth birthday, she went to Jenner's and bought him a little lace-collared dress in the Stewart tartan, and kept it hidden to surprise him on the day that he was due to be born.

She was so sure that he was going to be a girl that she played out imaginary scenes in her head, in which she taught Alice her first ballet steps; and in which they danced the opening scenes of *La Fille Mal Gardeé* to amuse their mother and father. And she imagined taking her for walks on winter mornings up to the Castle Mound, where strangers would stop and coo at Alice and think that Gillie was her mother, instead of her older sister.

But one January morning she heard her mother crying out; and there was a lot of running up and down stairs; and father drove mother off to the

Morningside Clinic, while the snow swarmed around them like white bees, and eventually swallowed them up.

She spent the day with Mrs McPhail, who was their cleaner, in her neat cold house in Rankeillor Street, with its ticking clocks and its strong smell of lavender polish. Mrs McPhail was tiny and disagreeable, and kept twitching her head like a chicken. She gave Gillie a bowl of greyish stew for lunch, with onions in it, and watched and twitched while Gillie miserably pushed it around and around, and the snow on the kitchen windowsill heaped higher and higher.

Mrs McPhail's rotary washing-line stood at an angle in the centre of her back yard, and that was clogged up with snow, too. It looked to Gillie like a seraph, with its wings spread; and as she looked, the sun suddenly broke out from behind the clouds, and the seraph shone, dazzling and stately, yet tragic, too, because it was earthbound now, and now could never hope to return to heaven.

"Do you no care for your dinner?" asked Mrs McPhail. She wore a beige sweater covered with pills of worn wool, and a brown beret, even indoors. Her face made Gillie think of a plate of lukewarm porage, with skin on, into which somebody had dropped two raisins for eyes, and drawn a downward curve with the edge of their spoon, for a mouth.

"I'm sorry, Mrs McPhail. I suppose I'm not very hungry."

"Good food going to waste. That's best lamb, and barley."

"I'm sorry," she said.

But then, unexpectedly, the disagreeable Mrs McPhail smiled at her, and said, "Don't fash yourself, darling. It's not every day that you get a new baby, now, is it? Now what do you think it'll be? A boy or a girl?"

The thought of it being a boy had never entered Gillie's head. "We're going to call her Alice," she said.

"But what if she's a he?"

Gillie put down her fork. The surface of her stew was floating with small globules of fat. But it wasn't the stew that made her feel nauseous. It was the unexpected idea that her mother might have been harbouring a brother, instead of a sister. A brother! A son and heir! Wasn't that what Grandma had always complained about, every time that they visited her? "Such a pity you never had a son and heir, Donald, to carry on your father's name."

A son and heir wouldn't want to learn ballet steps. A son and heir wouldn't want to play with her doll's house, which she had carefully brought down from the attic, and fitted with new carpets, and a dining-table, and three plates of tiny plaster-cast meals with sausages and fried eggs.

She had saved for so long for that tartan dress. Supposing the baby was a boy? She flushed at her own stupidity.

"You look feverish, pet," said Mrs McPhail. "Don't eat your dinner if you don't feel like it. I'll warm it up for later. How about some nice pandowdie?"

Gillie shook her head. "No, thank you," she whispered, and tried to smile. In the back yard, the sun had vanished, and the sky was growing grim; but the rotary clothes-line looked more like a wrecked angel than ever. She could hardly bear to think of it standing there, throughout the night, unloved, and abandoned, and unable to fly.

"Let's watch telly," said Mrs McPhail. "I can't miss *Take the High Road*. I wouldnie have a thing to talk about tomorrow, doon the bingo."

They sat on the clumpy brown sofa and watched television on Mrs McPhail's blurry ex-rental television set. But every now and then, Gillie would look over her shoulder at the seraph in the back yard, watching his wings grow larger and thicker as the snow fell faster still. Perhaps he would fly, after all.

Mrs McPhail was noisily sucking a humbug. "What do you keep keekin' at, pet?"

Gillie was embarrassed at first. But somehow she felt that she could tell Mrs McPhail almost anything, and it wouldn't matter. It wouldn't get "reported back", the way that her grandma had once reported her comments about school back to her mother and father.

"It's your clothes-line. It looks like an angel."

Mrs McPhail twisted herself around and stared at it. "With wings, you mean?"

"It's only the snow."

"But you're right, pet. That's just what it looks like. An angel. Seraphim and cherubim. But they always arrive, don't you know, when a baby arrives. It's their duty to take good care of them, those little ones, until they can stand on their own two feet."

Gillie smiled and shook her head. She didn't understand what Mrs McPhail was talking about, although she didn't like to say so.

"Every child has a guardian angel. You have yours; your new baby has hers. Or his. Whatever it's turned out to be."

It has to be Alice, thought Gillie, desperately. *It can't be a son and heir.*

"Would you like a sweetie?" asked Mrs McPhail, and offered her the sticky, crumpled bag.

Gillie shook her head. She was trying to give up sweeties. If she wasn't good enough to be a ballerina, she wanted to be a supermodel.

By four o'clock it was dark. Her father came at five o'clock and stood in the porch of Mrs McPhail's house with snow on his shoulders and whisky on his breath. He was very tall and thin, with a tiny sandy moustache and bright grey eyes like the shells you could find on Portobello Beach before they went dry. His hair was thinning on top and it was all sprigged up.

"I've come to take you home," he said. "Your mum's well and the baby's well and everything's fine."

"You've been celebrating, Mr Drummond," said Mrs McPhail, with mock disapproval. "But you've every right. Now tell us what it was and how much it weighed."

Dad laid both his hands on Gillie's shoulders and looked right into her eyes. "You've a baby brother, Gillie. He weighed seven pounds six ounces and we're going to call him Toby."

Gillie opened her mouth but she couldn't speak. Toby? Who was Toby? And what had happened to Alice? She felt as if Alice had been secretly spirited away, and her warm place in her mother's womb given to some strange and awful boy-baby whom she didn't know at all, the human equivalent of a cuckoo.

"That's grand!" said Mrs McPhail. "No wonder you've been taking the malt, Mr Drummond! And a cigar, too, I shouldn't be surprised!"

"Well, Gillie?" asked her father. "Isn't it exciting! Think of all the fun you'll be able to have, with a baby brother!"

Gillie was shaking with a genuine feeling of grief. Her eyes filled with tears and they ran down her cheeks into her tartan scarf. *Alice! They've taken you away! They never let you live!* She had thought of Alice so often that she even knew what she looked like, and what they were going to play together, and what they would talk about. But now there was no Alice, and there never would be.

"Gillie, what's the matter?" her father asked her.

"Are you feeling all right?"

Gillie's throat felt as if she'd swallowed one of Mrs McPhail's humbugs without sucking it. "I bought—" she began, and then she had to stop because her lungs hurt and every breath was a painful sob. "I bought – I bought her a dress! I spent my birthday money on it!"

Her father laughed and gave her a hug. "There now, don't you go worrying your wee head about that! We'll go back to the shop and swap it for a romper-suit, or maybe some trews! How about that? Come on now, this is such a happy day! No more greeting now, you promise?"

Gillie sniffed and sniffed again and wiped her eyes with her woolly gloves.

"Girls of that age," said Mrs McPhail, sagely. "She's been good today, though. She didn't eat much of her lunch, but she's an angel."

They crossed Clerk Street in the whirling snow. Her father had parked outside the Odeon cinema and already the car was beginning to look like an igloo on wheels. The Odeon was showing *Alice in Wonderland* and Gillie could almost believe that it wasn't a coincidence at all, but that the cinema management had arranged it with her parents in order to mock her.

They drove back towards the centre of the city. Above Princes Street, the castle rock was scarcely visible through the blizzard, and last-minute shoppers trudged along the gritty, salted pavements like lost souls struggling through a dream from which they could never wake up.

A year passed and it was winter again. She sat in front of her dressing-table mirror with a tablecloth on her head and wondered what it would be like to be a nun. She liked the look of herself as a nun. She was very thin, very small-boned for fourteen, with a pale complexion and large dark eyes – eyes that were rather soulful and droopy the way that some Scottish eyes are. She could work among the sick and homeless, selflessly bandaging their sores and giving them drinks of water.

The only trouble was, nuns had to give up men and she was very keen on John McLeod in the lower sixth, even though he had never noticed her (as far as she knew, anyway). John McLeod was very tall with raging red hair and he was the captain of curling. She had gone to watch him play and once she had given him a winter-warmer. He had popped it in his mouth and said "Ta."

The other trouble was that becoming a nun was a very Roman Catholic sort of thing to do and the Drummond family were Church of Scotland through and through.

She stood up and went to the window. The sky was the colour of pale gum, and the gardens of Charlotte Square were filled with snow.

"What do you think, Alice?" she asked. Alice was still alive, somewhere in the back of Gillie's mind –

somewhere dark and well-protected. She knew that if she ever forgot about Alice, then Alice would cease to exist, completely, as if she had never been thought of.

You want to become a nun? Alice replied. *Do it secretly. Take your holy orders without telling anybody.*

"But what's the point of that? What's the point of becoming a nun if nobody else knows?"

God will know. Devote your life to serving God and honouring the Virgin Mary, and to helping your fellow human beings even if they're drunk in doorways, and you will be rewarded in heaven.

"But what if John McLeod asks me to the pictures?"

In that case you may renounce your nunly vow, at least for one night.

She was still looking out of the window with the tablecloth on her head when her father unexpectedly came into her bedroom. "What's up with you?" he asked. "Are you playing at ghosts?"

Gillie dragged off the tablecloth and blushed.

"Your mother wants you to feed Toby his lunch while she gets the washing done."

"Do I have to? I'm supposed to be finishing my homework."

"Where? What homework? I don't see any homework. Come on, Gillie, Mum's awful busy with the house to keep and Toby to take care of. I do expect you to lend a hand."

Gillie reluctantly followed her father downstairs. They lived in a large four-storey house in Charlotte Square which they had inherited from Mum's parents when they died and which they could barely afford to keep up. Most of the decorations were still unchanged from Granny and Grandfather's day: brown floral wallpaper and brown velvet curtains, and large gloomy paintings of stags at bay. About the most cheerful picture was a view of Ben Buie in a thunderstorm.

Her mother was in the large, yellow-tiled kitchen, strapping Toby into his high chair. She was slender and slight, like Gillie, but she was fair-haired rather than dark, with very sharp blue eyes. Toby had inherited her fairness and her eyes, and he had a mop of curly blond hair as fine as cornsilk, which her mother refused to have cut. Daddy didn't like it much because he thought it made Toby look like a girl; but Gillie knew better. Alice would have been gentle and dark, like her, and they would have spoken together in giggles and whispers.

"His hotpot's ready," said Mum, and gave Gillie the open jar, wrapped in a cloth because it was hot. Gillie drew up a chair at the large pine kitchen table and stirred the jar with a teaspoon. Toby smacked his fat little hands together and bounced up and down on his bottom. He was always trying to attract Gillie's attention but Gillie knew who he was and she didn't take any notice. He was a cuckoo. Dear dark Alice had never been allowed to see the light of day, and here was this fat curly *thing* sitting in her place. He even slept in Alice's crib.

Gillie spooned up puréed hotpot and put it up against Toby's lips. The instant Toby tasted it he turned his head away. Gillie tried again, and managed to push a little bit into his mouth, but he promptly spat it out again, all down his clean bib.

"Mum, he doesn't like it."

"Well, he has to eat it. There's nothing else."

"Come on, cuckoo," Gillie cajoled him, trying another spoonful. She held his head so that he wouldn't turn away, and squeezed his fat little cheeks together so that he *had* to open his mouth. Then she pushed the whole spoonful on to his tongue.

There was a long moment of indignant spluttering, while Toby grew redder and redder in the face. Then he let out a scream of protest, and hotpot poured out of his mouth and sprayed all over the sleeve of Gillie's jumper.

Gillie threw down the spoon in fury. "You cuckoo!" she screamed at him. "You horrible fat cuckoo! You're disgusting and I hate you!"

"*Gillie!*" her mother protested.

"I don't care! I hate him and I'm not feeding him! He can die of starvation for all I care! I don't know why you ever wanted him!"

"Gillie, don't you dare say such a thing!"

"I dare and I don't care!"

Mum unbuckled Toby from his high-chair, picked him up and shushed him. "If you don't care you'd better get to your room and stay there for the rest of the day with no tea. Let's see how *you* like a bit of starvation!"

It started to snow again. Thick, tumbling flakes from the Firth of Forth.

"They really believe that I don't know what they did to you, Alice."

You must forgive them, for they know not what they do.

"I don't want to forgive them. I hate them. Most of all I hate them for what they did to you."

But you're a nun now. You've taken holy vows. You must forgive them in the name of the Father, and of the Son and of the Holy Spirit amen.

Gillie spent the afternoon lying on her bed reading *Little Faith* which was a novel about a nun who started a mission in the South Seas and fell in love with a gun-runner. She had read it twice already, but she still loved the scene where the nun, who has fasted for five days and five nights as a penance for her passionate feelings, is witness to a miraculous vision of St Theresa, "incandescent as the sun", who forgives her for feeling like a woman.

At five o'clock she heard her mother carrying Toby upstairs for his bath. At half-past five she heard mummy singing to him in his bedroom, across the corridor. She sang him the same lullaby that she always used to sing for Gillie, when she was small, and the sound of it made Gillie feel even more depressed and left out. She turned her face to the wall and stared miserably at the wallpaper. It was supposed to be roses, but it seemed to have a sly hooded face in it, medieval-looking and misshapen, like a leper.

"Dance to your daddy, my little babby. Dance to your daddy, my little lamb. You shall have a fishy, on a little dishy. You shall have a fishy when the boat comes in..."

Not long after her father opened her door. "Are you ready to say that you're sorry?" he asked her.

Gillie didn't answer. Her father waited at the door for a while, and then came in and sat on the side of the bed. He laid his hand gently on her arm, and said, "This is not like you, Gillie. You're not jealous of Toby, are you? You don't have to be. We love you just as much as ever. I know that Mum's busy with Toby a lot of the time, but she still cares for you, and so do I."

But what about me? said Alice.

"How about saying you're sorry, and coming down for some tea? There's fish fingers tonight."

You never cared about me.

"Come on, Gillie, what do you say?"

"You never cared about me! You wanted me dead!"

Her father stared at her in disbelief. "Wanted you dead? What put such a thought into your head? We love you; we wouldn't have had you otherwise; and if you want to know the truth you would have stayed our only child, and we would have been glad of it, if

311

only Toby hadn't been conceived by accident. We didn't mean to have him, but we did, and now he's here, and we love him. Just the same way that we love you."

Gillie sat up in bed with reddened eyes. "Accident?" she said. "Accident? Try telling Alice that Toby was an accident!"

"Alice? Who's Alice?"

"*You killed her!*" Gillie screamed. "*You murdered her! You murdered her and she never lived!*"

Alarmed, angry, her father stood up. "Now, come on, Gillie. I want you to calm down. Let me call Mum and we'll have a wee chat."

"I don't want to talk to either of you! You're horrible! I hate you! Go away!"

Her father hesitated for a moment. Then he said, "The best thing for you to do, my girl, is to have your bath and get yourself to bed. We'll talk some more in the morning."

"I don't want your stupid bath."

"Then go to sleep dirty. It makes no difference to me."

She lay on her bed listening to the noises in the house. She could hear her mother and father talking; and then the bath running. The cistern roared and whistled just above her room. She heard doors opening and closing, and the burbling of the television in her parents' bedroom. Then the door was closed and all the lights were switched off.

Outside the window, the city was so thickly-felted

in snow that it was totally silent, from Davidson's Mains to Morningside, and Gillie could almost have believed that everyone was dead, except for her.

She was woken by a bright light dancing on the wallpaper. She opened her eyes and frowned at it for a while, not quite sure where she was, or whether she was sleeping or waking. The light quivered and trembled and danced from side to side. Sometimes it was like a wide squiggly line and then it would suddenly tie a knot in itself, so that it formed the shape of a butterfly.

Gillie sat up. She was still fully dressed and her leg had gone dead because she had been sleeping in a funny position. The light was coming from under her door. First of all it was dazzling and then it was dim. It danced and skipped and changed direction. Then it retreated for a while, so that all she could see was a faint reflected glow.

Oh, no! she thought. The house is on fire!

She climbed off her bed and limped dead-legged to the door. She felt the doorknob to see if it was hot. The Fire Brigade had come to the school to give them all a lecture on do's and don'ts, and she knew that she wasn't to open the door if it was hot. Fire feeds on oxygen like a baby feeds on milk.

But the doorknob was cold, and the door-panels were cold. Cautiously, Gillie turned the knob, and opened the door, and eased herself into the corridor. Toby's room was directly opposite; and the light was

313

shining from all around Toby's door. At times it was so intense that she could scarcely look at it, and it shone through every crevice, and even through the keyhole.

She sniffed. The odd thing was that she couldn't smell smoke. And there was none of that crackling sound that you normally get with a fire.

She approached Toby's door and dabbed the door-knob with her fingertip. That, too, was quite cold. There was no fire burning in Toby's room. For a moment, she became dreadfully frightened. She had a cold, sliding feeling in her stomach as if she had swallowed something really disgusting and knew that she was going to sick it up again. If it wasn't a fire in Toby's room, what was it?

She was just about to run to her parents' room when she heard an extraordinary noise. A thick, soft, rustling noise; and then the sound of Toby gurgling and giggling.

He's laughing, said Alice. *He must be all right.*

"I wish it had been a fire. I wish he was dead."

No you don't; and neither do I. You're a nun now; you're in holy orders. Nuns forgive everything. Nuns understand everything. Nuns are the brides of Christ.

She opened Toby's door.

And Holy Mary! cried Alice.

The sight that met her eyes was so dramatic and so dazzling that she fell to her knees on the carpet, her mouth wide open in disbelief.

In the centre of Toby's nursery stood a tall white figure. It was so blindingly bright that Gillie had to shield her eyes with the back of her hand. It was so tall that it almost touched the ceiling, and it was dressed in swathes of brilliant white linen, and it seemed to have huge folded wings on its back. It was impossible for Gillie to tell if it were a man or a woman. It was so bright that she couldn't clearly see its face, but she could vaguely distinguish two eyes, floating in the brilliance like chicken embryos floating in egg-white; and the curve of a smile.

But what made Gillie tremble more than anything else was the fact that Toby was out of his crib, and standing on his cribside rug, *standing,* with this tall, dazzling creature holding his little hands for him.

"Toby," she whispered. "Oh God, Toby."

But all Toby did was turn towards her and smile his cheekiest smile, and take two unsteady steps across the rug, while the dazzling creature helped him to balance.

Gillie slowly rose to her feet. The creature looked at her. Although it was so bright, she could see that it wasn't staring at her aggressively. In fact there was something in its eyes that seemed to be appealing for understanding; or at least for calm. But then it lifted Toby up in its arms, right up in the air in its brilliant, flaring arms, and Gillie's composure fell apart like a jigsaw falling out of its box.

"*Mum!*" she screamed, running up the corridor

and beating on her parents' bedroom door. "Mum, there's an angel in Toby's room! Mum, Mum, Mum, come quick! There's an angel in Toby's room!"

Her father and mother came bursting out of the bedroom ruffled and bleary and hardly knowing where they were going. They ran to Toby's nursery and Gillie ran after them.

And there he was, tucked up in his blue-and-yellow blanket, sucking his thumb. Content, curly, and right on the edge of falling to sleep.

Dad turned and looked at Gillie with a serious face.

"I saw an angel," she said. "I'm not making it up, I promise you. It was teaching Toby to walk."

Dr Vaudrey laced his fingers together and swung himself from side to side in his black leather armchair. Outside his window there was a view of a grey brick wall, streaked with snow. He had a dry pot plant on his desk and a photograph of three plain-looking children in sweaters that were too small for them. He was half-Indian, and he wore very thick black-framed glasses and his black hair was brushed back straight from his forehead. Gillie thought that his nose looked like an aubergine. Same colour. Same shape.

"You know something, Gillie, at your age religious delusions are very common. To find a faith and to believe in its manifestations is a very strong desire for adolescent young women."

"I saw an angel," said Gillie. "It was teaching Toby to walk."

"How did you know it was an angel, what you saw? Did it say to you, 'Hello, excuse me, I am an angel and I have just popped in to make sure that your baby brother doesn't have to scurry about on his hands and knees for the rest of his life?'"

"It didn't say anything. But I knew what it was."

"You say you knew – but how? This is the point that I am trying to make to you."

Gillie lowered her eyes. Her hands were resting in her lap and somehow they didn't even look like hers. "The fact is I'm a nun."

Dr Vaudrey swung around to face her. "Did I hear what you said correctly? You are a *nun*?"

"In secret, yes."

"An undercover nun, is that what you're saying?"

Gillie nodded.

"May I ask to which order you belong?"

"It doesn't have a name. It's my own order. But I've given my life to God and the Blessed Virgin and to suffering humanity even if they're drunk in doorways."

Dr Vaudrey slowly took off his spectacles and looked across his desk at her with infinite sympathy, even though her head was lowered and she couldn't see him. "My dear young lady," he said, "you have the most laudable aims in life; and it is not for me to say what you saw or what you didn't see."

"I saw an angel."

Dr Vaudrey swung himself around in the opposite direction. "Yes, my dear. I believe that you probably did."

The young minister was waiting for her in the library. He was stocky, with thinning hair and fleshy ears, but she thought he was really quite good-looking for a minister. He wore a horrible sweater with reindeer leaping all round it and brown corduroy trousers.

"Sit down," he said, indicating a dilapidated sofa covered with cracked red leather. "Would you care for some coffee? Or maybe some Irn Bru? Mind you I'm fairly sure the Irn Bru's flat. They bought it in two Christmasses ago, and it's been sitting in the sideboard ever since."

Gillie sat pale and demure at the very far end of the sofa and gave the minister nothing more than a quick negative shake of her head.

He sat astride a wheelback chair and propped his arms across the top of it. "I can't say that I blame you. The coffee's no good, either."

There was a long silence between them. The library clock ticked so wearily that Gillie kept expecting it to stop, although it didn't.

"I suppose I ought to introduce myself," said the young minister. "I'm Duncan Callander, but you can call me Duncan if you want. Most of my friends called me Doughnuts. You know – Duncan Doughnuts?"

Another long silence. Then Duncan said, "You've

seen an angel, then? In the flesh so to speak?"

Gillie nodded.

"This Doctor Vaudrey ... this psychiatrist ... he thinks that you've been suffering some stress. It's partly due to your age, you see. Your mind and your body are going through some tremendous changes. It's only natural to look for something more to believe in than your parents and your school-teachers. With some girls it's a pop group; with other girls it's God. But Doctor Vaudrey thought your case was very interesting. He's had girls with religious visions before. But none like yours. He said he could almost believe that you really saw what you said you saw."

He took out his handkerchief and made an elaborate ritual out of wiping his nose. "That's why he passed you on to your own minister, and why your own minister passed you on to me. I'm a bit of specialist when it comes to visions."

"I saw an angel," Gillie repeated. She felt that she had to keep on saying it until they believed her. She would go on saying it for the rest of her life, if necessary. "It was helping Toby to walk."

Duncan said, "It was six-and-a-half to seven feet tall, dazzling white, and you could just about make out its eyes and its mouth. It may have had wings but you're not at all sure about that."

Gillie turned around and stared at him. "How did you know that? I haven't told that to anybody."

"You didn't have to. Yours is the twenty-eighth

sighting since 1973, and every single one sounds exactly like yours."

Gillie could hardly believe what she was hearing. "You mean – *other* people have seen them – as well as me?"

Duncan reached out and took hold of her hand and squeezed it. "Many other people, apart from you. It's not at all uncommon. The only uncommon thing about *your* seeing an angel is that you're just an ordinary girl, if you can forgive me for saying so. Most of the other manifestations have come to deeply religious people, ministers and missionaries and such, people who have devoted all of their life to their church."

"I have, too," Gillie whispered.

Duncan gave her an encouraging smile. "You have, too?"

"I took holy orders."

"Where did you do this? At St Agnes?"

Gillie shook her head. "In my bedroom."

Duncan laid his hand on her shoulder. "Then you're a very exceptional novice indeed. And you must be pure of heart, and filled with love, or else you couldn't have seen what you saw."

"Are angels dangerous?" asked Gillie. "Toby won't get hurt, will he?"

"Quite the opposite, as far as I know. In all of the sightings of angels that I've read about, they've been protecting people, particularly children. We don't really know for sure whether they come from heaven, or whether they're some kind of visible energy that comes out of the human mind. All kinds of people have been trying to prove their existence for years. Physicists, bishops, spiritualists ... you name them. Just think what a spectacular boost it would be if the church could prove that they were real, and that they had been sent by God!"

He reached across his desk and picked up a book with several marked pages in it. "You see these pictures? This is the closest that anybody has ever come to proving that angels exist. For forty years, paediatric studies of babies taking their first steps have proved beyond a shadow of doubt that they are technically in defiance of all the laws of physics when they begin to toddle. They don't have the physical strength, they don't have the balance. And yet – miraculously – they do it.

"In 1973 a team of doctors set up an experiment at Brigham & Women's Hospital in Boston, in America, using children who were just on the verge of walking. They took ultra-violet and infra-red photographs ... and here, you can see the results. In at least five of these pictures, there's a tall shadowy shape which appears to be holding the toddlers' hands."

Gillie studied them closely, with a prickling feeling down her back, as if centipedes were crawling inside her jumper. The shapes were very dim, and their eyes were barely visible. But they were just the same as the dazzling figure who had visited Toby's bedroom.

"Why hasn't anybody said anything about this before?" she asked. "If there have been twenty-seven other sightings, apart from mine, why hasn't anybody said so?"

Duncan closed the book. "Church politics. The Roman Catholics didn't want the sightings mentioned in case they proved not to be angels, after all, but simply some sort of human aura. And the Church of Scotland didn't want them mentioned because they frown on miracles and superstition and hocus-pocus. Nobody said anything because they were all monks or nuns or ordained clergy, and they were under strict instructions from their superiors to keep their visions to themselves."

"But I'm not a real nun! I could say something about it, and nobody could stop me!"

Duncan said, "First of all I have to speak to the kirk elders, to see what they think about it. After all, if a statement is made to the effect that one of our parishioners has witnessed an angel, then the church is going to be closely involved in all of the publicity that's bound to follow."

"You do believe me, though, don't you?" said Gillie. "I'm not mad or anything. I really saw it and it was really there."

"I believe you," smiled Duncan. "I'll talk to the elders tomorrow, and then I'll come around to your house and tell you what they've decided to do."

That evening, while they were having supper at the

kitchen table, lamb chops and mashed neeps, little Toby came wobble-staggering across the floor and clung to the edge of Gillie's chair. He looked up at her and cooed.

"Go away, cuckoo," she told him. "You'll have your Marmitey fingers all over my skirt."

For a split-second, she thought she saw his eyes *flash* – actually flash like somebody taking a photograph.

You'd better watch what you say, Alice warned her. *Toby's got a guardian angel, and you don't want to go upsetting* him.

A weak sun was shining through the dishrag clouds when Duncan Callander came to call the next afternoon. He sat in the best room and Mum gave him a cup of tea and a plateful of petticoat tails.

"I talked to the kirk elders this morning. We had a special meeting, in fact. I want to tell you that they all extend their warmest best wishes to young Gillie here, and that they very much appreciate her bringing such a delightful story to their attention."

"But it's not a story!" Gillie interrupted.

Duncan raised his hand to silence her. He didn't look her in the eye. He looked instead at the pattern on the carpet and spoke as if he had learned his words from a typewritten sheet of paper.

"As I say, they were very appreciative, and very amused. But they find that there is no evidence at all that what Gillie saw was anything more than an optical illusion; or a delusion brought on by the stress of having a new baby in the household. In other words, the most likely explanation is a little show of harmless attention-seeking by an older sister who feels jealous and displaced."

Gillie stared at him. "You said you believed me," she whispered. "You said you believed me."

"Well, yes, I'm afraid that I did, but it was wrong of me. I have a rather mystical turn of mind, I'm afraid, and it's always getting me into hot water. The kirk elders – well, the kirk elders pointed out that nobody has ever produced any conclusive proof that angels actually exist, and until that happens the kirk's official line is that they do not." He took a breath. "I apologize if I misled you."

"And that's all?" Gillie demanded. "That's all that's going to happen? I saw an angel and you're going to say that I was making it up because I was jealous of Toby?"

"If you want to put it that way, yes," Duncan told her, although he spoke so soft and ashamed that she could hardly hear him.

Mum took hold of Gillie's hand and squeezed it. "Come on, sweetie. You can forget it all now; put it behind you. Why don't I bake you your favourite cake tonight?"

Where are you going to sleep? asked Alice.

"I don't know. I'll find somewhere. Tramps have to."

You're not going to sleep in a doorway on a freezing-cold night like this?

"I'll find a squat. Anywhere's better than home."

Your supper's waiting on you. Mum baked that rich thick chocolate cake. Your warm bed's all turned down.

"I don't care. What's the point of cakes and warm beds if people say you're a liar? Even that minister said I was a liar, and who was the one who was doing the lying?"

She had trudged the whole length of Rose Street, between brightly-lit pubs and Indian restaurants, jostled by rowdy teenagers and cackling drunks. Maybe Mrs McPhail would have her for the night. Mrs McPhail believed in angels.

By the time she had crossed Princes Street and started the long walk up Waverley Bridge, it had started to snow again. Sir Walter Scott watched her from his Gothic monument as if he understood her predicament. His head, too, had been full of fancies. She was wearing her red duffel-coat and her white woolly hat, but all the same she was beginning to feel freezing-cold, and her toes had already turned numb.

At the top of the hill the streets were almost deserted. She crossed North Bridge Street but she decided to walk down the back streets to Mrs McPhail's in case Dad was out looking for her in the car.

She had never felt so desolate in her life. She had

known that people would find it difficult to believe her. She hadn't minded that. What had hurt so much was Duncan's betrayal. She couldn't believe that adults could be so cynical – especially an adult whose chosen calling was to uphold truth and righteousness and protect the weak.

She was half-way down Blackfriars Street when she saw a young man walking very quickly toward her. He was wearing a tam and an anorak and a long Rangers scarf. He was coming toward her so fast that she wondered if somebody were chasing him. His face was wreathed in clouds of cold breath.

She tried to step to one side, but instead of passing her he knocked her with his shoulder, so that she fell back against a garden wall.

"What did you do that for?" she squealed at him; but immediately he seized hold of the toggles of her duffel-coat and dragged her close to him. In the streetlight she could see that he was foxy-faced and unshaven, with a gold hoop earring in each ear, and skin the colour of candlewax.

"Give us your purse!" he demanded.

"I can't!"

"What d'you mean you can't? You have to."

"I'm running away. I've only got six pounds."

"Six pound'll do me. You can always run away again tomorrow. I don't even have anywhere to run away from."

"No!" screamed Gillie, and tried to twist away from him. But he clung on to her duffel-coat and wrenched her from side to side.

"Out with your purse or it'll be the worse for you, bonny lass!"

"Please," she swallowed. "Please let me go."

"Then let's have your purse and let's have it quick."

His face was so close to hers that she could smell the stale tobacco on his breath. His eyes were glassy and staring. She reached into her pocket, took out her furry Scottie-dog purse and handed it to him. He glanced down at it in disdain.

"What's this? A dead rat?"

"It's my p-p-p –"

He thrust the purse into his pocket. "Trying to make me look stupid, is it? Well, how about a little souvenir to make *you* look even stupider?"

He dragged off her woolly hat, seized hold of her hair, and wrenched her from side to side. She couldn't scream. She couldn't struggle. All she could do was gag with fear.

But it was then that she felt the pavement vibrating beneath her feet. Vibrating, as if a heavy road-roller were driving past. She heard a deep rumbling noise, that rapidly grew louder and louder, until she was almost deafened. The young man let go of her hair and looked around in alarm.

"What in the name of–" he began. But his words were drowned out by a thunderous blast of sound, and then a dazzling burst of white light. Right in front of them, a tall incandescent figure appeared, crackling with power, a figure with a crown of sizzling static and immense widespread wings.

It was so bright that the entire street was lit up, as if it were daylight. The falling snow fizzed and evaporated against its wings. Gillie stayed with her back to the garden wall, staring at it in disbelief. The young man stood staring at it, too, paralysed with fear.

The wings flared even wider, and then the figure reached out with one long arm, and laid its hand on top of the young man's hand, as if it were blessing him, or confirming him.

There was a sharp crack which echoed from one side of the street to the other. The young man screamed once; and then smoke started to pour out of his mouth and his nose; and he exploded. Fragments of tattered anorak were strewn all over the pavement, along with smoking ashes and dismembered shoes.

Almost immediately, the figure began to dim. It folded its wings, turned, and vanished into the snow, as quickly and completely as if it walked through a door. Gillie was left with nothing but the young man's scattered remains and an empty street, although she could see that curtains were being pulled back, and people were starting to look out of their windows to see what had happened.

She picked up her purse. Next to it, there were six or seven white feathers – huge and soft and fluffy as snow, although some of them were slightly scorched.

She picked those up, too, and started to walk quickly back toward North Bridge Street, and then to run. By the time she heard the fire engines she was well on her way home.

She pushed Toby through the kirkyard gate and up between the snow-topped gravestones. Duncan was standing in the porch, pinning up some notices. He gave her an odd look as she approached, although he didn't turn away.

"What have you come for?" he asked her. "An explanation, or an apology? You can have both if you like."

"I don't need either," she said. "I know what I saw was true and I don't need to tell anybody else about it. I know something else, too. Everybody has a guardian angel of their own, especially the young, because everybody has to do something impossible, now and again, like learning to walk, or learning that your parents do care about you, after all."

"You seem to be getting on better with your little brother," Duncan remarked.

Gillie smiled. "God must have wanted him, mustn't he, or else he wouldn't have sent him an angel. And God must have wanted me, too."

Duncan gave her a questioning look. "There's something you're not telling me. You haven't seen another angel, have you?"

"Did you hear about the lad who was struck by lightning last night, in Blackfriars Street?"

"Of course. It was on the news."

"Well, I was there, and it wasn't lightning. Whoever heard of lightning in a snowstorm?"

"If it wasn't lightning, then what?"

Gillie reached into her pocket and took out a handful of scorched feathers, which she placed in Duncan's open hand. "There," she said. "Evidence of angels."

He stood in the porch for a long time, watching her push Toby away down the street. The wintry breeze stirred the feathers in his hand and blew them one by one across the kirkyard. Then he turned around and went inside, and closed the door.

HOSPITAL TRUST

Dennis Hamley

MORLEY CARTWRIGHT SAT IN THE DOCTORS' WAITING room feeling gloomy. He hated the place, always full of old men who wheezed and young women, usually pregnant, surrounded by shrieking children with snotty noses.

The fog outside had worsened as he trudged along the road. Now it seemed to seep through the windows. He couldn't bear to read three-year-old copies of *Country Life*. He scanned the notices, scowled at the exhortation not to smoke (how *long* would he be trapped in here?), read all the "Well Woman" posters, looked in vain for anything for the "Well Man".

Yes, he felt very unhappy. A sudden spasm in his side reminded him he felt ill as well.

Why did he still come to this unsalubrious place? Why hadn't he changed his doctor after that unfortunate business five years before? Everyone he knew went to the cheerful young doctors at the gleaming new Health Centre. Why had he stuck with ancient Dr Grimes and decrepit Dr Hough in this creaking Victorian slum? Especially when they were always ill themselves and he saw a succession of locums.

A locum had caused all the trouble. Dr Grout. Filling in for Dr Hough, absent with one of her frequent and seemingly untreatable complaints. Dr Grout, incredibly tall, unnaturally thin, black-suited like a badly-dressed spider, leaning over Morley and his mother like a broken arch in a ruined castle.

"Come in with me, Morley," his mother had said. "You know I'm afraid of doctors."

So, after the examination, he had joined his sixty-five year old mother in the surgery. They waited to hear what this scrawny lamppost of a medical man with his long jaw and yellow teeth would say.

"Well, I've examined your mother thoroughly, Mr Cartwright. And I'm happy to assure you both that there's nothing to worry about." He grinned yellowly at Morley. "She's fitter than you or I are."

A week later his mother had been rushed screaming to hospital and operated on at once.

Well, she had survived – and she was still living in the house at the top of Glass Street. Here, she was surrounded by photographs of her long-dead husband, long-married daughter and grandchildren. She had no need of photographs of her middle-aged, unmarried son who still lived in the house. Sometimes she quietly worried about him.

She had worried even more about him after that episode. Morley had been so *angry*.

"Everyone makes mistakes," she had said.

334

"This one nearly killed you," he raved. "I'll *sue!*"

He didn't. But he felt better after writing a strong letter of complaint to the Family Practitioners' Council and having a good shout at ancient Dr Grimes and decrepit Dr Hough.

"We are so very sorry," Dr Hough muttered, toying curiously with her stethoscope as if it were a device totally new to her.

"That Dr Grout should be struck off," yelled Morley. "He's a menace. He'll kill somebody. Probably has already. Hundreds."

Dr Grimes stood in front of his dusty bookcase, hands behind his back.

"I can assure you," he had said, "that Dr Grout will never work in this practice again. Never. Take it from me. *NEVER.*"

With that outcome, Morley had to be content.

And here he was, on a foggy November morning, with a nagging pain in his side, remembering Dr Grimes' assurance so not feeling worried when the receptionist said, "Neither Dr Grimes nor Dr Hough is available this morning. I'm afraid it's a locum."

Par for the course, he thought. But I don't mind as long as competence comes with the deal. So he sat in the waiting room and gave way to gloomy thoughts.

"Mr Cartwright?"

The receptionist's voice interrupted his reverie.

"Surgery two, please."

He walked down the corridor and knocked on the door.

"Enter," came a voice.

He turned the handle and walked in.

The locum stood behind the desk, black-suited, yellow-toothed, bending over like a broken arch in a ruined castle.

It was Dr Grout.

For a moment, Morley was too shocked to speak.

"But Dr Grimes said..." he eventually spluttered.

"Needs must when the devil drives," said Dr Grout. "Any port in a storm."

Morley nearly stormed out.

"Don't worry, Mr Cartwright. There'll be no mistake this time." The long jaw wagged as he spoke: the yellow teeth seemed to have a life of their own.

Suddenly, Morley's anger turned to doubt. He would be well-advised to stay on the right side of this man.

"Now," said Dr Grout. "What seems to be the matter?"

Morley told him about sharp pains in chest and side, cold sweats, frequent and sudden dizziness, nausea welling though his whole body.

"I see," said Dr Grout. "Let's have a closer look at you."

Dr Grout's hands were extraordinarily cold: Morley shrank at their touch. The blood-pressure gauge gripped his arm like the coils of a small boa constrictor, the thermometer lay like brass on his tongue, the stethoscope like hard pebbles on his chest.

"Oh, no," said Dr Grout when he had finished. "I'm making no mistake this time."

"What's the matter with me?"

"It could be a number of things. I can't be definite. You need more tests."

He smiled at Morley: the effect was that of opening the lid of an old piano.

"I'd like to refer you straight away to the local hospital," he said. "But they're chock-a-block: you'd have to wait."

"I don't *want* to wait," said Morley.

"They'd fit you in at St Sebastian's," said Dr Grout.

"Where?"

"In Clagbury."

"But that's thirty miles away."

"We can send patients where we like nowadays."

"It would be hard for Mother to visit."

"Do you want this sorted out quickly or not?"

"Yes, but..."

"Then St Sebastian's it is. They'll take you straight away. I'll get in touch with them this morning."

"But..."

"They'll give you some tests, poke around a bit, might open you up and explore inside. Perhaps even take something out. Don't worry, they'll see you're all right."

"But why can't I..."

"Good morning, Mr Cartwright."

Morley suddenly found himself in the corridor looking at a closed door.

Dr Grout worked fast. Morley saw him on Monday: on Tuesday the letter plopped through the letterbox. Morley tore open the envelope.

The paper was creamy. *St Sebastian's, Clagbury* was embossed at the top. Underneath this wraith-like inscription appeared, in bright red, the words *Hospital Trust*.

He read:

> *Dear Mr Cartwright,*
>
> *A bed has been reserved for you for today, (Tuesday). Please report to Reception at 2.30p.m. May I extend my best wishes for the pleasant stay enjoyed by all who enter here.*
>
> *Yours sincerely.*
> *Anthea Bandon-Hope*
> *(Senior Hospital Manager)*

Morley's first thought was cheerful. What a nice letter.

"I'll drive you to Clagbury," said Mother.

Morley looked outside.

"Not in this fog," he said.

The grey blanket outside was, if anything, worse.

"What shall we do?" he groaned. "I can't *not* go. I've psyched myself up for it."

"Ring St Sebastian's."

The "burr-burr" at the other end sounded clicky and deep, like a geriatric lion purring. A faraway voice answered, "St Sebastian's. How may I help you?"

"How can I get to you in this fog?" Morley babbled.

"Have no fear. *We* will collect *you.*"

The phone went dead. Morley looked at it.

"Hello! Hello! Are you there?" he shouted.

He put the phone down and looked wildly at his mother.

"I never told them who I was," he said.

"Ring again," said his mother.

He rang and rang and the geriatric lion purred and purred but no other voice said, "St Sebastian's. How may I help you?"

Morley was distraught.

Suddenly, the doorbell rang. On the porch, dim in the swathing fog, stood two figures, a man and a woman. The man wore a white, high-necked jacket and black trousers: the woman a dark blue dress with a broad belt and a strangely elaborate white head-dress.

"Mr Cartwright?" said the woman.

"St Sebastian's," said the man. "We knew where to find you."

They ignored Morley's surprise and each took one of his arms. The man carried his case. Morley managed to give Mother a peck on the cheek before he was hustled down the garden path by these two strong, tight-gripping people. The thick, dirty fog choked so much that Morley was coughing uncontrollably by the time they reached the vehicle outside the front gate. His companions were not affected.

They opened the rear double doors of a big, blue van with windows. Morley found himself sitting on a seat with his guides on either side of him. The man pulled Morley's safety-belt out of its reel and passed it across to the woman. She slotted it home and said, "Must have you well fastened in."

All Morley could see of the driver were broad shoulders covered in dark grey and the back of a grey peaked cap. The van started with a judder and crept cautiously along the road. Morley looked fixedly through the window and saw nothing but rolling greyness.

The journey was noisy, bumpy and without talk. Morley was rocked, deafened and disoriented. The very first objects he could discern outside the windows – after a full hour of this – were huge black iron gates. In the scrollwork he saw, plainly enough, *ST SEBASTIAN'S HOSPITAL*.

"Thank God," he said to himself. *"I have arrived."*

Just after Morley had left, the phone rang in Mrs Cartwright's house. She picked it up.

"This is Dr Grimes' secretary speaking. Can I speak to Mr Morley Cartwright, please?"

"I'm sorry. He's just gone to his appointment at the hospital."

"Are you sure?"

"Oh, yes."

Silence – then: "I'll ring you back, Mrs Cartwright."

* * *

The female nurse undid his safety-belt. The male nurse picked up his case. Together they swung him down the step at the van's rear and bundled him out towards the hospital's main doors. They passed notices with arrows pointing the way: *ACCIDENT, CASUALTY, OUTPATIENTS, RECEPTION*. The exterior walls were dark, dripping bricks. The doors were huge, black and peeling. They were set in a high archway, like a Gothic church. Once inside, he blinked in the cold gloom. His companions took him to the reception desk.

"New patient," said the male nurse.

The grip on his arms relaxed, was gone. Morley looked round to say his farewells and thank yous. But the two were nowhere to be seen.

The woman behind the desk had *VOLUNTARY HELPER* pinned to her woollen shawl. Her face was wrinkled with incredible age, her mouth was virtually toothless, the fingers with which she tapped the keys of her computer were hooked and thin with sharp little nails.

"Name?" she croaked.

He told her.

A skittery tap on the keys.

"Ah yes," she said. "A porter will escort you."

Morley sat on a chair opposite the reception desk and looked round him. The ceilings were very high. A steady, cold wind blew down the corridor towards him.

Faintly he heard far-off rumbles, crashes, cries: an undercurrent of myriad conversations. Steadily below it all he could hear a perpetual, unchanging rhythmic beating, like a giant heart far underground. His unrelieved wait seemed very long. Gloom and far-off but insistent noise combined to send him into an uneasy trance.

"Let's be havin' you, sir."

The voice made Morley jump.

A little man with a sharp, birdlike face stood by him, with an empty wheelchair. His badge said *J. LARKIN, PORTER.*

"In we get, sir."

Morley shook himself back to consciousness.

"I can walk," he said.

"Hospital rules, sir," said Mr Larkin. "If you're here, you're a patient. If you're a patient, you're ill. If you're ill, you could spark out any minute. And then where would you be, sir? And where would we be for letting you, sir? In court, sir, that's where."

If Mr Larkin's speech was meant to reassure, it failed. Morley stood and tried irritatedly to push Mr Larkin off as the porter took his arm and guided him down. He failed: the birdlike little man was, in strength, more eagle than sparrow. Morley subsided into the depths of the chair: its deep sides and big armrests made him feel he was sitting at the bottom of a well. Mr Larkin disappeared completely as he pushed the chair through long, featureless, echoing corridors. Morley heard only his disembodied voice.

"Oh, yes, sir. We do everything at St Sebastian's. Heart surgery? Why, Mr Murdo, the cardiac man, he'd take your heart out soon as look at you and put three back in its place if he could. And Mr Grillparzer, the plastic surgeon – a few hours with him and your own mother wouldn't know you. In fact, she wouldn't want to. But the best of all is Mr Maledict Unthank. He's the real top man."

"What's his speciality?" croaked Morley from the bottom of the chair.

"Anything!" cried Mr Larkin delightedly. "If he finds it there inside you and takes a shine against it, he'll have it out clean as a whistle before you've had time to tie your gown up."

Morley was silent as the catalogue of St Sebastian's medical expertise continued. The corridor along which Mr Larkin wheeled him seemed endless. The background noises grew louder as they approached the hospital's heart.

At last Mr Larkin stopped in front of double lift doors. As he darted forward and touched a button beside the door, Morley saw him in silhouette for the first time since the journey started – a jerky, sharp-nosed, knock-kneed little creature.

The lift doors opened with a wheeze and discordant clank.

"Third floor," said Mr Larkin.

The lift shook, juddered and groaned its way slowly upwards, as if its tenuous hold on the cable would plummet them to unimaginable depths and squashed deaths on iron floors at any moment.

Morley shook his head angrily. *Snap out of this. You're in a British National Health Service hospital at the end of the twentieth century. Medicine is* miraculous *compared to what it was. You are* safe. SAFE.

The doors opened. Now Mr Larkin traversed another long corridor. The clangs, bumps, and cries were very close now, though the regular beating sound was still far away and even further below. An indefinable smell, sweet, sour and antiseptic all at once, stung Morley's nostrils. Huge rubber double doors swung open as Mr Larkin pushed the wheelchair through into a vast, arched chamber.

"Here we are. Your ward," he said.

A large, forbidding woman with a hooked nose met them. She wore a dark blue dress. Her name badge said *SISTER SACRAMENT.*

"Mr Cartwright? This way to your bed," she said.

Now came the last stage of Morley's journey, past beds lined up either side full of thin, still men who stared dully at them.

Sister Sacrament tugged at the curtains of a high, empty bed towards the end. "Get yourself ready and hop in," she said.

"I'll leave you to it then, sir," said Mr Larkin. "Good luck till I come to wheel you out again."

He was gone. Morley slowly put his pyjamas on and climbed into the high, creaking bed.

Without realizing, he sank into a doze.

He woke to find the bed curtains drawn back. The misty, vaulted ward was dimly lit. He looked from side to side. To right and to left, beside him and opposite, beds stretched. Surely there could be no more than forty all told – but it seemed as though rank on rank of beds were ranged to infinity. All held still forms. Several slept, some covered entirely by blankets, others with heads lolling to one side. Some sat up, leaning back against high banks of pillows, gasping or moaning. All were male: all were emaciated, grizzled, grey about the face.

He looked to his immediate left. The patient was asleep, head on the pillow canted towards Morley, breathy snores coming from the open mouth. He looked to his right.

A man, black, about his own age, sat up, reading a paper. He saw Morley was watching him and put the paper down.

"Hi, man," he said. "The name's Clyde Brightway."

"Good evening," replied Morley guardedly. "Morley Cartwright."

"Are you here for tests, Morley?"

"I fear so."

"Me too," said Clyde. "Dr Grout said he couldn't find what was the matter with me."

"Dr Grout?" said Morley in surprise.

"I reckon everyone here's been referred by Dr Grout," said Clyde.

"He certainly gets around," said Morley. "I never thought I'd see him again since I had trouble with him a few years ago."

"Me neither," said Clyde. "He sent my little girl for an operation she didn't need. I complained..."

"...And got nowhere –" Morley finished the sentence for him – "except that your usual doctor said he'd never use him as a locum again."

Clyde's eyes opened wide.

"That's right," he said. "How did you know?"

"Because that's what happened to me," said Morley.

There was no time to continue the conversation. Sister Sacrament approached Morley's bed, snapped the curtains shut round it and stood beside him. She glowered down on him from a great height.

"I will take your temperature and blood pressure," said, Sister Sacrament. "We'll get you done and out of here quickly."

She shoved a thermometer in Morley's mouth. It tasted of brass and felt like a small, cold snake. Then she wound the belt of the blood-pressure gauge round his arm and squeezed the bulb. Her black eyes fixed Morley with a stare as she rhythmically squeeze-squeeze-squeezed the little bulb. Morley felt his arm was tightened in a vice. His head swam and his ears filled with the sound of a roaring sea and his heartbeat clanging like submerged wrecks colliding in its depths.

She stopped squeezing: all was quiet. Morley shook his head to clear it. She unwound the belt and took the thermometer from his mouth. She pointed to the blood-pressure gauge.

"High," she said.

She looked at the thermometer.

"Low," she said.

She looked down at him and then intoned: "Nil by mouth. In view of what you have to go through tomorrow, you shall take no solid or liquid refreshment."

Even the water jug she carried away.

As soon as Sister Sacrament had left, the supper trolley was wheeled through the ward by two pale, attenuated people of indeterminate gender. Morley watched, depressed and deprived. It was his impression that while he wanted food and could not have it, everybody else in the ward could have food but didn't want it.

"If I ate that slop, I couldn't keep it down, man," said Clyde.

Light waned still further: the yellow light bulbs flickered. Morley could see nothing through the high, arched windows opposite. The grey cotton wool of the day's fog had been replaced by the black sludge of the night's. St Sebastian's seemed to be sailing like a huge ocean liner through wide and deserted seas.

He shivered. He was very cold.

Sister Sacrament marched up to him. She carried two plastic beakers. One sloshed with water, the other rattled with pills.

"One pill to get your blood pressure down, another to put your temperature up," she said.

Morley swallowed them. The water was bitter and brackish.

"What did you mean about what I was to go through tomorrow?" he said.

"No more and no less than anyone else on this ward," she replied.

"What's that?"

"Tomorrow morning you will be taken to X-ray and after that to Pathology, where blood will be taken from you."

"What for?" cried Morley, alarmed. Why should he feel so worried? He'd had blood tests before.

"It is needed."

"Then what?"

"You'll be visited by the consultant in charge of your case."

"Who's that?"

"Mr Maledict Unthank."

Mr Larkin's hero.

She left. Morley watched her tall form with its gigantic shadow dwindle away to nothing at the far end of the ward.

He was suddenly so tired. The patient on his left still snored, though now his head was lolling the other way. Clyde too was asleep.

No one to talk to, nothing to read, nothing to watch or listen to – he was alone with disturbed thoughts in an unsettling place. He closed his eyes – to a vivid mental vision of a Dracula figure with white fangs, red eyes and dripping mouth, black cloak draped over him like creaking wings. He had a sudden conviction that this was a premonition of the consultant in charge of his case – Mr Maledict Unthank.

He slept. But not for long. He woke: his watch said 1.30. The ward seemed no different from daytime. Dark figures moved stealthily at the far end where the office was: the night staff. Snores, cries of pain and fear sounded close to him. Echoing subterranean thuds and clanks sounded from unseen regions far off. The regular heart-like beat pumped away far below. A cold, dead wind touched his face: the air seemed full of rushing, invisible presences trying in vain to seize him. For a long time he lay stock still, rigid with terror. Then sleep returned – and with it came nightmares. He was chased by panthers, wild dogs, crocodiles, snakes, all of which were called Mr Maledict Unthank.

The phone rang again.
  "Mrs Cartwright?"
  "Yes."
  "Which hospital did you say your son was admitted to?"
  "I don't think I told you. It was St Sebastian's, Clagbury."
  "Who referred him there?"
  "Dr Grout."
  Silence again – then: "I'll ring you back later."

*   *   *

Next day dawned. Mr Larkin arrived and helped Morley into the wheelchair.

"X-ray first, is it?"

He wheeled Morley along yet more corridors.

"Have a good night?" he asked.

"Terrible," Morley groaned.

"They all say that," said Mr Larkin. "But I promise you this. Nobody who comes here ever has more than one night which they can just call terrible."

X-ray was easy. Morley had had lots of them over the years. Even so, he had never been able to *feel* the radiation before. Next, Pathology. A woman with red lips, long black hair and overpowering scent breathed, "Let me take your arm." She produced a syringe of such proportions as to make Morley even dizzier. He turned away while she found the vein. He waited.

Her shout nearly made him keel over.

"No blood. I can get no blood."

A door opened: another woman, uncannily like the first, flew out.

"Don't worry. I'll get blood out of him."

The new arrival took his other arm. Morley turned his head again, closed his eyes and held his breath. The silence seemed to last for ever. Then Morley felt the needle withdrawn and the cold dressing and tiny plaster placed over the skin.

"You see?" said the second woman. "He did have blood. And now I have it."

"Couple of right little ravers in Pathology, aren't

they?" said Mr Larkin as he wheeled Morley back to the ward.

Back in his bed, Morley looked round. To his left, the patient still slept.

To his right was an empty, stripped bed.

Where was Clyde? What would he do without the only sane person he'd met in the place so far?

Even as he wondered, Sister Sacrament arrived and remade the bed, another porter wheeled in another wheelchair and a small, grey-haired man was helped into Clyde's bed. The curtains were drawn: Morley waited until they were opened again and leaned over.

"Good morning," he said. "My name is Morley Cartwright."

The new arrival spoke at once.

"I am Mr Gupta," he said. "And I am here for tests. I am being sent here by Dr Grout..."

For the second time Morley interrupted someone. "...Who told you he couldn't find out what was wrong and you were surprised to see him because you had complained about him before and were told he would never be a locum at your usual doctor's again."

"This is all most true," said Mr Gupta. "And I am asking you how you are knowing these details."

"How indeed," said Morley. "How indeed."

The phone rang again.

"Mrs Cartwright?"

"Yes."

351

"Are you sure *that what you told us is correct?"*

"Definitely. Dr Grout got Morley a bed at very short notice in St Sebastian's. I'm very grateful to him."

"I see. I'll ring you back later."

Nobody seemed to want to eat off the plates piled with brown, green and grey cylindrical objects which passed up and down the ward on the lunch trolley. Morley remembered the last time he was in hospital. The food had been lovely. He was quite glad after all of the *NIL BY MOUTH* notice.

He slipped into a doze. He had no idea how long it was before a quiet, low, insinuating voice beside him said, "Mr Cartwright?"

A tall, thin man stood by the bed. Morley thought there was something familiar about his long face, bony wrists, tapered fingers. But his dark, burning eyes were unlike anything Morley had ever seen before. Next to him stood another, younger doctor, a clip-board loaded with notes in his hand. Behind him was a gaggle of white-coated and very young men and women – medical students, Morley supposed. Behind them was Sister Sacrament.

As Morley opened his eyes, they regrouped in a semi-circle round his bed, all looking down on him intently. Morley was aware that Mr Larkin was dodging round the outside of the group, like a little boy trying to find a place to look through a crowd of people at the ritual killing that was going on in secret.

The tall man spoke. Once again, Morley could not

place the familiar inflection in his voice.

"My name is Mr Maledict Unthank. I am the consultant surgeon in charge of your case."

"How do you do?" said Morley diffidently and proffered his hand. It was ignored.

"I have read your notes," said Mr Maledict Unthank. "The prognosis is not good."

"What's wrong with me?" asked Morley.

Mr Maledict Unthank proceeded as if Morley had not spoken.

"However, it would be wrong of me to continue solely on the words of others. Let me see for myself."

Whereupon he prodded, poked, listened to and gravely stared at various parts of Morley's anatomy. The rest watched him impassively.

After some minutes, he stepped back.

"As I feared," he said. "There are few things right, many things wrong. Organs exist in there which must come *out*. There must be no delay. Sister, prepare him for theatre. *At once*."

There was a sudden delighted giggle and Mr Larkin rushed out of the ward as if to make some preparations of his own.

The phone rang. A new voice.

"Mrs Cartwright? This is Dr Grimes speaking."

"Yes, doctor?"

"Mrs Cartwright, we're very worried about Morley. Our receptionist says he left the surgery yesterday without seeing a doctor."

"That's not true. He saw Dr Grout."

"And Morley told you Dr Grout was sending him to St Sebastian's?"

"Yes."

"Mrs Cartwright, something seems to have gone badly wrong."

"Don't be silly, Dr Grimes. Dr Grout has been very efficient. My Morley's being safely taken care of in hospital."

Silence – then: "I'll ring you back later."

Morley was too shocked to argue. Mr Maledict Unthank and the students left. Sister Sacrament drew the curtains round the bed and then seized Morley. She pulled his pyjamas off and wrapped him in a starchy, frayed white operating gown. She sat him up and pushed his head forward while she tied the knots at the back. Then she stepped outside the curtain, to return pushing a small trolley bearing phials of different coloured liquids and a syringe.

"Pre-med time," she said and, with her knee in the small of his back, held him down with iron strength while she selected a phial, filled the syringe from it and plunged the needle into his terrified skin.

"That will calm you down," said Sister Sacrament.

It did no such thing. Morley was half-paralysed: his arms and legs could hardly move. He tried to shriek out his stark fear: not a sound could he make. He was a prisoner inside himself. This was nothing like the pleasant drowsiness the pre-med injection had given him the last time he had an operation.

Time stood still as Morley lay in horrified dumbness. It might have been years before the curtains were pulled back again. Now Mr Larkin stood there, with a trolley instead of a wheelchair.

"Aren't you the trussed-up chicken for the pot, then?" he said as he took hold of Morley.

"One-two-three," said Mr Larkin. "And *ups*-a-blooming-daisy." Morley found himself swung helplessly off the bed and on to the trolley, on his back, staring upwards, unable to stir.

"And off we go," said Mr Larkin. "Along the twisty road to kingdom come."

The trolley moved. Mr Larkin started to whistle, a perky little tune in a minor key. Above Morley's head, the lights hanging from the ceiling flickered down. He found himself counting them – one, two, three – as the procession passed down corridors, up ramps, through wards – twenty-eight, twenty-nine. The counting made a sort of rhythmic accompaniment to Mr Larkins's whistling and the perpetual beating from far below. They went in lifts, round corners, down more ramps – seventy-three, seventy-four – and finally through big green double doors into the operating theatre. At last Mr Larkin's whistling stopped. So did the trolley. Morley was lifted off and on to the operating table. He was surrounded by green-robed, masked figures who crowded round, looked down on him, muttered wordlessly. Above them shone white lights of extraordinary intensity.

The tallest figure took its mask away.

"Ah, Mr Cartwright. The moment of truth has come. Let there be no mistake this time," said Mr Maledict Unthank.

Morley was held down on each side. A mask was placed over his face.

"Soon off to bye-byes," said Mr Maledict Unthank.

Morley breathed deeply. Nothing seemed to happen.

The mask was removed.

Morley was still awake.

"I'm still awake," he tried to say.

No sound came out.

He tried to sit up.

He was now completely paralysed.

"He's well away," said the anaesthetist. She put the mask to one side and studied the monitor over Morley's head.

"No, I'm not," Morley tried uselessly to shout.

"Then let us proceed," said Mr Maledict Unthank.

Morley watched what he did next, helpless and terrified.

"An incision *here*," said Mr Maledict Unthank, warming to his task. Morley knew something was passing over and cutting through his skin, though he felt no pain. "Now, let's have a look."

All the green-robed figures peered forward to see for themselves what Mr Maledict Unthank was looking at.

"You know what it is as well as I do," said Mr Maledict Unthank. There was a low murmur of agreement. "As I thought, we are too late."

"Too late for what?" Morley tried vainly to shout.

"Poor fellow," said Mr Maledict Unthank. "Sew him up and let him go. We have done all we can."

The anaesthetist was still looking at the monitor.

"We've lost him," she suddenly said.

She turned to Morley and lifted his wrist. Despite all Morley's efforts, it fell limply back when she let it go.

"Yes," she said. "He's gone."

"No, I haven't," Morley tried to scream.

"Ah, well," said Mr Maledict Unthank, stripping off his operating gloves. "There's only one place for him now. Come, let us away. Our work is done."

The stately crew filed out. Morley was left, rigid and silently shrieking, on the operating table.

The phone rang.

"Mrs Cartwright?"

"Yes?"

"This is Dr Grimes again. I don't want to worry you, but may Dr Hough and I come round to see you? We need to talk in person. We have information which may come as a bit of a shock."

"Of course you may, Dr Grimes."

"We'll be with you in fifteen minutes."

"Lovely. I'll put the kettle on."

*   *   *

A whistle sounded from outside. Mr Larkin re-entered.

"Here we are again, me old mate," he said. "I know you can't hear me but we mustn't be downhearted, must we? It comes to us all."

"I *can* hear you." Morley hadn't given up trying to make himself heard.

"I guide 'em all in," said Mr Larkin. "And I guide 'em all out again. No one would get anywhere in this place if it weren't for me."

He rolled Morley's limp body off the operating table on to the same trolley he had brought him on and covered him with a white sheet. Then they set off down corridors again, down lifts, deeper and deeper towards the very bowels of the hospital. That regular beating which had never left Morley's ears since he had been here grew louder the deeper they plumbed – as if they approached a monstrous heart at the centre of the earth. Yet it did not get hotter the closer they approached. Rather, cold encroached: freezing, numbing, thrice-Arctic cold which Mr Larkin ignored but which bit deeper and deeper into Morley until he thought his blood would solidify within him. Now the beating was loudest of all: it deafened and echoed like huge drums being played in a vast vault.

"Not far now, me old mate," said Mr Larkin.

He leant across and twitched the sheet away from Morley's face.

"I always do that," he said. "I know everyone I

wheel down here's as dead as a doornail, but I like to think that if they did have eyes to see with they could get a look at what they're in for next."

Morley saw more double doors ahead. Over them, in big white letters, was one word.

MORGUE

The doors opened. The lights inside were blinding. Trolleys like those he was on were lined up in a row. Morley knew who lay on the nearest. Clyde. He could just make out another. Mr Gupta.

In front of them was a wall of square metal doors. One, he saw, was labelled M. CARTWRIGHT.

"No point hanging around," said Mr Larkin. He opened the door with Morley's name on.

"Into the freezer with you," he said.

He pushed the trolley up to the door. Morley saw the long, coffin-shaped box he was to be shut up in, thought of the door clanging behind him as he lay paralysed but conscious, thought of an eternity of freezing, immobile darkness.

Yesterday, he had been at home.

This was impossible.

"*I DON'T BELIEVE THIS IS HAPPENING,*" he tried to shout.

And he made it. Words sounded.

"Oh, yes it is, mate," said Mr Larkin. He was pushing Morley in: already his legs up to the knees were in the coffin.

"IT ISN'T!" Morley had found his voice. *"I'VE GOT TO SNAP OUT OF THIS."*

Suddenly, he had movement as well.

"In you go, mate." Mr Larkin was pushing hard.

"NO! NO! NO! NO!"

Morley was properly alive now. He prepared to spring off the trolley.

And then he realized the noise like a beating heart which had been in his ears since he arrived had stopped. There was complete silence. A third figure stood in the room, taller than Mr Maledict Unthank, sterner than Sister Sacrament. Its mouth opened and yellow teeth waggled.

"I said there would be no mistake this time," said Dr Grout.

"You can't keep me here. I'm going," Morley screamed.

"Are you, now?" said Dr Grout.

"YES!"

"Try," said Dr Grout. "Go on, try."

Morley tried. There was strength in his limbs – but he could not seem to use it to get off the trolley. In front of him was the freezer compartment with his name on the door: behind him was a corridor leading upwards to the open air and freedom. These were the only alternatives left him and all he could do was thrash his legs until one or the other claimed him.

Dr Grout's mouth widened into a piano keyboard smile.

"Keep at it, Morley," he said. "We have all the time

in the world – and there's no one you can complain to."

Dr Grimes and Dr Hough sat in Mrs Cartwright's sitting room.

"We don't understand what has happened," said Dr Hough.

"I told your son I would never employ Dr Grout again," said Dr Grimes. "And no more I did. Nor did anyone else. There were so many complaints about him that he was struck off the register. Poor fellow killed himself soon afterwards. Left a note swearing vengeance on everyone who'd helped to bring him to his end."

"Well, perhaps this Dr Grout is his brother," said Mrs Cartwright. "My Morley's safe in St Sebastian's."

"There's no such hospital," said Dr Hough. "There was – it was demolished thirty years ago when the district hospital was built. Dr Grout was Senior Registrar. There's a Sainsbury's and a multi-screen cinema on the site now."

Morley's mother did not answer for a while. Then she said, "Oh dear. What are we going to do?"

"I wish I knew," answered Dr Grimes. "I wish I knew."